Americo R

LABORUM DULCE LENIMEN

G. SCHIRMER

COSÌ FAN TUTTE

WOMEN ARE LIKE THAT

An Opera in Two Acts

Libretto by

LORENZO DA PONTE

Music by

W. A. MOZART

VOCAL SCORE

Including the Secco Recitatives

English Version by

RUTH AND THOMAS MARTIN

As Produced by the Metropolitan Opera Company, New York

With an Essay on the
Story of the Opera by
NATHAN BRODER

Ed. 2038

G. SCHIRMER, INC., NEW YORK

42735
Printed in the U. S. A.

DRAMATIS PERSONAE

FIORDILIGI }
DORABELLA } Ladies from Ferrara and Sisters, living in Naples. . Sopranos

GUGLIELMO, Officer, betrothed to Fiordiligi . . . . Baritone

FERRANDO, Officer, betrothed to Dorabella . . . . Tenor

DESPINA, Chambermaid to the Ladies . . . . Soprano

DON ALFONSO, An old Philosopher . . . . Bass

Soldiers, Servants, Sailors, Wedding-Guests, Townspeople

The action takes place in Naples

COSÌ FAN TUTTE

Towards the end of 1789—two years before his death—Mozart was, as usual during this period of his career, in dire financial straits. On December 29 he wrote to his friend and fellow-Mason, Michael Puchberg, "According to the present arrangement I am to receive from the management next month 200 ducats for my opera. If you can and will lend me 400 gulden until then, you will be rescuing your friend from the greatest embarrassment . . . I invite you, you alone, to come on Thursday at 10 o'clock in the morning to hear a short rehearsal of my opera. I am only inviting Haydn and yourself." The obliging Puchberg, who had already answered several appeals of this sort from his friend, sent 300 gulden.[1] (A gulden was worth about 45 cents and a ducat about two dollars; Mozart was therefore to be paid approximately $400 for his work.)

The opera in question was *Così fan tutte, osia la scuola degli amanti* (*All Women Behave Like That, or The School for Lovers*). Mozart had been since 1787 official composer to the Imperial Court at Vienna, at a salary of 800 gulden a year, but had been given little to do besides writing dances. A successful revival of *Le Nozze di Figaro* in Vienna in 1789 (it was given twelve times from August to November), however, had impressed the music-loving but undiscriminating Emperor Joseph II, and Mozart was commissioned to write a new opera. He set to work immediately and completed the music in January 1790.

The librettist was the same man who had written the texts for *Figaro* and *Don Giovanni*—Lorenzo da Ponte. Since his career is not as familiar as is Mozart's, the biographical sketch given in the Introduction to the Schirmer edition of the vocal score of *Figaro* is here repeated.

His real name was Emanuele Conegliano and he was born March 10, 1749, at Ceneda, a small town in northeastern Italy. His father, a Jew, was left a widower, and when Emanuele was fourteen had himself and his three sons baptized so that he could marry a young Catholic girl. In accordance with a custom of the time, the eldest son took the name of the sponsor, Monsignor Lorenzo da Ponte, bishop of Ceneda. Young Lorenzo studied in the seminary of the town and later at Portogruaro. By the time he was twenty-two he was giving instruction in rhetoric and the Italian language and had taken minor orders for the priesthood. From Portogruaro he went to Venice, where he eked out a precarious living by teaching and writing poetry and by less legitimate activities, plunging zestfully into the dissolute life of the Venetian Republic. He got into, and out of, one scrape after another until, in 1779, the patience of even the lenient authorities of Venice was overtaxed, and they banished da Ponte from all Venetian territories. He made his way to Vienna, armed with a letter of introduction to Antonio Salieri, court composer to Joseph II. There Salieri helped to get him appointed theater poet and da Ponte enjoyed some years of success, writing many librettos (including the

[1] Emily Anderson, *Letters of Mozart and His Family*, London, 1938, III, 1391.

three for Mozart) as well as poems for special occasions. After the death of Joseph II (1790) da Ponte left Vienna. Most of the next thirteen years (1792-1805) were spent in London, where he was for part of the time poet of the King's Theatre. In 1805 da Ponte, as a result of one of his frequent financial crises, came to the United States. He tried the grocery business, first in New York and then in Elizabethtown, N. J., returned to New York to teach Italian, attempted for eight years to establish himself as a business man in Sunbury, Pa., and for a year in Philadelphia, but came back in 1819 to New York. Here he taught Italian again and in 1825 was appointed professor of Italian Literature at Columbia College (a post that gave him prestige but no salary). In the same year Manuel Garcia and his daughter Maria Malibran came to New York and da Ponte persuaded them to produce *Don Giovanni* (for the first time in America) at the Park Theater. In the 1820s da Ponte wrote his memoirs, which still make lively reading today, even though the author understandably glossed over or omitted the less savory episodes in his life, and his memory of events that took place thirty or forty years before he wrote about them is not reliable. He died in New York on August 17, 1838, at the age of eighty-nine.

While the libretto for *Figaro* was derived from a play by Beaumarchais and that for *Don Giovanni* from an opera by Bertati and Gazzaniga and other sources, the plot of *Così fan tutte* seems to have been invented by da Ponte.[2] A brief outline of it follows:

Act I: Don Alfonso, a cynical old philosopher, declares to his young friends Ferrando and Guglielmo that no women can be trusted, including their respective fiancées, the sisters Dorabella and Fiordiligi. Enraged at this slur, they accept his offer to wager 100 *zecchini* that he can prove his point in twenty-four hours if they will agree to follow his instructions unquestioningly. Don Alfonso then announces to the two sisters that their sweethearts have been ordered off to the wars. There is a touching scene of farewell and the two officers ostensibly sail off, to the cheers of the villagers. Despina, maid to the sisters, finds them prostrated by their loss and pooh-poohs their lamentations, saying that one man is pretty much like another. To further his scheme Don Alfonso enlists Despina's aid and introduces to her two young and wealthy "Albanians" who are enamored of her mistresses. She does not recognize Ferrando and Guglielmo in their disguise and supports their suit. Fiordiligi and Dorabella are outraged at this intrusion upon their sorrow and angrily order the two foreigners to leave. When the young men pretend to take poison in their despair, the sisters relent somewhat. Despina appears in the disguise of a doctor and revives the "Albanians" by means of a huge magnet. They renew their ardent attack on the young ladies' affections but are again repulsed.

Act II: After Despina derides their constancy, the sisters, especially Dorabella, weaken and decide a flirtation will do no harm. Dorabella chooses Guglielmo and Fiordiligi Ferrando. As the couples stroll in the garden Guglielmo wins Dorabella's love and gives her a golden locket in return for a picture of Ferrando. Fiordiligi, however, refuses to yield to Ferrando and decides to disguise herself as a man and join her betrothed at the front. But when Ferrando threatens to slay himself, she too gives in. Both Guglielmo and Ferrando are now utterly cast down by the clear evidence of their sweethearts' fickleness; but the triumphant Don Alfonso promises them that he will fix everything. He arranges a ceremony in which Ferrando is to marry Fiordiligi and her sister

[2]The statement, found in many books on Mozart, that this plot was built, at the request of the Emperor, around an actual occurrence is based on nothing more than a rumor reported many years after the première.

Guglielmo. In the midst of the ceremony, which is conducted by Despina in the guise of a notary, the military music to which the two officers marched off to war is heard again and it is announced that they have returned. In the confusion Ferrando and Guglielmo leave the stage and come back without their disguises, explaining that they had received royal permission to return to the arms of their loved ones. The officers pretend to fly into a rage when they find the marriage contract, the sisters blame Don Alfonso and Despina for leading them astray, their lovers reveal that they were the "Albanians," Guglielmo returns Ferrando's picture to Dorabella and gets his locket back, the sisters are properly chastened, and all ends happily.

Così fan tutte was performed for the first time on January 26, 1790, at the Burgtheater in Vienna with the following cast:

Fiordiligi..............Adriana Ferraresi del Bene
Dorabella.......................Louise Villeneuve
Guglielmo........................Francesco Benucci
Ferrando.........................Vincenzo Calvesi
Despina.............................Mme. Bussani
Don Alfonso......................Francesco Bussani

As usual, Mozart was thoroughly familiar with the capabilities of the singers for whom he wrote. He had no high opinion of Mme. Ferraresi's powers, but she was the current mistress of da Ponte, and Mozart, probably to oblige his friend, had composed two concert arias for her (K. 577, 579). For Louise Villeneuve, Mme. Ferraresi's sister in real life as well as in the opera, Mozart had written three concert arias (K. 578, 582, 583). Calvesi had sung the tenor part of a vocal quartet (K. 479) and trio (K. 480) composed by Mozart in 1785. Benucci had created the role of Figaro and Bussani those of Bartolo and Antonio; and both men had also sung in the first Vienna performance of *Don Giovanni* (Leporello and Commendatore-Masetto, respectively). Mme. Bussani had been the first Cherubino.

The opera seems to have been fairly successful at first. Even Count von Zinzendorf, who had found *Figaro* a bore, thought "Mozart's music charming and the subject very amusing." After five performances the theater was closed for two months because of the death of Joseph II (February 20). When it was reopened, *Così fan tutte* was given five times more and then was dropped. But the following year it was performed in German at Frankfort and Mainz and in Italian at Prague, Leipzig, and Dresden; and after Mozart's death it spread beyond Central Europe. Strangely enough, the first New York performance does not seem to have taken place until 1922.

For some peculiar reason, many 19th-century critics who did not balk at the most far-fetched coincidences in opera librettos, at the most absurd and obscure plot-convolutions, at singing dragons and informative birds, found da Ponte's plot unrealistic. What bothered these writers in the age of Romanticism even more was what they considered a flippant attitude towards love in his libretto. Many attempts to "improve" it were made, and Mozart's music was mauled and distorted to fit more edifying tales. The work was performed with an entirely new libretto at Copenhagen in 1826; two years later Mozart's opera was given in London as *Tit for Tat or The Tables Turned*, with the music "arranged" by one W. Hawes; in Paris in 1863 it turned up as *Peines d'Amour perdues*, with a text based on Shakespeare's *Love's Labour's Lost*; and as late as 1909 it appeared in Dresden as *Die Dame Kobold*, with a libretto taken from a comedy by Calderon.

The charges of incredibility and an irreverent attitude towards love are of course wholly beside the point. Mozart and da Ponte were not dealing here with recognizable human figures, as in *Figaro*, or with the creation of flesh-and-blood characters out of universal types, as in *Don Giovanni*. They were engaged in telling an amusing tale, for which a small group of stock characters was perfectly adequate. And even some of these come alive. Don Alfonso and Despina are as "real" as any characters in opera, and Fiordiligi is far from a puppet. The truth, as it seems to us, about the matter was seen as early as 1805 by a writer in a Berlin musical periodical.

> The theme of this opera [he wrote] was a satire on the highly praised fidelity of the female sex and an innocent playing with the sanctity of love. That this evidence of the infidelity of all women was regarded merely as a jest is precisely the delicate charm of the whole opera, and that this infidelity, on the other hand, is let off so easily is proof of the playful sense of beauty on the part of the composer. Everything is only masquerade, playfulness, jest, dallying, and irony . . . Mozart was not at all serious about the serious moments that crop up now and then; they served him merely as a means of shaping the form and, one might say, of darkening, of shading the prank; even though one cannot deny that he let himself go too much in such passages, as if they had, in the process of working on them, grown in spite of himself. They should have been there merely as contrasts, to be treated, like some of the asides, not without irony.[3]

Certain it is that Mozart lavished on this work some of his most delightful music, his most exquisite craftsmanship. If some of the arias are not perhaps as telling as the best in his other mature operas, they are outnumbered by the ensembles, which are wonderfully varied in style and construction. The orchestration is Mozart at his most sparkling—in other words, the finest to be found in 18th-century music. Occasionally a mock-serious piece, aping the style of the lamenting or heroic aria of the *opera seria*, underscores the gentle irony of the work. The sly humor extends even into the Overture, which unlike that to *Figaro*, employs several themes from the opera. A subtle touch is the appearance here, as a tailpiece to one of the themes, of a jolly figure sung by Basilio in *Figaro* (Act I, No. 7) to the words "così fan tutte le belle." It is difficult to see why *Così fan tutte* has not always been accepted, and especially in our times, for what it is—a musical lark that is one of the gems of *opera buffa*.

Nathan Broder

NOTE

In performances of the opera Nos. 7, 24, and 27, with their preceding recitatives, are often omitted.

[3]Quoted in Otto Jahn, *W. A. Mozart*, Leipzig, IV, 1859, 497.

INDEX

INDEX (*continued*)

Così fan tutte

Women Are Like That

Lorenzo da Ponte
English version by
Ruth and Thomas Martin

Wolfgang Amadeus Mozart

Overture

Andante

f
p
f
ten.
ten.

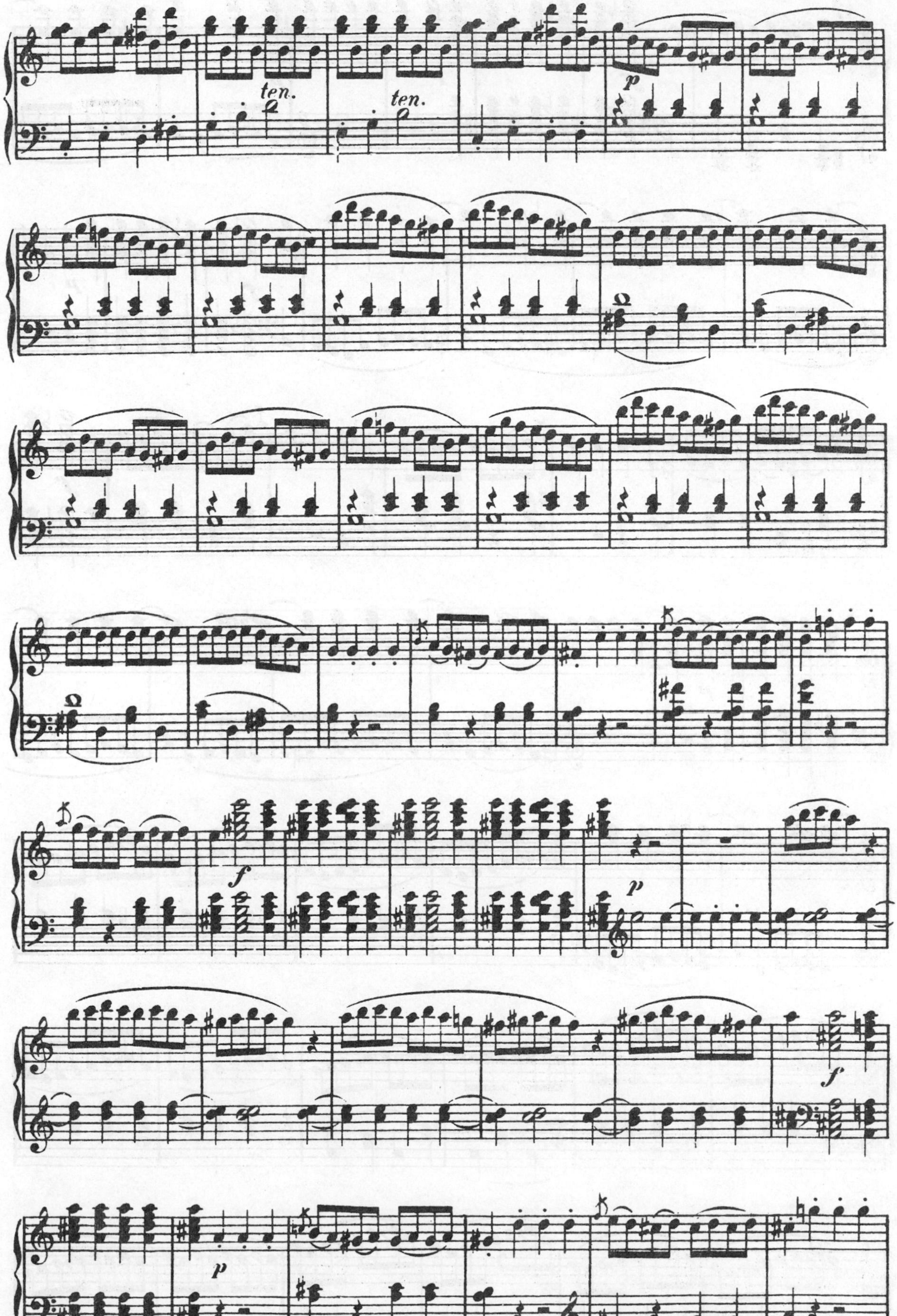
ten.
ten.
p
f
p
f
p

f
p
f
p
f

p
f
p
cresc.
f
ff

ATTO PRIMO
SCENA I

ACT I
SCENE I

Nº 1. Terzetto

li _ gi tra_dir _ mi non sa, tra_dir _ mi non sa, u _ gua _ le in lei
li- gi would no more be right, would no more be right, than try- ing to
tr
tr
mf
p
cre _ do co_stan _ za e bel _ tà, u _ gua _ le in lei cre _ do costan_za e bel_
tell you the sun shines at night, than try- ing to tell you the sun shines at
3
3
3
mfp
DON ALFONSO
tà. Ho i cri _ ni gia grigi ex ca _ thedra parlo,
night. I'm well o- ver six- ty, I speak from ex- per- ience,
mf
p
mf
p
mf
f
ma ta _ li li _ ti _ gi fi_ni _ sca_no quà, ma ta _ li li_
but since you won't heed the ad- vice of a friend, at least let us
p

FERR.
No, det - to ci a - ve - te che in fi - de esser
With no shred of proof you de- clared them un-
GUGL.
ti - gi fi - ni - sca - no quà. No, det - to ci a - ve - te che in fi - de esser
bring this dis- pute to an end. With no shred of proof you de- clared them un-
mf p mf p
pon - no, pro - var cel' do - ve - te, se a - ve - te o - ne - stà.
faith- ful. An in- sult like that we could nev- er ig- nore.
D. ALF.
pon - no, pro - var cel' do - ve - te, se a - ve - te o - ne - stà. Tai pro - ve la -
faith- ful. An in- sult like that we could nev- er ig- nore. Don't ask me to
cresc. p
(Ferrando and Guglielmo put their hands on their swords.)
No, no le vo - gliamo: o fuo - ri la spa - da, o fuo - ri la
That's just what we ask you, we want sat- is- fac- tion, we want sat- is-
GUGL.
sciamo... No, no le vo - gliamo: o fuo - ri la spa - da, o fuo - ri la
prove it... That's just what we ask you, we want sat- is- fac- tion, we want sat- is-
f p f p

spa_da, o fuo_ri la spa_da rompiam l'a_mi_stà.
fac- tion, or else choose your wea- pon to set- tle the score.
D. ALF.
spa_da, o fuo_ri la spa_da rompiam l'a_mi_stà. O paz_zo de_
fac- tion, or else choose your wea- pon to set- tle the score. You both must be
f
tr
p
FERR.
Sul vi_vo mi tocca, sul vi_vo mi
I can't take it light-ly! I can't take it
D. ALF.
si_re! o paz_zo de_si_re!
cra- zy! You both must be cra- zy!
GUGL.
Sul vi_vo mi tocca, sul vi_vo mi
I can't take it light- ly. I can't take it
tocca, chi lascia di bocca sorti_re un ac_cen_to che tor_
light- ly. You slan- der un- right- ly the high-mind- ed wom-an I wor-
cercar di scopri_re quel mal che tro_va_to me_schi_
I on- ly was try- ing to save you some troub- le and warn
tocca, chi lascia di bocca sorti_re un accen_to che tor_
light- ly! You slan- der un- right- ly the high- mind- ed wom-an I wor-

to, che tor - to le fa, chi lascia di
ship, ad- mire, and a- dore. My hon- or is
- ni, me_schi - ni ci fa, cer_car di
— you of what is in store. I on- ly
to, che tor - to le fa, chi lascia di
ship, ad- mire, and a- dore. My hon- or is
bocca sor_tire un ac_cen_to che tor - to, che
slight- ed— our friend-ship is blight- ed— you wound- ed my
-sco_pri - re quel mal che tro_va_to me_schi - ni, me_
was try- ing to save you some troub- le and warn you of
bocca sor_ti - re un ac_cen_to che tor - to, che
slight- ed— our friend- ship is blight- ed— you wound- ed my
tor - to le fa, che tor - to le
pride to the core, my pride to the
schi - ni ci fa, meschi - ni, me_schi - ni ci
what is in store, and warn you of what is in
tor - to le fa, che tor - to, che tor - to le
pride to the core! you wound - ed my pride to the
sf
p
f

fa, che tor - - - to le fa, che tor - to le
core, my pride to the core, my pride to the
fa, meschi - - ni, meschi - ni ci fa, me - schi - ni ci
store, and warn you of what is in store, of what is in
fa, che tor - to, che tor - to le fa, che tor - to le
core! you wound - ed my pride to the core, my pride to the
p
f
fa, che tor - to le fa.
core, my pride to the core!
fa, me - schi - ni ci fa.
store, of what is in store!
fa, che tor - to le fa.
core, my pride to the core!
cresc.
f
tr.

Recit.
GUGL.
D. ALF. (calmly)
Fuor la spa_da! scie_gliete qual di noi più vi pia_ce. Io son uo - mo di pa_ce,
Choose your weap- on! You'll ren- der us com- plete sat- is- fac- tion. I'm a peace- - lov- ing bach'- lor,
FERR.
e duel_li non fo, se non a men_sa. O bat_ter_vi, o dir su_bi_to, perchè d'in_fe_del-
and get my sat- is- fac- tion when I'm din- ing. Ei- ther fight with me, or a- pol- o- gize for cast- ing all those
D. ALF.
tà le no_stre a_man_ti so_spet_ta_te ca_pa_ci. Ca_ra sem_pli_ci_tà,
slurs up- on our sweet- hearts and their good rep- u- ta- tion. How can you be so blind!
FERR.
D. ALF.
quan_to mi pia_ci! Ces_sa_te di scher_zar, o giu_ro al cie_lo_ Ed
You make me laugh! This joke has gone too far! I will not stand for it! My
io, giu_ro al_la ter_ra, non scherzo, a_mi_ci mi_ei: so_lo sa_per vor_re_i che
friends, I can as- sure you, I spoke in bit- ter ear- nest. May I ask one ques- tion: what
raz_za d'a_ni_ma_li son que_ste vo_stre bel_le, se han co_me tut_ti noi car_ne,
strange, un- com- mon spe- cies do your la- dy- loves be- long to? Would you say they are god- dess- es,

Nº 2. Terzetto

si_a, do_ve si_a, nes_sun lo
prove it, who can prove it? Name me one
pp
FERR.
con fuoco
GUGL.
con fuoco
FERR.
sa. La fe_ni_ce è Do_ra_bel_la, La fe_ni_ce è Fior_di_li_gi, Do_ra_
name! I have proof in Do- ra- bel- la, I have proof in Fior- di- li- gi, Do- ra-
f
p
FERR.
bel_la, la fe_ni_ce è Do_ra_bel_la!
bel- la! No one else but Do- ra- bel- la!
GUGL.
Fior_di_li_gi, la fe_ni_ce è Fior_di_li_gi!
Fior- di- li- gi! No one else but Fior- di- li- gi!
cresc.
f
fp
D. ALF.
Non è questa, non è quel_la, non fu mai, non vi sa_rà, non vi sa_
Fid- dle fad- dle, fid- dle fad- dle, you are wrong, they're all the same, they're all the
p
cresc.

rà, non vi sa - rà. È la fe - de del - le femmine co - me l'a - ra - ba fe -
same, they're all the same! I re- peat that wom-an's con- stan- cy is the pur- est sort of
FERR.
La fe - ni - ce è Do - ra - bel - la, Do - ra - bella è la fe - ni - ce.
I be- lieve in Do- ra- bel- la, you can't weak- en my con- vic- tion!
GUGL.
D. ALF.
ni - ce. La fe - ni - ce è Fiordi - li - gi, Fior - di - li - gi è la fe - ni - ce, Che vi
fic- tion. I be- lieve in Fior- di- li- gi, you can't weak- en my con- vic- tion! Is that
FERR.
GUGL.
D. ALF.
sia, ciascun lo di - ce, Do - ra - bel - la, Fior - di - li - gi, do - ve
all you have to of- fer? Do- ra- bel- la! Fior- di- li- gi! Are you
cresc.
GUGL.
D. ALF.
FERR.
D. ALF.
si - a. Fior - di - li - gi, do - ve si - a, Do - ra - bella, nes - sun lo
ser- ious? Fior- di- li- gi! Can you prove it? Do- ra- bel- la! No, no, you
pp

FERR. sotto voce
GUGL. sotto voce
D. ALF.
Recit.
FERR.
sa, Do_ra_bel_la. Fior_di_li_gi. nes - sun lo sa. Sciòc_che_rie di Po-
can't! Do- ra- bel- la! Fior- di- li- gi! I say you can't! The- o- ret- i- cal
f
GUGL.
D. ALF.
e_ti. Scem_piag_gi_ni di vec_chi. Or be_ne; u_di_te, ma
bom- bast! The talk of sen- ile cyn- ics! I'm flat- tered! How- ev- er, you
f
sen_za an_dar in col_le_ra: qual pro_va a_ve_te voi, che og_nor co-
say that they are vir- tu- ous. To- day that may be true, but will it be to-
p
stan - ti vi sien le vostre a_man_ti; chi vi fè si_cur_tà,
mor- row? How can you be so cer- tain? Have you an- y guar- an- tee
p
FERR.
GUGL.
che in_va_ria_bi_li so_no i lor co_ri? Lunga es_pe_rien_za_ No_bil e-
that the love they pro- fess is e- ter- nal? Im- pec- ca- ble mor- als. Old- fash- ioned

FERR.
GUGL.
FERR.
du_ca_zion_ Pen_sar su_bli_me_ A_na_lo_gia d'u_mor_ Dis_in_te_
prin- ci- ples. Loft- y i- de- als. High- mind- ed way of life. Ut- ter un-
GUGL.
FERR.
GUGL.
res _ se_ Im_mu_ta_bil ca_rat_te_re_ Pro_mes_se_ Pro_te_ste_
sel- fish- ness. The firm- est of char- ac- ters! Her prom- ise! Her hon- or!
FERR.
D. ALF.
Giu_ra_men_ti_ Pian_ti, so_spir, ca_rez_ze, sveni_men_ti. Lascia_te_mi un po'
Her de- vo- tion! Kiss- es and tears, ca- ress- es, fits of swoon- ing! What could be more ri-
fp
FERR.
D. ALF.
ri_de_re_ Co_spet_to! fi_ni_te di de_ri_der_ci? Pian
di- cu- lous! Dam- na- tion! When will there be an end to this? Be
f
pia_no: e se toc_car con ma_no og_gi vi fo che
pa- tient! What if I could con- vince you this ve- ry day that

GUGL.
FERR.
D. ALF.
co - me l'al - tre so - no? Non si può dar! Non è! Gio -
they're like all the oth- ers? That is a lie! Of course! Will you
p
FERR.
D. ALF.
GUGL.
chiam! Gio - chia - mo! Cen - to zec - chi - ni. E mil - le, se vo -
bet? I'm will- ing. One hun- dred sov- 'reigns! A thou- sand, if you
D. ALF.
FERR.
D. ALF.
le - te. Pa - ro - la. Pa - ro - lis - si - ma. E un cen - no, un
wish. A- greed? On my hon- or! But prom- ise: no
mot - to, un ge - sto, giu - ra - te, di non far di tut - to
ink- ling, no men- tion, not e- ven a sug- ges- tion of our
FERR.
D. ALF.
que - sto al - le vo - stre Pe - ne - lo - pi. Giu - ria - mo. Da sol -
wa- ger to your glo- ri- ous par- a- gons! We prom- ise. On your

GUGL.
D. ALF.
da_ti d'o_no_re. Da sol_da_ti d'o_no_re. E tut_to quel fa_
hon- or as sol- diers? On our hon- or as sol- diers! And till to- mor- row
FERR.
Tut_to! Bra_
Glad- ly! My
GUGL. D. ALF. GUGL.
re_te ch'io vi di_rò di far. Tut_tis_si_mo! Bra_vis_si_mi! Bra_
eve- ning you will do what I say? Most will- ing- ly! Your hand on it! My
vis_si_mo! Sig_nor Don Al_fon_set_to! A spe_se vo_stre
hand on it! You con- nois- seur of wom- en! To see you beat- en
vis_si_mo! Sig_nor Don Al_fon_set_to!
hand on it! You con- nois- seur of wom- en!
or ci di_ver_ti_re_mo.
will be ex- treme- ly fun- ny!
(to Ferrando)
E de' cen_to zec_chi_ni, che fa_
Let us plan how to spend all that

Nº 3. Terzetto

vi _ to io vo _ glio far. in o _ nor di Ci _ te _ re _ a un con
bet we made be- fore, I shall give a ga- la din- ner for the
vi _ to _ io vo_glio far.
sweet- heart that I a- dore.
D. ALF.
Sarò anch'
May I
io de' con_vi_ta_ti?
al- so join the par- ty?
cresc.
FERR.
Ci sa _ re_te, si Si _ gnor, ci sa _ re_te, si Si _ gnor, ci sa _ re_te, si Si _ gnor.
Why, of course, that's on- ly fair! Don Al- fon- so, you'll be there. Don Al- fon- so, you'll be there.
GUGL.
Ci sa _ re_te, si Si _ gnor, ci sa _ re_te, si Si _ gnor, ci sa _ re_te, si Si _ gnor.
Why, of course, that's on- ly fair! Don Al- fon- so, you'll be there. Don Al- fon- so, you'll be there,
tr

FERR. sotto voce
E che
While the
D. ALF. sotto voce
E che
While the
GUGL. sotto voce
E che
While the
tr
brin - dis re - pli - ca - ti far vo - glia - mo al dio d'a -
sound of clink- ing glass- es ech- oes gai- ly through the
brin - dis re - pli - ca - ti far vo - glia - mo al dio d'a -
sound of clink- ing glass- es ech- oes gai- ly through the
brin - dis re - pli - ca - ti far vo - glia - mo al dio d'a -
sound of clink- ing glass- es ech- oes gai- ly through the
f
mor, e che brin - dis re - pli - ca - ti far vo -
air, we shall sing the end- less prais- - es of true
fp

glia _ mo al dio d'a _ mor, e che brin _ dis re _ pli _ ca _ ti,
wom — — en ev- 'ry- where, while the sound of clink- ing glass — — es
glia _ mo al dio d'a _ mor, e che brin _ dis re _ pli _ ca _ ti,
wom — — en ev- 'ry- where, while the sound of clink- ing glass — — es
glia _ mo al dio d'a _ mor, e che brin _ dis re _ pli _ ca _ ti,
wom — — en ev- 'ry- where, while the sound of clink- ing glass — — es
fp
f
p
cresc.
f
sotto voce
f
far vo _ gliamo al dio d'a _ mor, e che brin _ dis re _ pli _ ca _ ti,
ech- oes gai- ly through the air, while the sound of clink- ing glass- — es
s. v.
f
far vo _ gliamo al dio d'a _ mor, e che brin _ dis re _ pli _ ca _ ti,
ech- oes gai- ly through the air, while the sound of clink- ing glass- — es
s. v.
f
far vo _ gliamo al dio d'a _ mor, e che brin _ dis re _ pli _ ca _ ti,
ech- oes gai- ly through the air, while the sound of clink- ing glass- — es
p
f
p
cresc.
f
sotto voce
f
far vo _ gliamo al dio d'a _ mor, far vo _ gliamo al dio d'a _ mor, far vo _ glia _ mo al
ech- oes gai- ly through the air, ech- oes gai- ly through the air, ech- oes gai- ly
s. v.
f
far vogliamo al dio d'a _ mor, far vogliamo al dio d'a _ mor, far voglia _ mo al
ech- oes gai- ly through the air, ech- oes gai- ly through the air, ech- oes gai- ly
s. v.
f
far vogliamo al dio d'a _ mor, far vogliamo al dio d'a _ mor, far voglia _ mo al
ech- oes gai- ly through the air, ech- oes gai- ly through the air, ech- oes gai- ly
p
f

SCENA II SCENE II

Nº 4. Duetto

(Curtain. A garden at the seashore.)

ser_va tu un po - co, os - ser - va, che
one of Fer- ran- do— I love it! What
fo - co ha ne' sguar_di, se fiam_ma, se dar_di non
light in his glanc- es! It spar- kles, and danc- es, and
stacc.
sembran scoc_car, se fiam_ma, se dar_di non sembranscoc_car,
lends him such grace! It spar- kles, and danc- es, and lends him such grace,
FIORD.
non sem_bran scoc_car. Si ve_de un sem_bian_te guer.
and lends him such grace! The face of a he- ro, au-

a piacere
DORAB.
rie_ro ed_a_man_te. Si vede u_na fac_cia, che al_
da- cious, yet dis- arm- ing! His face is ex- press- ive — so
f
p
let_ta, che al_let_ta, che al_let_ta, e mi_nac_cia, e mi_
gra- cious, so kind- ly and charm- ing, yet he is man- ly and pos-
f
p
FIORD.
Fe_li_ce son i_o, fe_li_ce son i_
I'm ev- er so hap-py, con- tent- ed and hap-
DORAB.
nac_cia, e mi_nac_cia. Io so_no, io so_no fe_li_
ses- sive, so pos- ses- sive! I'm ev- er so hap- py, so hap-
cresc.
f
p
cresc.
f
Allegro
o!
py.
Se questo mio co_re mai cangia de_
If this love of mine ev- er fails in af-
ce!
py.
Se questo mio co_re mai cangia de_
If this love of mine ev- er fails in af-
Allegro
p

si_o, mai cangia, mai cangia de_si_o, A_mo - - -
fec- tion, or turns in an- oth- er di- rec- tion, my dar- - - -
si_o, mai cangia, mai cangia de_si_o, A_mo - - -
fec- tion, or turns in an- oth- er di- rec- tion, my dar- - - -
Adagio
a tempo
- re, A_mo - - - - - re, mi fac_cia vi_
- ling, my dar- - - - - ling, may Fate take re-
- re, A_mo - - - - re, mi fac_cia vi_
- ling, my dar- - - - - ling, may Fate take re-
Adagio
a tempo
ven - - do pe_nar, mi fac_cia vi_ven - - do pe_nar.
venge on my heart, may Fate take re- venge on my heart.
ven - - do pe_nar, mi fac_cia vi_ven - - do pe_nar, A
venge on my heart, may Fate take re- venge on my heart. Be-

Se que_sto mio co_re mai cangia de_
If ev- er my feel- ings should wa- ver or
mo_re, mi fac_cia ri_ ven_do pe_ nar.
lov- ed, may Fate take re- venge on my heart,
si_ o. A_ more mi faccia ri_vendo pe_nar. A_ mo_re mi faccia ri_
al- ter, if ev- er a dis- cord should tear us a- part, my dar- ling, may Fate take re-
A_ mo_re mi faccia ri_
my dar- ling, may Fate take re-
ven_do pe_ nar. A_ mo_re mi fac_cia ri_ ven_do pe_ nar,
venge on my heart, be- lov- ed, may Fate take re- venge on my heart,
ven_do pe_ nar.
venge on my heart.
Se que_sto mio
If ev- er my

A-
my
co-re mai cangia de-si-o, A-more mi faccia vi-vendo pe-nar, A-
can-dor should weak-en or fal-ter, if ev-'er my fer-vor should fail or de- part, my
mo-re mi fac-cia vi-ven-do pè-nar, vi-ven - - do pe-
dar-ling, may Fate take re- venge on my heart, re- venge on - my
mo-re mi fac-cia vi-ven-do pe-nar, vi-ven - - do pe-
dar- ling, may Fate take re- venge on my heart, re- venge on my
nar, vi-ven - - do pe-nar, mi faccia pe-nar, mi faccia pe-
heart, re- venge on my heart, re- venge on my heart, re- venge on my
nar, vi-ven - - do pe-nar, mi faccia pe-nar, mi faccia pe-
heart, re- venge on my heart, re- venge on my heart, re- venge on my

nar, A_mo_re mi fac_cia vi_ven_do pe_nar!
heart, be- lov- ed, may Fate take re- venge on my heart!
nar, A_mo_re mi fac_cia vi_ven_do pe_nar!
heart, be- lov- ed, may Fate take re- venge on my heart!
cresc.
f
Recit.
FIORD.
Mi par che sta_mat_ti_na vo_lon_tie_ri fa_rei la paz_za_rel_la: ho un cer_to
On such a love- ly morn- ing I can't help feel- ing just a lit- tle ro- guish. I can't ex-
p
fo_co, un cer_to piz_zi_cor en_tro le ve_ne_ quan_do Gu_gliel_mo vie_ne_ se sa_
plain it, but some- how I could do some harm- less mis- chief. When my Gu- gliel- mo gets here, how I'd
DORAB.
pes_si, che bur_la gli vo far. Per dir_ti il ve_ro, qualche co_sa di nuo_vo anch'
love to tease him just a bit! To be quite hon- est, I my- self have a feel- ing that

FIORD.
io nell' al_ma pro_vo, io giu_re_re_i, che lon_ta_ne non siam dagli I_me_ne_i. Dam_mi la
some-thing's bound to hap-pen. I al-most think we are soon to be mar-ried to our sweethearts. Give me your
ma_no: io voglio astro_lo_gar_ti: uh, che bell' Em_me! e questo e un Pi: va
hand, dear, I want to read your fu-ture. Look at that M there! And here a P! That's
DORAB.
FIORD.
be_ne: ma_tri_mo_nio pre_sto. Af_fè, che ci a_vrei gu_sto. Ed io non ci a_vrei
eas-y! Mat-ri-mo-ny pend-ing! That's one thing I would wel-come! I would not mind it
DORAB.
rab_bia. Ma che dia_vol vuol dir che i no_stri spo_si ri_tar_da_no a ve_nir? son già le
ei-ther. But where in the world are our two sweet-hearts? What's keep-ing them so long? It's get-ting
(Enter Don Alfonso.)
SCENA III
SCENE III
FIORD.
DORAB.
FIORD.
se_i — Ec_co_li. Non son es_si: è Don Alfon_so, l'a_mi_co lor. Ben venga il Si_gnor Don Al_
late — There they are! You're mis-tak-en, it's Don Al-fon-so, our mu-tual friend. Good morn-ing to you, Don Al-

Nº 5. Aria

Allegro agitato

Che fa_re_te? Che fa_rò? oh chegran fata_li_
How ex- plain it? What to say? Oh, ac- curs- ed,trag- ic
tà! dar di peg-gio non si può,ah non si può, ho di
day! When you know, you will a- gree, you will a- gree. Noth- ing
voi, di lor pie_tà, ho di voi, di lor pie_
worse could ev- er be! All your joys are done and
cresc.
p
tà, ho di voi, di lor pie_tà, di
past. Poor dear boys, the die is cast, the
cresc.
p
voi pie_tà, di lor pie_tà.
die is cast, the die is cast.

Recit.
FIORD.
Stel_le! per ca_ri_tà, Si_gnor Al _ fon_so, non ci fa _ te mo _
Good- ness! What can it be, dear Don Al- fon- so? Do not keep us in sus-
fp
D. ALF.
DORAB.
rir. Con_vien ar_mar_vi, figlie mie, di co_stan_za. Oh De_i! qual
pense. You must have cour- age, be pre- pared for a shock. Good Heav- ens! What's
FIORD.
ma_le è ad_di_ve_nu_to mai, qual ca_so ri_o? forse è mor_to il mio bene? È morto il
hap- pened to our fi- an- cés? Are they in troub- le? Is my Fer- ran- do dead? Or my Gu-
f
p
D. ALF.
DORAB.
D. ALF.
FIORD.
mi_o? Mor_ti non son, ma po_co men che morti. Fe_ri_ti? No. Amma_la_ti?
gliel- mo? Dead they are not, but not much less than that. In pris- on? No. Are they ill?
D. ALF.
FIORD.
D. ALF.
FIORD.
DORAB.
Nep_pur. Che co_sa dunque? Al marzial campo or_din re_gio li chiama. Ohi_
No, no. What could it be then? By roy- al or- der they must leave for the front. Oh,
D. ALF.
FIORD.
DORAB.
D. ALF.
mè! che sen_to! e par_ti_ran? Sul fat_to. E non v'è modo d'im_pe_dir_lo? Non
dear! How dread- ful! When do they leave? At once! And is there no way to ex- empt them? No

FIORD.
D. ALF.
vè. Ne un so_lo addio? Gli in_fe_li_ci non hanno co_rag_gio di ve_der_vi; ma se
way. And no good-byes? Wretch-ed fel-lows, they don't have the cour-age to face you. But if
DORAB.
D. ALF.
voi lo bramate, son pronti_ Dove son? A_mi_ci, en_tra_te!
you both can bear it, I'll call them. Oh, please do! Com- in, now, my he-roes!
Nº 6. Quintetto
SCENA IV
SCENE IV
(Enter Ferrando and Guglielmo, in traveling clothes.)
Andante
GUGL.
Sen_to,o Di_o, che que_sto
All is o-ver, the blow has
piede è re_stio nel gir_le a_vante.
fall-en, all my hopes de-stroyed and shat-tered.
FERR.
Il mio labbro
I am speech-less,
pal_pi_tan_te non può det_to pronun_ziar.
shocked and bat-tered! You be-hold a bro-ken man!
D. ALF.
Nei mo_
In the
f
p

men_ti i più ter _ ri _ bi_li sua vir_tù l'e _ roe pa _
face of this ca- tas- tro- phe, steel your heart and be cou-
FIORD.
Or che abbiam la nuova in_te _ sa, or che abbiam la nuova in
Now that all has been de- cid- ed, now that all has been de-
DORAB.
le_sa. Or che abbiam la nuova in_te _ sa, or che abbiam la nuova in_
ra- geous! Now that all has been de- cid- ed, now that all has been de-
te _ sa, a voi re_sta a fa_re il me_no; fa_te co_re, fa_te
cid- ed, you must do me one last fa- vor: be a sto- ic, be her-
te_sa, a voi re_sta a fa_re il me_no; fa_te co_re, fa_te
cid- ed, you must do me one last fa- vor: be a sto- ic, be her-
co_re, a entrambe in se_no im_mer_ge _ te_ci l'ac_ciar, im _ mer_
o- ic, with- out a wa- ver plunge your sword right through my heart, plunge your
co_re, a entrambe in se_no im_mer_ge _ te_ci l'ac_ciar, im _ mer_
o- ic, with- out a wa- ver plunge your sword right through my heart, plunge your

FERR.
ge_te_ci l'ac_ciar. I dol mi_o! la sorte in_col_pa
sword right through my heart. Dear- est an- gel! The worst has hap- pened!
GUGL.
ge_te_ci l'ac_ciar. I_dol mi_o! la sorte in_col_pa
sword right through my heart. Dear- est an- gel! The worst has hap- pened!
DORAB.
FIORD.
se__ ti deggio ab_ban_do_nar! Ah, no, no, non par_ti_ra_i, No cru_
Fate__ de- crees that we must part! No, no, no, I can- not bear it! I will
se__ ti deggio ab_ban_do_nar!
Fate__ de- crees that we must part!
fp
fp
del, non tene an_drai, pria ti vo mo_ri_re ai
die of grief I swear it! Let me die right here be-
DORAB.
voglio pria ca_varmi il co_ re.
Let me per - ish, I im- plore you!
fp
fp

FIORD.
FERR.
GUGL.
D. ALF.
piedi. (Co_sa di_ci?) (Te n'av_ve_di?) (Saldo a_
fore you! (Are we win- ning?) (Are we los- ing?) (The be-
mi_co, saldo a_mi_co, finem lauda, finem lauda!)
gin- ning is a- mus- ing, but to- mor-row comes the sor-row!)
FIORD.
sotto voce
Il de_ stin, il de_
So does Fate take a-
DORAB.
sotto voce
Il de_ stin, il de_
So does Fate take a-
FERR.
sotto voce
Il de_
Gone is
D. ALF.
sotto voce
Il destin co_sì de_
So the sud- den hand of
GUGL.
sotto voce
Il destin co_sì de_
So the sud- den hand of

stin co _ sì de _ frau _ da le
way the joy of liv- ing, end
stin co _ sì de _ frau _ da le
way the joy of liv- ing, end
stin co _ sì de _ frau _ da
all the joy of liv- ing,
frau _ da le speran _ ze de' mor _ ta _ li,
Fate will take a- way the joy of liv- ing,
frau _ da le speran _ ze de' mor _ ta _ li,
Fate will take a- way the joy of liv- ing,
spe _ ran _ ze, le spe _ ran _ ze de' mor
for- ev- er all the hopes and dreams we
spe _ ran _ ze, le spe _ ran _ ze de' mor
for- ev- er all the hopes and dreams we
le spe _ ran _ ze de' mor _
all the hopes and dreams we
il destin co _ sì de _ frau _ da le speran _ ze de' mor _
So the sud- den hand of Fate will take a- way the joy of
il destin co _ sì de _ frau _ da le speran _ ze de' mor _
So the sud- den hand of Fate will take a- way the joy of

cresc.
ta_li. Ah chi mai fra tan_ti ma_li, chi mai può la vi_ta a_
cher-ished. Bowed by grief, a-lone in sor-row, who would care to live at
ta_li. Ah chi mai fra tan_ti ma_li, chi mai può la vi_ta a_
cher-ished. Bowed by grief, a-lone in sor-row, who would care to live at
ta_li. Ah chi mai fra tan_ti ma_li, chi mai può la vi_ta a_
cher-ished. Bowed by grief, a-lone in sor-row, who would care to live at
ta_li. Ah chi mai fra tan_ti ma_li, chi mai può la vi_ta a_
liv-ing. Bowed by grief, a-lone in sor-row, who would care to live at
ta_li. Ah chi mai fra tan_ti ma_li, chi mai può la vi_ta a_
liv-ing. Bowed by grief, a-lone in sor-row, who would care to live at
mar, chi? chi? chi? chi? chi può
all, to live at all? Who would
mar, chi? chi? chi? chi? chi può
all, to live at all? Who would
mar, chi? chi? chi? chi? chi può
all, to live at all? Who would
mar, chi? chi? chi? chi? chi può
all, to live at all? Who would
mar, chi? chi? chi? chi? chi può
all, to live at all? Who would

mai la vi_ta a_mar, chi?
care to live at all, who?
mai la vi_ta a_mar, chi? Ah, no, no, non par_ti_
care to live at all, who? No, no, no, I can- not
mai la vi_ta a_mar, chi?
care to live at all, who?
mai la vi_ta a_mar, chi?
care to live at all, who?
mai la vi_ta a_mar, chi?
care to live at all, who?
fp
FIORD.
DORAB.
ra_i, No cru_del, non te_ne an_dra_i. vo_glio pria ca_varmi il
bear it! I will die of grief, I swear it! Let me per- ish, I im-
fp
fp
FIORD.
pria ti vo mo_ri_re ai piedi.
Let me die right here be- fore you!
FERR.
GUGL.
co_re. (Co_sa di_ci?) (Te n'av_
plore you! (Are we win- ning?) (Are we
fp

D.ALF.
ve_di?) (Sal_do a_mi_co, saldo a_mi_co, finem lauda, finem
los- ing?) (The be- gin- ning is a- mus- ing, but to- mor- row comes the
FIORD. sotto voce
Il de_
So does
DORAB.
lau_da!)
sor- row!)
sotto voce
Il de_
So does
FIORD.
stin, il de_stin co_sì de_
Fate take a- way the joy of
DORAB.
stin, il de_stin co_sì de_
Fate take a- way the joy of
FERR.
sotto voce
Il de_stin co_sì de_
Gone is all the joy of
D. ALF. sotto voce
Il de_stin co_sì de_frau_da le speran_ze de' mor_
So the sud- den hand of Fate will take a- way the joy of
GUGL. sotto voce
Il de_stin co_sì de_frau_da le speran_ze de' mor_
So the sud- den hand of Fate will take a- way the joy of

frau _ da le spe -
liv- ing, end for-
frau _ da le spe -
liv- ing, end for-
frau _ da
liv- ing,
ta _ li,
liv- ing.
ta _ li,
liv- ing.
ran _ ze, le spe _ ran _ ze de' mor _ ta _ li. Ah chi
ev- er all the hopes and dreams we cher- ished. Bowed by
ran _ ze, le spe _ ran _ ze de' mor _ ta _ li. Ah chi
ev- er all the hopes and dreams we cher- ished. Bowed by
le spe _ ran _ ze de' mor _ ta _ li. Ah chi
all the hopes and dreams we cher- ished. Bowed by
il de_stin co_sì de_frau_da le speran_ze de' mor_ta_li. Ah chi
So the sud- den hand of Fate will take a- way the joy of liv- ing. Bowed by
il de_stin co_si de_frau_da le speran_ze de' mor_ta_li. Ah chi
So the sud- den hand of Fate will take a- way the joy of liv- ing. Bowed by
sf
p

cresc.
f
mai fra tan - ti ma - li, chi mai può la vi - ta a - mar, chi?
grief, a- lone in sorrow, who would care to live at all, to
mai fra tan - ti ma - li, chi mai può la vi - ta a - mar, chi?
grief, a- lone in sor- row, who would care to live at all, to
mai fra tan - ti ma - li, chi mai può la vi - ta a - mar, chi?
grief, a- lone in sor- row, who would care to live at all, to
mai fra tan - ti ma - li, chi mai può la vi - ta a - mar, chi?
grief, a- lone in sor- row, who would care to live at all, to
mai fra tan - ti ma - li, chi mai può la vi - ta a - mar, chi?
grief, a- lone in sor- row, who would care to live at all, to
tr
sf
p
chi? chi? chi? chi può mai la vi - ta a -
live at all, who would care to live at
chi? chi? chi? chi può mai la vi - ta a -
live at all, who would care to live at
chi? chi? chi? chi può mai la vi - ta a -
live at all, who would care to live at
chi? chi? chi? chi può mai la vi - ta a -
live at all, who would care to live at
chi? chi? chi? chi può mai la vi - ta a -
live at all, who would care to live at

mar, ah— chi mai può la vi_ta a_mar, ah— chi mai
all, ah,— who would care to live at all, ah,— who would
mar, chi mai può, chi mai può la vi_ta a_mar, chi mai può, chi mai
all,— who would care, who would care to live at all,— who would care, who would
mar, chi mai, chi mai può la vita a_mar, chi mai, chi mai
all, who would who would care to live at all, who would, who would
mar, chi mai, chi può la vi_ta a_mar, chi mai, chi
all, yes, who would care to live at all, yes, who would
mar, chi mai, chi può la vi_ta a_mar, chi mai, chi
all, yes, who would care to live at all, yes, who would
sf p
può la vi_ta a_mar, chi mai può la vi_ta a_
care to live at all, who would care to— live at
può la vi_ta a_mar, chi mai può la vi_ta a_
care to live at all, who would care to— live at
può la vi_ta a_mar, chi mai può la vi_ta a_
care to live at all, who would care— to live— at
può la vi_ta a_mar, chi mai può la vi_ta a_
care to live at all, who would care to live at
può la vi_ta a_mar, chi mai può la vi_ta a_
care to live at all, who would care to live at
sfp

sf p
mar, chi mai può la vi ta a mar, chi mai
all, who would care to live at all, who would
sf p
mar, chi mai può la vi ta a mar, chi mai
all, who would care to live at all, who would
mar, chi mai può la vi ta a mar, chi mai può la
all, who would care to live at all, who would care to
mar, chi mai può la vi ta a mar, chi mai può la
all, who would care to live at all, who would care to
mar, chi mai può la vi ta a mar, chi mai può la
all, who would care to live at all, who would care to
sfp
f
può la vi ta a mar?
care to live at all?
può la vi ta a mar?
care to live at all?
vi ta a mar?
live at all?
vi ta a mar?
live at all?
vi ta a mar?
live at all?
p

Recit.

GUGL.
FERR.
Non pian_ge_re, i_dol mi_o! Non di_spe_rar_ti, a_do_ra_ta mia
Take cour- age, my be- lov- ed! My lit- tle sweet- heart, do not yield to de-
p
D. ALF.
FIORD.
spo_sa! Lascia_te lor tal sfo_go: è troppo giu_sta la ca_gion di quel pianto. Chi
spair. My friends, you must be pa- tient, do not con- sole them, let them have a good cry. Per-
DORAB. (they embrace tenderly)
FIORD.
sa, s'io più ti veggio! Chi sa, se più ri_tor_ni! La_sciami questo fer_ro: ei mi dia
haps we part for- ev- er! How can I live with- out you! Lend me your sword, I beg you, to end my
fp
DORAB.
mor_te, se mai bar_ba_ra sor_te in quel se_no a me ca_ro_ Mor_rei di
tor- ture. Since for- tune is so cru- el, on- ly death can con- sole me! I'll die of
FERR.
duol, d'uopo non ho d'ac_cia_ro. Non far_mi, a_ni_ma mi_a, quest'in_fau_sti pre_
grief, I shall not need a weap- on. For- get these om- i- nous fan- cies, and re- mem- ber, I
GUGL.
Non far_mi, a_ni_ma mi_a, quest'in_fau_sti pre_
For- get these om- i- nous fan- cies, and re- mem- ber, I
fp

Nº 7. Duettino

di - scon tur - bar. Il ci - glio se - re - no, mio be - ne, a me gi - ra, mio
bow to its reign. So wait and be pa- tient; no space can di- vide us, no
di - scon tur - bar. Il ci - glio se - re - no, mio be - ne, a me gi - ra, mio
bow to its reign. So wait and be pa- tient; no space can di- vide us, no
be - ne, a me gi - ra; fe - li - ce al tuo se - no io spe - ro tor -
space can di- vide us. We'll soon be u- nit- ed and hap- py a-
be - ne, a me gi - ra; fe - li - ce al tuo se - no io spe - ro tor -
space can di- vide us. We'll soon be u- nit- ed and hap- py a-
cresc.
colla parte
nar, fe - li - ce al tuo se - no io spe - ro tor - nar, io
gain, we'll soon be u- nit- ed and hap- py a - gain, and
nar, fe - li - ce al tuo se - no io spe - ro tor - nar, io
gain, we'll soon be u- nit- ed and hap- py a - gain, and
mfp
mfp

spe - ro tor - nar, io spe - ro tor -
hap - py a- gain, and hap - py a-
spe - ro tor - nar, io spe - ro tor -
hap - py a- gain, and hap - py a-
mfp
mfp
nar, io spe - ro tor - nar, io spe - ro tor - nar.
gain, and hap - py a- gain, and hap - py a- gain.
nar, io spe - ro tor - nar, io spe - ro tor - nar.
gain, and hap - py a- gain, and hap - py a- gain.
cresc.
f
Recit.
D. ALF.
(La co - me - dia è gra - zio - sa, e tut - ti du - e fan ben la lo - ro
(The per- form- ance is charm- ing! The way they're act- ing ex- ceeds my ex- pec-
f
FERR.
par - te.) O cie - lo! que - sto è il tam - bu - ro fu - ne - sto, che a di - vi - der mi vien dal mio te -
ta- tions!) O- heav- ens! That is the om- i- nous sig- nal which will tear me a- way from my be-
(A drum is heard.)
fp
D. ALF.
FIORD.
DORAB.
so - ro. Ec - co a - mi - ci, la bar - ca. Io man - co. Io mo - ro.
lov- ed. And the boat is ar- riv- ing. Gu- gliel- mo! Fer- ran- do!
f

No. 8. Coro

Maestoso

(Enter soldiers, village men and women. The military march is heard in the distance. A barge arrives at the landing.)

dì si cangia lo_co og_gi mol_to, do_man po_co, ora in
free of care and sor- row, here to- day and there to- mor- row, o- ver
terra ed or sul mar. Il fra_gor ditrombe e pif_fe_ri,
land and o- ver sea! We are march- ing on to vic- to- ry,
lo sparar di schioppi e bom_be forza ac_
with the flags and ban- ners fly- ing for our
cre - sce al brac - cio, e all' a_ni_ma va_ga sol di tri_on_
coun- try's hon- or, while trum- pets are sound- ing and our spir- its

far. Bel - la vi - ta mi-li - tar, bel - la vi - ta mi-li - tar!
soar. On — to glo- - ry, on to war, on — to glo- - ry, on to war!
Recit.
D. ALF.
Non v'è più tem-po, a - mi - ci, an-dar con-vie - ne, o - ve il de -
My friends, it's time you start- ed. You must be go- ing, du- ty is
f
FIORD. DORAB. FERR. GUGL.
sti - no, an-zi il do-ver v'in - vi - ta. Mio cor - I - do - lo mi - o - Mio ben - Mia
call- ing, des- ti- ny has de- cid- ed. My love! My dear be- lov- ed! My life! My
p
FIORD. D. ALF.
vi - ta - Ah per un sol mo-men - to - Del vo-stro reg-gi-men-to già è par -
trea- sure! Stay just a mo- ment long- er! The first one of the barg- es has al-
ti - ta la bar - ca, raggiun - ger - la con - vien coi pochi a - mi - ci che su
read- y de- part- ed. Hur- ry to meet the sol- diers who are wait- ing to es-

Nº 9. Quintetto

mi _ a! sii ___ co _ stan _ _ te a me
prom- ise? Swear ___ you'll al- - - ways be
se puo _ i, _
please, will you.
cer _ ta; o ca _ ra _
prom- ise, dear an- gel!
tar, mio ___ be _ ne!
my dear ___ an- gel!
ri _ do, io cre _ po se non ri _ do.
sil- ly, this real- ly is too sil- ly!
DORAB.
FERR.
sol _ Ser _ ba _ ti fi _ _ _ _ do. Ad _
true! Think of me al- - - - ways! I
FIORD.
Ad _ di _ o!
Fare- well, then!
GUGL.
DORAB.
di _ _ o! Ad _ di _ _ o! Ad _ di _ o!
prom- - - ise! I prom- - - ise! Fare- well, then!
cresc.
f

FIORD.
Mi si di - vi - - - de il
How I shall grieve and
DORAB.
Mi si di - vi - - - de il
How I shall grieve and
FERR.
Mi si di - vi - - - de il
How I shall grieve and
GUGL.
Mi si di - vi - - - de il
How I shall grieve and
p
cor, bell' i - dol mi - - - o, mi si di -
mourn when we are part- - - - ed, how I shall
cor, bell' i - dol mi - - - o, mi si di -
mourn when we are part- - - - ed, how I shall
cor, bell' i - dol mi - - - o, mi si di -
mourn when we are part- - - - ed, how I shall
cor, bell' i - dol mi - - - o, mi si di -
mourn when we are part- - - - ed, how I shall
cresc.
f

vi - - de il cor, bell' i - dol mi - - -
grieve and mourn when we are part- - - -
vi - - de il cor, bell' i - dol mi - - -
grieve and mourn when we are part- - - -
vi - - de il cor, bell' i - dol mi - - -
grieve and mourn when we are part- - - -
vi - - de il cor, bell' i - dol mi - - -
grieve and mourn when we are part- - - -
p
o! Ad - di - o, ad -
ed! I love you for-
o! Ad - di - o, ad -
ed! I love you for-
o! Ad - di - o, ad -
ed! I love you for-
o! Ad - di - o, ad -
ed! I love you for-
D. ALF.
Io cre - po se non ri - do, io cre - po se non
This real- - ly is too sil- ly, this real- - ly is too

di - o, ad - di - - - - - o!
ev- - er, for- ev- - - - - er!
di - o, ad - di - - - - - o!
ev- - er, for- ev- - - - - er!
di - o, ad - di - - - - - o!
ev- - er, for- ev- - - - - er!
di - o, ad - di - - - - - o!
ev- - er, for- ev- - - - - er!
ri - do, io cre - po se non ri - do, se non ri - do, se non ri - do.
sil- ly, this real- ly is too sil- ly, sil- ly, sil- ly, sil- ly, sil- ly!
Maestoso
(Ferrando and Guglielmo board the boat. The two women stand at the landing, motionless. The boat gradually recedes in the distance, to the sound of the drums.)
Sopr.
Alt.
Coro
Ten.
Bass
Bel - la vi - ta mi - li - tar, bel - la vi - ta mi - li - tar! O - gni
On to glo- ry, on to war, on to glo- ry, on to war! We are
Maestoso
dì si cangia lo - co, og - gi molto, do - man po - co, ora in terra ed or sul
free of care and sor- row, here to- day and there to- mor- row, o- ver land and o- ver

mar. Il fra_gor di trombe e piffe_ri, la spa_
sea! We are march- ing on to vic- to- ry with the
rardischioppi,e bombe, for_za ac_cre _ sce al
flags and ban- ners fly- ing for our coun- try's
brac _ cio, e all' a_ni_ma va_ga sol di tri_on _far. Bel _ la
hon- or, while trum- pets are sound- ing and our spir- its soar. On to
vi _ ta mi_li_tàr, bel _ la vi _ ta mi_li_tar!
glo- ry, on to war, on to glo- ry, on to war!
(Exit Chorus.)

Recit.
SCENA VI
SCENE VI
DORAB.
(as if awaking from a trance)
D. ALF.
FIORD.
Do_ve son? Son par_ti_ti. Oh di = par_ten_za cru_de_
Are they gone? They are gone. This sep- a- ra- tion is a
D. ALF.
(the waving of a handkerchief in the distance)
lis_si_ma a_ma_ra! Fa_te co_re, ca_ris_si_me fi_gliuole; guar_da_te, da lon_
ter- ri- ble blow! Be cou- ra- geous, it's not as bad as that. Look there, now; in the
FIORD.
DORAB.
ta_no vi fan cen_no con man o i ca_ri spo_si. Buon viaggio, mia vi_ta! Buon
dis- tance, on the ship you can see your sweet- hearts wav- ing. God keep you, my trea- sure! Safe
FIORD.
viaggio! Oh Dei! co_me ve_lo_ce se ne va quel_la bar_ca! già spa_ri_sce!
jour- ney! How rap- id- ly the ves- sel dis- ap- pears in the dis- tance! In one mo- ment
DORAB.
già non si ve_de più. Deh faccia il cie_lo ch'abbia pro_spe_ro corso. Fac_cia che al campo
they will be out of sight. Heav- en pro- tect them on their per- il- ous jour- ney! How I will miss my
D. ALF.
giunga con for_tu_na_ti au_spi_ci. E a voi sal_vi gli a_man_ti, e a me gli a_mi_ci.
dar- ling, a- way in for- eign lands! I will miss them no less — my two best friends.

No. 10. Terzettino

ni - gno ri - spon - da ai no - stri de -
faith- - ful- ly guide you, be- lov- - - ed so
ni - gno ri - spon - da ai no - stri de -
faith- - ful- ly guide you, be- lov- - - ed so
ni - gno ri - spon - da ai no - stri de -
faith- - ful- ly guide you, the loves they hold
sir. So - a - ve sia il ven - to, tran -
dear. May For- - tune di- rect you and
sir. So - a - ve sia il ven - to, tran
dear. May For- - tune di- rect you and
sir. So - a - ve sia il ven - to, tran -
dear. May For- - tune di- rect you and
quil - la sia l'on - da, ed o - gni e - le - mento be - ni - gno ri -
jour- ney be- side you, watch o- ver and pro- tect you, be- nign and re-
quil - la sia l'on - da, ed o - gni e - le - men - to be - nigno ri -
jour- ney be- side, you, watch o- - - ver, pro- tect you, be- nign and re-
quil - la sia l'on - da, ed o - gni e - le - mento be - nigno ri -
jour- ney be- side you, watch o- ver and pro- tect you, be- nign and re-

spon - da ai no - stri de - sir, ai
spon- - sive to love so sin- cere, to
sponda ai no - stri de - sir, ai
spon- sive to love so sin- cere, to
sponda ai no - stri de - sir, ai
spon- sive to love so sin- cere, to
no - stri de - sir, be -
love so sin- - cere, be-
no - stri de - sir, be -
love so sin- - cere, be-
no - stri de - sir, be -
love so sin- - cere, be-
cresc.
ni - gno ri - spon - - - - - - -
nign and re- spon- - - - - - - -
ni - gno ri - spon - - - - - - -
nign and re- spon- - - - - - - -
ni - gno de - sir, be - ni - gno ri - spon - da ai no - stri de -
nign, so be- nign be- nign and re- - spon- sive to love so sin-
p
f

- - - da ai no - stri de - sir, ai
- - - sive to love so sin- cere, to
- - - da ai no - stri de - sir, ai
- - - sive to love so sin- cere, to
sir ai no - stri de - sir, ai
cere, to love so sin- cere, to
no - stri de - sir, ai no - stri de -
love so sin- cere, to love so sin-
no - stri de - sir, ai no - stri de -
love so sin- cere, to love so sin-
no - stri de - sir, ai no - stri de -
love so sin- cere, to love so sin-
sir, ai no - stri de - sir!
cere, to love so sin- cere!
sir, ai no - stri de - sir!
cere, to love so sin- cere!
(Exeunt Fiordiligi and Dorabella.)
sir, ai no - stri de - sir!
cere, to love so sin- cere,
cresc.
f
p

Recit.
SCENA VII
SCENE VII
D.ALF.
Non son cat_ti_vo co_mi_co! va be_ne; al con_cer_ta_to
I have a flair for com- e- dy! My act- ing, to judge from my suc-
lo_co i due cam_pio_ni di Ci_pri_gna,e di Mar_te mi sta_ran_no at_ten_
cess, has been con- vinc- ing. But Fer- ran- do and Gu- gliel- mo, can they e- qual my per-
den_do; or senza in_du_gio, raggiun_ger_li con_vie_ne. Quan_te smor_fie, quan_te buf_fo_ne_
form- ance? I'll go and meet them to coach them for their roles. And the la- dies! Much a- do a- bout
fp
ri_e! Tan_to meglio per me, cadran più fa_cil_men_te: que_sta raz_za di gente è la più
noth- ing. That means on- ly one thing—they'll weak-en so much soon- er! They're the kind of wo- men who are
pre_sta a can_giar_si d'a_mo_re. Oh po_ve_ri_ni! per fem_mi_na gio_car cen_to zec_
quick- est to re- verse their af- fec- tion. O you poor fel- lows! You risk a hun- dred sov-'reigns on two
fp

Allegro moderato
chi_ni!" Nel ma - - - - re
wo- men! A man in
p
cresc.
sol - ca, e nell' a - re - na
dan- ger, lost in the jun- - gle's
f
p
se_mi_na, e il va_go ven_to spe_ra in re_te ac_
wil- der- ness, or in a ship- wreck, is saf- er than the
cresc.
f
p
co_glie_re chi fon - - - da
sim- ple- ton who founds his
cresc.
sue spe - ran_ze in cor di fem_mi_na.
hopes on wo- man and her fi- del- i- ty!
(Curtain)
f

Recit. SCENA VIII — SCENE VIII

(A pretty room, with several chairs, a little table, three doors: one left, one right, one in the middle. Despina alone.)

Nº 11. Recit. ed Aria

o - dio me stessa!
e- ven my- self!
p
Chi scher_ni_sce il mio duol,
Who would mock my de- spair?
chi mi con_so_la?
Who dares con- sole me?
Deh fuggi, per pie_tà,
A- way from me at once!
fuggi,
Hur- ry,
fuggi,
hur- ry!
f
Maestoso
fug_gi, per pie_tà,
far from where I am!
la_scia_mi so_la.
Leave me a- lone here!
ARIA
Allegro agitato
Sma_nie im_pla_ca_bi_li,
Come, end- less ag- o- ny,
che m'a_gi-
come and pos-
3
3
p

ta - te en - tro quest'a - ni-ma più non ces -
sess___ me, en - ter this heart of mine, burn and ob -
sa - te, fin-chè l'an - go - scia mi fa mo -
sess___ me, tor - ment and goad___ me un - til I
rir. mi fa mo - rir.
die, un - til I die.
f p f
E - sem - pio mi - se-ro
My love is trag - e- dy
p f p f p f
d'a - mor fu - ne - sto, d'a - mor fu -
with none to share it, with none to
p f p

ne - sto, da-rò all'Eu - me - ni-di se vi - va
share it. Should cru- el Des- ti- ny force me to
re - sto col suono or - ri - - - - - bi -
bear it Till Death re- leas- - - - - es
le de' miei so - spir, de' miei so -
me, I'll mourn and sigh, I'll mourn and
spir, de' miei so - spir.
sigh, I'll mourn and sigh.
cresc.
Sma - nie im-pla-ca - bi-li, che m'a-gi -
Come, hope- less mis- er- y, de- ride and

ta - te, en - tro quest' a - ni - ma più non ces
taunt me, en - ter this soul of mine, pur- sue and
sa - te, fin - chè l'an - go - scia mi fa mo -
haunt me, pierce and cor- rode me un- til I
mfp
rir, mi fa mo - rir.
die, un- til I die.
f p f
E - sem - pio mi - sero
My love is mar- tyr- dom,
p f p f p f
d'a - mor fu - ne - sto, d'a - mor fu -
a storm that rag- es, a storm that
p f p

ne - sto, da - rò all' Eu - me - ni_di se
rag- es. Should Fate pro- long my life through
mf p mfp
vi - va re - sto col suo_no or - ri - - -
count- less ag- - es, I'll grieve the years
mf p mfp
- - bi - le de' miei so - spir, da -
a- way un- til I die, should
cresc.
f p
rò all' Eu - me - ni_di, se vi - va re - sto,
Fate pro- long my life through count- less ag- - es,
cresc.
f
col suo_no or - ri - bi - le
I'll grieve the years a- way
p

de' miei so - spir, da - rò all' Eu - me - ni - di,
un- til I die. My love is mar- - tyr- dom,
cresc.
se vi - va re - sto,
a storm that rag- - es.
col suono or -
I'll grieve the
f
p
ri - bi - le, col suono or - ri - bi - le, de' miei
years a- way, I'll grieve the years a- way un- til
sf
p
so - spir, de' miei so - spir, de'
I die, un- til I die, un-
miei 'so - spir.
til I die!
(Both women collapse in their chairs, in utter despair.)

Recit.

DESP.
Signo_ra Do_ra_bel_la, Signo_ra Fiordi_li_gi, di_te_mi, che co_sa è
Dear mis- tress Do- ra- bel- la, dear mis- tress Fior- di- li- gi, tell me, what has
DORAB DESP. FIORD.
sta_to? O ter_ri_bil dis_grazia! Sbriga_te_vi in buon' o_ra. Da Na_po_li par-
hap- pened? A ter- ri- ble dis- as- ter! Please tell me all a- bout it! Our fi- an- cés left
DESP. (laughing) DORAB. DESP.
ti_ti so_no gli a_manti nostri. Non c'è altro? ri_tor_ne_ran. Chi sa! Co_me, chi
Na- ples, and we are both de- sert- ed! Oh, is that all! They will be back! Who knows? Why do you
DORAB. DESP.
sa? do_ve son i_ti? Al cam_po di bat_ta_glia. Tanto meglio per lo_ro: li ve_
say that? Where have they gone? They both have gone to war. So much the bet- ter! In that
FIORD. DESP.
dre_te tor_nar car_chi d'al_lo_ro. Ma ponno anche pe_rir. Al_lo_ra po_i tan_to
case they'll re- turn cov- ered with laur- els! But if they should die? Well, what a- bout it? All the
FIORD. (Stands up, raging.) DESP.
me_glio per voi. Sciocca, che di_ci? La pu_ra ve_ri_tà, due ne per_de_te, vi
bet- ter for you! How dare you say that? I mere- ly tell the truth! What if you lose them? There

FIORD.
DORAB.
restan tuttigli al_tri. Ah, perdendo Gu_glielmo, mi pa_re ch'io mor_re_i! Ah. Fer-
still are all the oth- ers. Ah, with- out my Gu- gliel- mo I could not go on liv- ing! Ah, if
fp
DESP.
ran_do perdendo, mi par, che vi_va a se_pel_lir_mi an_dre_i. Brave, vi
I would lose Fer- ran- do, then for me al- so death would be more than wel- come. Well spo- ken, in-
fp
par ma non è ver: an_ co_ra non vi fu donna, che d'a_mor sia morta. Per un
deed, but you are wrong. I've nev- er heard of a wo- man dy- ing out of love. To
DORAB.
uo_mo mo_rir! al_tri, ve n'hanno, che compen_sa_no il danno. E cre_di che po-
die for a man, when thou- sand oth- ers can be had for the ask- ing! You real- ly mean to
DESP.
tri_a altro uom amar, chi s'ebbe per a_mante un Gu_glielmo, un Ferrando? Han gli altri an-
tell me that there are men com- par- ing e- ven vague- ly with a Gu- gliel- mo, a Fer- ran- do? They are no
co_ra tut_to quello ch'han es_si. un uom a_des_so a_ma_te, un al_tro n'a_me-
bet- ter, nor are they worse than the oth- ers. To- day you're lov- ing one man, to- mor- row an-

re_te, u_no val l'al_tro, per_chè nessun val nul_la; ma non par_liam di
oth- er. One's worth the oth- ers, be- cause they all are worth- less! Why waste your time on
ciò, so_no ancor vi_vi, e vi_vi tor_neran; ma son lon_ta_ni, e più tos_to che in va_ni
tears? They're still a- live, and will be for some time. But they're a- way now, and rath- er than la-
FIORD.
(furiously)
DESP.
pianti per_de_re il tempo, pen_sa_te a divertirvi. Diver_tir_ci? Si_cu_ro! e quel chè
ment in sack- cloth and ash- es, for- get them and be gay! For- get them? Ex- act- ly! By far the
meglio far all'a_mor co_me as_sas_si_ne, e co_me fa_ranno al campo i vo_stri ca_ri a_
best cure for lone- ly hearts is a new ro- mance. What else do you think your sweet hearts are do- ing while they're a-
DORAB.
man_ti. Non of_fen_der co_sì quelle alme bel_le, di fedel_tà, d'in_tatto a_mo_re e_
way? You dare to of- fend those no- ble spir- its, mod- els of faith, and par- a- gons of
fp
fp
DESP.
sem_pi. Via, via, pas_sa_ro i tem_pi da spac_ciar queste fa_vo_le ai bam_bi_ni.
vir- tue? You think that men are sta- ble? That's no more than an old wo- man's fa- ble!
f
p

Nº 12. Aria

Allegretto
DESP.
In uo_mi_ni, in sol_da_ti,
Sta- bil- i- 'ty in a sol- dier
p
spe_ra_re fe_del_tà? in
and vir- tue in a man? Who
uo_mi_ni spe - ra_re fe_del_tà? in sol_da - ti spe
ev- er saw it since the world be- gan? Give me one good ex-
(laughing)
ra re fe_del - tà, fe del - tà, fe_del - tà? non vi
am- ple if you can, if you can, if you can! Who'd be-
mf
p
fa_te sen - tir per ca_ri - tà! non vi fa_te sen - tir per ca_ri-
lieve such a sen- ti- men- tal tale of the per- fect and ev- er- lov- ing

Allegretto
tà! Di pa_sta si_mi_le son tut_ti quan_ti,
male! Dealing with wo- man- kind all men are broth- ers —
son tut_ti quan_ti: le fronde mo_bi_li, l'aure in_co_stan_ti han più de_
one like the oth- ers! Don't be a feath- er- brain ev- er to trust them. E- ven a
gli uomi_ni sta_bi_li_tà. Men_ti_te la_gri_me, fal_la_ci
weath- er- vane chang- es much less. All men's du- pli- ci- ty pass- es be-
sguar_di, vo_ci in_gan_ne_vo_li, vez_zi bu_giar_di, son le pri_
liev- ing. Feign- ing sim- plic- i- ty, ly- ing, de- ceiv- ing, and when they
ma_rie lor qua_li_tà, son le pri_ma_rie lor qua_li_
fool you, O what fi- nesse! And when they fool you, O what fi-
mf
p
cresc.

tà. In noi non a_ma_no che il cor di_let - to, poi ci di -
nesse! Let him be glam- or- ous, clev- er or hand- - some, gal- lant and
spre_giano, ne_ganci af_fet - to, nè val da' bar_bari chieder pie -
am- or- ous, strong- er than Sam- - son! Do not be gul- li- ble, trust- ing his
cresc.
tà, nè val da' bar_bari chie_der pie_tà, chie - der pie -
lies! He wants to pull the wool o- ver your eyes, o- ver your
f
p
tà, chie_der pie - tà. Paghiam,o
eyes, your trust- ing eyes! Pay them in
p
fem_mi_ne, d'u_gual mo_ne_ta que_sta ma_le_fi_ca razza indi -
kind when they flirt and phil- an- der. Sauce for the goose is the same for the

scre _ ta; a _ miam per co _ mo _ do, per va _ ni _ tà, a _ miam per
gan- der! E- ven the best of them, 'neath his ve- neer, is like the
co _ mo _ do, per va _ ni _ tà, a _ miam per
rest of them, nev- er you fear! Per- ish the
tr tr tr
co _ mo _ do, per va _ ni _ tà, la ra la, la ra la, la ra la la, amiam per
thought of a man who is true, la ra la, la ra la, la ra la la, do un- to
tr
co _ mo _ do, per va _ ni _ tà, a _ miam per
them as they do un- to you! Per- ish the
tr tr tr
co _ mo _ do, per va _ ni _ tà, la ra la, la ra la, la ra la
thought of a man who is true, la ra la, la ra la, la ra la
tr tr tr tr

SCENA X SCENE X

lar_le; in_fin che van_no i due cre_du_li spo_si, com' io lo_ro com_
blame them. Mean- while, I'll go and meet my two friends. In their pres- ent dis-
mi_si, a mascherar_si, pen_siam co_sa può farsi_ temo un po' per Despina,_
guise I'm op- ti- mis- tic my strat- e- gy is fool- proof! But that ras- cal Des- pi- na!
espr.
p
quella fur_ba po_trebbe ri_co_no_scerli: po_trebbe ro_vesciar_mi le
She is clev- er — she might see through the mas- quer- ade. She e- ven might up- set the whole
mac_chi_ne, ve_dre_mo_ se mai fa_rà bi_so_gno un
ap- ple- cart. How- ev- er . . . I know just how to han- dle a
re_galetto a tempo, un ze_chi_netto per u_na came_riere è un gran scongiuro. Ma per
girl like Des- pi- na. A lit- tle mon- ey al- ways goes a long way in such a case. But to
p

es _ ser si _ cu _ ro, si po _ tri _ a met _ ter _ la in par _ te a par _ te del se _
fur- ther my pur- pose, I could e- ven ask her to be a part- ner in my
(Knocks at the door.)
cre _ to. Ec _ cellente è il pro _ get _ to _ la sua ca _ mera è questa _ De _ spi _
proj- ect. With- out los- ing a min- ute I will knock at her door. Des- pi-
espr.
p
f
fp
DESP.
D. ALF.
DESP.
D. ALF.
(entering)
net _ ta! Chi bat _ te? Oh! Ih! De _ spi _ na mi _ a, di
net- ta! Who's knock- ing? I! Oh! My dear Des- pi- na, I
DESP.
D. ALF.
te bi _ so _ gno a _ vrei. Ed io nien _ te di vo _ i. Ti vo fa _ re del
want to ask a fa- vor. I don't give an- y fa- vors! Won't you lis- ten to my
p
DESP.
ben. A u _ na fan _ ciul _ la un vec _ chio co _ me lei non può far
of- fer? To girls of my age, a man of your vin- tage of- fers ver- y

D. ALF. (Shows her a gold piece.)
DESP.
D. ALF.
nul_la. Par_la pia_no ed os - ser_va. Me lo do_na? Sì,
lit- tle. This might change your o- pin- ion. A gold piece? Yes.
DESP.
se me_co sei buo_na. E che vo_reb - be? è lo_ro il mio giu_
It's yours for the ask- ing. What are you ask- ing? For gold I might
D. ALF.
DESP.
leb_be. Ed o_ro a_vra_i; ma ci vuol fe_deltà. Non c'è al_tro? son quà.
do it. The mer- est tri- fle — your good- will and your help. Is that all? Go on!
D. ALF.
DESP.
Pren_di ed as_col_ta. Sai. che le tue pa_drone han per- du_ti gli a_manti. Lo so.
Well, then, here's my prob- lem. Doubt- less- ly you have heard what has hap- pened to your la- dies? I have.
f
fp
D. ALF.
DESP.
Tut_ti i lor pian_ti, tut_ti de_li - ri lo - ro an - cor tu sa_i. So
Then you have no- ticed that they are o- ver- come by des- per- a- tion. What a-
fp

D. ALF.
tut_to. Or ben; se mai per con_so_lar_le un po_co, e trar, co_me di_
bout it? Now, then! sup- pose, in or- der to dis- tract them, or, as the say- ing
p
ciam chio _ do per chio _ do, tu ri_tro_vas_si il mo_do, da
goes, make the best of a bad bar- gain, help me to per- suade them to
met _ ter in lor gra_zia due sog _ get _ ti di gar_bo che vor_
meet two nice young gen- tle- men with ro- man- tic in- ten- tions, who are
rie_no provar, già mi ca_pi _ sci. C'è u_na man_cia per te di ven_ti
here from a- broad. You un- der- stand me, if you make them suc- cess- ful, I shall
DESP.
scu_di, se li fai ri _ u _ scir. Non mi dis_pia _ ce questa
give you a most gen- er- ous re- ward. That sounds ap- peal- ing. It's an at-

pro_po_si_zi_o_ne. Ma con quel_le buf_fo_ne basta, u_di_te: son
tractive prop-o-si-tion. But those two sil-ly fe-males! Tell me — your vis-i-tors, these
fp
gio_va_ni? son bel_li? e sopra tut_to han_no una buo_na
for-eign-ers, are they hand-some? And, more im-por-tant, have they well-lined
D. ALF.
bor_sa i vos_tri con_cor_ren_ti? Han tut_to quel_lo che pia_cer
pock-ets — these two pro-spec-tive lov-ers? They are most el-i-gi-ble young
DESP.
può al_le don_ne di giu_di_zio. Li vuoi ve_der? E do_ve
men an-y wo-man could dream of! Is that e-nough? Where are they
D. ALF.
DESP.
son? Son lì: li posso far entrar? Di_rei di sì.
now? Right here. So may I ask them in? A good i-de-a!
(Don Alfonso opens the door and the disguised lovers step in.)

SCENA XI SCENE XI

Nº 13. Sestetto

ba - cio, per quei rai di gra - zia pie - ni, fa che volga a me se -
hon- ored at the com- pli- ment you paid me, be- ing kind e- nough to
ba - cio, per quei rai di gra - zia pie - ni, fa che volga a me se -
hon- ored at the com- pli- ment you paid me, be- ing kind e- nough to
re - ni i be - gli oc - - - chi il mio te -
aid me win the god- - dess of my
re - ni i be - gli oc - - - - chi il mio te -
aid me win the god- - - dess of my
DESP. (laughing to herself)
sor. Che sem - bian - ze! che ve - sti - ti! che fi -
soul. Good- ness, gra- cious! How lo- qua- cious! That re-
sor.
soul.

gu - re! che mu_stac_chi! Io non so, se son Val -
ga- lia! Those mus- tach- es! Did they come from Pat- a-
lac_chi? o se Tur_chi son co - stor? Val_lac_chi.
go- nia, or per- haps from Tim- buc- too? The Con- go?
D.ALF. (softly to Despina)
Turchi, Turchi, Val_lacchi? Che ti par di quell' a -
Chi- na? Tur- key? Ma- lay- a? Don't you think they have some
DESP.
spet_to? Per par_lar - vi schiet_to, schiet - to, han_no un
vir- tue? Though I do not like to hurt you, they're fan-
mu - so fuor dell' u - so, ve_ro an_ti - do_to d'a -
tas- tic, far too dras- tic, and as lov- ers, they won't
fp
fp

DESP. (laughing to herself)
mor. Che fi_gu_re, che mu_stacchi! Io non
do! Too out-land-ish, too ex-ot-ic, pos-i-
FERR. sotto voce
Or la co_sa è appien de_ci_sa,
She is fooled by our dis-guis-es!
D. ALF. sotto voce
Or la co_sa è appien de_ci_sa,
She is fooled by our dis-guis-es!
GUGL. sotto voce
Or la co_sa è appien de_ci_sa,
She is fooled by their dis-guis-es!
f p
so, se son Val_lacchi? o se Turchi son co_
live-ly Don Quix-ot-ic! I am quite sur-prised at
se co_stei non ci rav_vi_sa, non c'è
Bar-ring un-fore-seen sur-pris-es, there is
se co_stei non ci rav_vi_sa, non c'è
Bar-ring un-fore-seen sur-pris-es, there is
se costei non ci rav_vi_sa,
Bar-ring un-fore-seen sur-pris-es,

stor? io non so, se son Val_lacchi, o se Turchi son co_
you. Don Al- fon- so, just be- tween us, did you find them on the
più nessun ti_mor, non c'è più nes_sun ti_
noth- ing more to fear, there is noth- ing more to
più nessun ti_mor, non c'è più nes_sun ti_
noth- ing more to fear, there is noth- ing more to
non c'è più nessun ti_mor, non c'è più nes_sun ti_
there is noth- ing more to fear, there is noth- ing more to
cresc.
f
p
FIORD.
(from within)
stor, io non so, se son Val_lacchi, o se Tur_chi son co_stor? Ehi, De_
moon, or per- haps on Mars or Ve- nus, did they land in a bal- loon? Eh, Des-
(from within)
DORAB.
mor, non c'è più nes_sun ti_mor. Ehi, De_
fear, there is noth- ing more to fear. Eh, Des-
mor, non c'è più nes_sun ti_mor.
fear, there is noth- ing more to fear.
mor, non c'è più nes_sun ti_mor.
fear, there is noth- ing more to fear.

DESP.
D. ALF. (to Despina)
spi_na! o_là De_spi _ na! Le pa_dro_ne. Ec_co l'i -
pi- na, come here, Des- pi- na! I am com- ing! Now, you take
spi_na! o_là De_spi _ na!
pi- na, come here, Des- pi- na!
cresc.
f
p
Allegro (He retires. Enter Fiordiligi and Dorabella.)
stan_te! fa con ar_te: io qui m'a _ scondo.
o- ver, and re- mem- ber, I'll join you lat- er.
f
FIORD.
Ragaz_zac_cia tra_co_tan_te! che fai lì con si_mil
I must say this is the lim- it! You're for- get- ting your po-
DORAB.
Ragaz_zac_cia tra_co_tan_te! che fai lì con si_mil
I must say this is the lim- it! You're for- get- ting your po-
gen_te; ra_gaz_zac _ cia tra_co_tan _ te, che fai lì con si_mil
si- tion. Who has giv- en you per- mis- sion to in- dulge in sil- ly
gen_te; ra_gaz_zac _ cia tra_co_tan_ te, che fai lì con si_mil
si- tion. Who has giv- en you per- mis- sion to in- dulge in sil- ly
p

gente, con si - mil gente, con si - mil gente: falli u - sci - re imman - ti -
bab- ble with to- tal stran- gers and com- mon rab- ble? Put them out this ver- y
gente, con si - mil gente, con si - mil gente: falli u - sci - re imman - ti -
bab- ble with to- tal stran- gers and com- mon rab- ble? Put them out this ver- y
cresc.
f
nen - te, immanti - nen - te, imman - ti - nen - te, o ti so pen -
min- ute, put them out this ver- y min- ute, put the crea- tures
nen - te, immanti - nen - te, imman - ti - nen - te, o ti so pen -
min- ute, put them out this ver- y min- ute, put the crea- tures
p
tir con lor, o ti so pentir con lor, o ti so pentir con
out the door, noth- ing less and noth- ing more, noth- ing less and noth- ing
tir con lor, o ti so pentir con lor, o ti so pentir con
out the door, noth- ing less and noth- ing more, noth- ing less and noth- ing
f
p
f
p

DESP.
(All three kneel down.)
lor. Ah, ma_da_me, perdo_na_te! al bel piè lan_guir mi_
more! Ah, dear la- dies, how un- feel- ing! Here be- fore your feet are
FERR.
lor. Ah, ma_da_me, perdo_na_te! al bel piè lan_guir mi_
more! Ah, dear la- dies, how un- feel- ing! Here be- fore your feet are
GUGL.
Ah, ma_da_me, per_do_na_te! al bel piè lan_guir mi_
Ah, dear la- dies, how un- feel- ing! Here be- fore your feet are
ra_te due me_schin, di vostro mer- - - to, spa_si_
kneel- ing two poor slaves, beg- ging your mer- - - - cy, that is
ra_te due me_schin, di vo_stro mer- - - to, spa_si_
kneel- ing two poor slaves, beg- ging your mer- - - cy, that is
ra_te due me_schin, di vo_stro mer_to, spa_si_
kneel- ing two poor slaves, beg- ging your mer- - cy, that is
man_ti a_do_ra_tor, spa_si_manti a_do_ra_tor.
all we're ask- ing for, that is all we're ask- ing for.
man_ti a_do_ra_tor, spa_si_manti a_do_ra_tor.
all we're ask- ing for, that is all we're ask- ing for.
man_ti a_do_ra_tor, spa_si_manti a_do_ra_tor.
all we're ask- ing for, that is all we're ask- ing for.

FIORD.
Giu - sti nu - mi! co - sa sen - to? dell' e -
What an out- rage! What pre- ten- sions! Who would
DORAB.
Giu - sti nu - mi! co - sa sen - to? dell' e -
What an out- rage! What pre- ten- sions! Who would
nor - me tra - di - men - to, chi fu mai l'in - degno au-
force un- wished at- ten- tions on us now, a- mid our
nor - me tra - di - men - to, chi fu mai l'in - degno au-
force un- wished at- ten- tions on us now, a- mid our
cresc.
tor? chi fu, chi fu
woe? Who? Who? Who would
tor? chi fu, chi fu
woe? Who? Who? Who would
DESP.
Deh cal - ma - te, deh cal - ma - te, quel - lo sde - gno,
Dear- est la- dies, they are gen- tle, sen- ti- men- tal.
FERR.
Deh cal - ma - te, deh cal - ma - te, quel - lo sde - gno,
Dear- est la- dies, we are gen- tle, sen- ti- men- tal.
GUGL.
Deh cal - ma - te, deh cal - ma - te, quel - lo sde - gno,
Dear- est la- dies, we are gen- tle, sen- ti- men- tal.
f p
f p
f p

FIORD.
DESP.
mai l'in - de-gno autor? deh cal - ma - te, quello sde-gno.
dare de- scend so low? They are gen- tle, sen- ti- men- tal!
DORAB.
FERR.
mai l'in - de-gno autor? deh cal - ma - te, quel - lo sdegno.
dare de- scend so low? We are gen- tle, sen- ti- men- tal!
GUGL.
deh cal - ma - te, quel - lo sdegno.
We are gen- tle, sen- ti- men- tal!
Molto Allegro
FIORD.
Ah, che più non ho ri - te - gno! tut - ta
Now I'm thor- ough- ly dis- gust- ed. You are
DORAB.
Ah, che più non ho ri - te - gno! tut - ta
Now I'm thor- ough- ly dis- gust- ed. You are
Molto Allegro
f
fp
f
fp
DESP.
sotto voce
pie - na ho l'al - ma in pet - to di di - spetto e di ter - ror! Mi da un
bra- zen and re- volt- ing! Stop mo- lest- ing us and go! I've a
pie - na ho l'al - ma in pet - to di di - spetto e di ter - ror!
bra- zen and re- volt- ing! Stop mo- lest- ing us and go!
cresc.
f
p

DESP.
po_co di so_spet_to, quella rab_bia e quel fu_
cer- tain strong sus- pi- cion that their fu- ry is all for
FERR. sotto voce
Qual di_let_to è a questo pet_to, quel_la rab_bia
I am cer- tain their op- po- si- tion and their fu- ry
DALF. sotto voce
(from the doorway)
Mi da un po_co di so_spetto, quel_la rab_bia e
I've a cer- tain strong sus- pi- cion that their fu- ry
GUGL. sotto voce
Qual di_let_to è a questo pet_to, quel_la rab_bia
I am cer- tain their op- po- si- tion and their fu- ry
FIORD. sotto voce
Ah, per_don mio bel di-
Ah, dear love, the pangs I
DORAB. sotto voce
Ah, per_don mio bel di_
Ah, dear love, the pangs I
ror! Mi da un po_co di so_
show. I've a cer- tain strong sus-
e quel fu_ror!
is not for show.
quel fu_ror, mi da un po_co di so_spet_to, quel_la rabbia e quel fu_
is for show. I've a cer- tain strong sus- pi- cion that their fu- ry is for
e quel fu_ror!
is not for show.

letto, in - no - cen - te è que - sto cor.
suf- fer you will nev- er, nev- er know.
letto, in - no - cen - te è que - sto cor.
suf- fer you will nev- er, nev- er know.
spetto, mi da un po - co di so - spetto, quella rabbia e quel fu - ror,
pi- cion, I've a cer- tain strong sus- pi- cion that their fu- ry is for show.
Qual di - let - to è a questo pet - to, quella rabbia e quel fu -
I am cer- tain their op- po- si- tion and their fu- ry is sin-
ror, mi da un po - co di so - spetto, quella rabbia e quel fu - ror,
show, I've a cer- tain strong sus- pi- cion that their fu- ry is for show.
Qual di - let - to è a questo pet - to, quella rabbia e quel fu -
I am cer- tain their op- po- si- tion and their fu- ry is sin-
Tut - - ta pie - - na ho l'al - ma in
You are bra- - zen and re-
Tut - - ta pie - - na ho l'al - ma in
You are bra- - zen and re-
mi da un po - co di so -
I am sure they won't stay
ror, e quel fu - ror, qual di - letto è a que - sto
cere and not for show. I am cer- tain they are
mi da un po - co di so -
I am sure they won't stay
ror, e quel fu - ror, qual di - let - to è a que - sto
cere and not for show. I am cer- tain they are

pet_to di di _ spetto e di ter _ ror. Ah, che più non ho ri _ tegno,
volt- ing with the in- sults you pro- pose. We are thor-ough- ly dis- gust- ed.
pet_to di di _ spetto e di ter _ ror. Ah, che più non ho ri _ tegno,
volt- ing with the in- sults you pro- pose. We are thor- ough- ly dis- gust- ed.
spetto, quella rabbia e quel fu _ ror! Mi da un
faith- ful and their fu- ry is a pose. Their re-
pet _ to, quel _ la rabbia e quel fu _ ror! Qual di _
faith- ful and their fu- ry is a pose. Their re-
spet_to, quel _ la rabbia e quel fu _ ror! Mi da un
faith- ful and their fu- ry is a pose. Their re-
pet _ to, quel _ la rabbia e quel fu _ ror! Qual di _
faith- ful and their fu- ry is no pose. Their re-
fp fp f
DESP. FIORD. DESP.
po_co di so _ spetto. ah, che più non ho ri _ tegno, quella rabbia e quel fu _
sent- ment can't be trust- ed. We are thor- ough- ly dis- gust- ed. And this fu- ry is a
FERR. DORAB. FERR.
letto è a questo pet_to, ah, che più non ho ri _ tegno, quella rabbia e quel fu _
sent- ment can't be trust- ed. We are thor- ough- ly dis- gust- ed. and this fu- ry is no
po_co di so _ spetto, quella rabbia e quel fu _
sent- ment can be trust- ed. And this fu- ry is a
letto e a questo pet_to, quella rabbia e quel fu _
sent- ment can't be trust- ed, and this fu- ry is no
fp fp f

FIORD.
ror, tut_ta pienaho l'al_ma in pet_to di di_spettoe di ter_ror,
pose. I re- fuse to stay and lis- ten to the in- sults you pro- pose.
DESP.
sotto voce
DORAB.
ror, tut_ta pienaho l'al_ma in pet_to di di_spettoe di_ter_ror, mi da un
pose. I re- fuse to stay and lis- ten to the in- sults you pro- pose. I've a
ror,
pose.
ror,
pose.
p
cresc.
f
p
FIORD.
sotto voce
DORAB.
sotto voce
FIORD.
tut_ta pienaho l'al_ma in pet_to tut_ta pienaho l'al_ma in pet_to di di_
I re- fuse to stay and lis- ten, I re- fuse to stay and lis- ten to the
DESP.
po_co di so_spet_to, quel_la rab_bia
cer- tain strong sus- pi- cion that this fu- ry
FERR.
sotto voce
qual di_let_to è a que_sto pet_to, quel_la
How_ I rel- ish the op- po- si- tion that_ this
sotto voce
mi da un po_co di sospet_to, quel_la
I've a cer- tain strong sus- pi- cion that this
qual di_let_to è a que_sto pet_to, quel_la
How_ I rel- ish the op- po- si- tion that_ this

FIORD.
spetto e di ter - ror! Ah, che più non ho ri -
insults you propose. What a shame-less impo-
DORAB.
di di - spetto e di ter - ror Ah, che
to the insults you propose. What a
DESP.
e quel fu - ror, mi da un po - co di so -
is all a pose. I am nursing a sus-
rab - bia e quel fu - ror, qual di - let - to
fury so clearly shows. Their behavior
rab - bia e quel fu - ror, mi da un po - co di so -
fury is a pose. I am nursing a sus-
rab - bia e quel fu - ror, qual di - let - to
fury so clearly shows. Their behavior
f
te - gno, tut - ta piena ho l'al - ma in pet - to di di - spetto e di ter - ror!
sition! Your offensive proposition only adds to all our woes.
più non ho ri - te - gno, tut - ta piena ho l'al - ma in pet - to di di - spetto e di ter -
shameless imposition! Your offensive proposition only adds to all our
cresc.
spet - to, quel - la rab - bia e quel fu - ror,
picion they're pretending, as we suppose.
cresc.
è a questo pet - to, quel - la rab - bia e quel fu -
is an admission they are faithful as we sup-
cresc.
spet - to, quel - la rab - bia e quel fu - ror,
picion they're pretending, as we suppose.
cresc.
è a questo pet - to, quel - la rab - bia e quel fu -
is an admission they are faithful as we sup-
f

sotto voce
Ah, per_don mio bel di_let_to,
Ah, my love, the pangs I suf- fer
s. v.
ror. Ah, per_don mio bel di_let_to,
woes. Ah, my love, the pangs I suf- fer
s. v.
mi da un po_co di so_spetto, mi da un
I've a cer- tain strong sus- pi- cion, I've a
s. v.
ror, qual di_
posc. I am
sotto voce
mi da un po_co di so_spetto, quel_la rabbia e quel fu_ror, _ mi da un
I've a cer- tain strong sus- pi- cion that their fu- ry is for show, I've a
s. v.
ror, qual di_
pose. I am
p
in_no_cen_te è que_sto cor.
you will nev- er, nev- er know.
in_no_cen_te è que_sto cor.
you will nev- er, nev- er know.
po_co di so_spet_to, quella rabbia e quel fu_ror,
cer- tain strong sus- pi- cion that their fu- ry is for show.
f
let_to è a questo petto, quella rabbia e quel fu_ror, e quel fu_
cer- tain their op- po- si- tion and their fu- ry is sin- cere and not for
po_co di so_spet_to, quella rabbia e quel fu_ror,
cer- tain strong sus- pi- cion that their fu- ry is for show,
f
let_to è a questo petto, quel_la rabbia e quel fu_ror, e quel fu_
cer- tain their op- po- si- tion and their fu- ry is sin- cere and not for
f

Tut - ta pie - - na ho l'al_ma in pet_to di di -
You are bra- - - zen and re- volt- ing! Stop mo-
Tut - ta pie - - na ho l'al_ma in pet_to di di -
You are bra- - - zen and re- volt- ing! Stop mo-
mi da un po - co di so - spetto, quel_la
I am sure they won't stay faith- ful and their
ror, qual di - letto è a que_sto pet - to, quel - la
show. I am hap - py they are faith- ful and their
mi da un po - co di so - spet_to, quel_la
show. I'm sure they won't stay faith- ful and their
ror, qual di - let - to è a que - sto pet - to, quel - la
show. I am hap - py they are faith- ful and their
spetto e di ter - ror, di di - spetto e di ter - ror, di di -
lest- ing us and go, we will spite you un- til you go, we will
spetto e di ter - ror, di di - spetto e di ter - ror, di di -
lest- ing us and go, we will spite you un- til you go, we will
rabbia e quel fu - ror, quel_la rabbia e quel fu - ror, quel_la
fu- ry is a pose. They will spite you un- til you go, they will
rabbia e quel fu - ror, quel_la rabbia e quel fu - ror, quel_la
fu- ry is no pose. They will spite us un- til we go, they will
rabbia e quel fu - ror, quel_la rabbia e quel fu - ror, quel_la
fu- ry is a pose. They will spite you un- til you go, they will
rabbia e quel fu - ror, quel_la rabbia e quel fu - ror, quel_la
fu- ry is no pose. They will spite us un- til we go, they will

spetto e di ter - ror. di di _ spetto e di ter _ ror, di di _
spite you un- til you go, and the an- swer will be No, and the
spetto e di ter - ror, di di _ spetto e di ter _ ror, di di _
spite you un- til you go, and the an- swer will be No, and the
rabbia e quel fu - ror, quella rabbia e quel fu _ ror, quella
spite you un- til you go, and the an- swer will be No, and the
rabbia è quel fu - ror, quella rabbia e quel fu _ ror, quella
spite us un- til we go, and the an- swer will be No, and the
rabbia e quel fu - ror, quella rabbia e quel fu _ ror, quella
spite you un- til you go, and the an- swer will be No, and the
rabbia e quel fu - ror, quella rabbia e quel fu _ ror, quella
spite us un- til we go, and the an- swer will be No, and the
3
3
3
3
spetto e di ter _ ror, di di _ spetto e di ter _ ror.
an- swer will be No, and the an- swer will be No!
spetto e di ter _ ror, di di _ spetto e di ter _ ror.
an- swer will be No, and the an- swer will be No!
rabbia e quel fu _ ror, quella rabbia e quel fu _ ror.
an- swer will be No, and the an- swer will be No!
rabbia e quel fu _ ror, quel _ la rabbia e quel fu _ ror.
an- swer will be No, and the an- swer will be No!
rabbia e quel fu _ ror, quel _ la rabbia e quel fu _ ror.
an- swer will be No, and the an- swer will be No!
rabbia e quel fu _ ror, quel _ la rabbia e quel fu _ ror.
an- swer will be No, and the an- swer will be No!

Recit.
D. ALF. (entering)
Che su_sur_ro! che strepi_to, che scompi_glio è mai questo! sie_te pazze,
What com-mo- tion! What ex- cite- ment! And why all this con- fu- sion? My dear la- dies,
f
p
ca_re le mie ragaz_ze? vo_le_te sol_le var il vi_ci_na_to? cosa a_ve_te? ch'è
have you lost your minds? You're li- a- ble to rouse all the neigh- bors! What has hap- pened, I
fp
DORAB (furiously)
(not noticing the two men)
D. ALF.
FIORD.
na_to? Oh ciel! mi_ra_te uo_mi_ni in ca_sa nostra? Che ma_le c'è? Che
ask you? Good Lord! An out- rage! Men in a house like ours? Is that so bad? So
fp
(enraged)
Allegretto
D. ALF.
ma_le? in questo giorno? do_po il ca_so fu_nesto? Stelle! so_gno, o son
bad? It is un- heard of — on this trag- ic oc- ca- sion! Bless me! It can't be! Am I
p
de_sto? a_mi_ci mie_i, miei dol_cis_si_mi a_mi_ci! Voi qui?
dream- ing? I can't be- lieve it! My two ver- y best friends! You here?
p

co_me? perchè! quando! in qual modo! Numi! quanto ne go_do! (Secon-
Real- ly? How so? You here! Of all peo- ple! Tell me, when did you get here? (Play a-
(rapturously embracing each other)
FERR.
GUGL.
D. ALF.
da_te_mi.) A_mi_co Don Al_fonso! A_mi_co ca_ro! O, bella improvi_
long with me!) I'm o- ver- joyed to see you. My ben- e- fac- tor! What a ver- y small
DESP.
D. ALF.
sa_ta! Li co_no_sce_te voi? Se li co_ no_sco! questi so_no i più dolci a_
world! You've seen these men be- fore? Oh, have I seen them! I have known them since they were
mi_ci ch'io m'ab_bia in que_sto mon_do, e vo_stri an_cor sa_
ba- bies! I love them like a fa- ther, and you will love them
FIORD.
GUGL.
ran_ no. E in ca_sa mia che fan_no? Ai vostri pie_di due
al- so. What do they want in my house? Two hum- ble crea- tures, two
FIORD.
FERR.
rei, due de_lin_quenti, ec_co Ma_da_me! A_mor_ Nu_mi! che sen_to? A_
slaves, two wretch- ed wretch- es lie at your feet and love — Heav- ens! How dare you? And

(The women draw back, weakly, followed by the persistent lovers.)
sempre a tempo colla parte
GUGL.
mor, il nu_me, si pos_sen_te per voi, qui ci con_du_ce. Vi_sta ap_pe_na la
Love, our i- dol, leads us on- ward to you, in- to your pow- er. O- ver- come by your
FERR.
lu_ce di vostre ful_gi_dis_si_me pu_pil_le_ che al_le vi_ve fa_vil_le_
beau-ty, the dev- as- ta- ting splen- dor of your eyes — Like two flut- ter- ing but- ter- flies —
f
p
fp
GUGL.
FERR.
far_fal_let_te a_mo_ro_se e ago_niz_zan_ti_ vi vo_lia_mo da_
ir- re- sist- i- bly drawn in- to your or- bit — like two bees by two
van_ti_ per im_plo_rar pie_ta_
rose- buds — and hum- bly ask for mer-
GUGL.
ed ai la_ti ed a re_tro per im_plo_rar pie_ta_
There we hov- er, a- dor- ing, and hum- bly ask for mer-
fp
cresc.
FIORD.
DORAB.
de in fle_bil me_tro! Stel_le! che ar_dir! So_rel_la! che fac_
cy and con- so- la- tion! That is e- nough! O sis- ter, what to
de in fle_bil me_tro!
cy and con- so- la- tion!
f

Nº 14. Recitativo ed Aria

die_de
ai ca_ri a_man_ti
al- ways
to our be- lov- eds
saprem lo_ro ser_bar
in_fi_no a morte,
till the day of our death,
pure and un- fail- ing,
a di_spet_to del mondo
e del_la sor_te.
in the face of mis- for- tune
ev- er pre- vail- ing.
Aria
Andante maestoso
Co_ me scoglio
im_
Strong- ly found- ed,
a
f
p
tr
mo_ to re_sta
con_tra i ven_ti e la tem_
mar- ble tow- er,
safe- ly guard- ed from ev- 'ry

Allegro
pe_sta, e la tem_pe - - - - sta, co - sì o_gnor quest'
foe and hos- tile pow- - - - er, so my heart, for-
f
p
al - - - ma è forte nel - - la fe_de, e
ev- - - - er faith- ful, bears an ar- mor no
nell' a_mor. Con noi nac - que
force can rend. It is love, com-
quel - - la fa_ce, che ci pia - - ce, e
plete, un- fail- ing, bring- ing joy and
cresc.
ci con_so_la; e po_trà la morte
sweet- est com- fort, o- ver e- vil force pre-
f
p

so_la, la mor - - - te so_la,
vail- ing, for- ev- - - er pre- vail- ing,
far che can_gi af - fet - to il cor,
love that on- ly death can end,
far che can_gi, far che can_gi af - fet - to il cor, far che
love that on- ly, love that on- ly death can end, love that
can - gi af- fet - - - - - -
on- ly death
cresc.
- to il cor.
can end.
cresc.

Co _ me scoglio im _ mo _ to re_sta con _ tra i
Strong- ly found- ed, a mar- ble tow- er, safe- ly
venti e la _ tem _ pe_sta, co _ sì o _
guard- ed from hos- tile power, so my
gnor quest'al _ _ ma è forte nel _ la fe_de e
heart, for- ev- er faith- ful, bears an ar- mor no
nell' a _ mor, nella fe _ de e nell' a _ mor.
force can rend, bears an ar- mor no force can rend.
p
cresc.

Più Allegro
Rispet_ta_te, a_nime in_
You will nev- er win our
grate,
fa- vor.
questo e_sempio di co_
Bear the truth with res- ig-
stan_za,
e u_na bar - ba_ra spe_ran_za non vi
na- tion.
We are proof a- gainst temp- ta- tion, we are
ren_da auda - ci an_cor,
e una bar - bara spe_ran - - -
deaf when you im- plore,
we are proof a- gainst temp- ta- - - -
f
fp
p

za non vi ren da au
tion. Cast your i- dle
da ci an_cor, non vi ren da au_da ci an-
hopes a- way, cast your i- dle hopes a-
cor, non vi renda audaci an_cor, non vi
way. There is noth- ing more to say. We are
renda au_da_ci an_cor, non vi ren
deaf when you im- plore we are faith-
da au da ci an_cor, au
ful ev- er-more, for-

da - ci an - cor, au - da - ci an -
ev- er- more, for- ev- er-
fp fp cresc.
(The women start to leave: Ferrando and Guglielmo try to detain them.)
cor.
more!
f
Recit.
FERR.
GUGL. (to Dorabella)
(to Don Alfonso)
Ah, non par_ti_te! Ah, bar_ba_ra re_sta_te! (Che vi
Please do not leave us! How can you be so cru- el! (See, I
D. ALF.
pa_re?) (A_spetta_te!) Per ca_ri_tà ra_gazze, non mi fa_te più far tri_sta fi_
told you!) (Wait till lat- er!) Dear la- dies, I im- plore you, your out- bursts em- bar- rass me se-
p
DORAB. (angrily)
D. ALF.
gu_ra. E che preten_de_re_ste? Eh nul_la... ma mi pa_re che un pocchin di dol_
vere- ly. Just what are you sug- gest- ing? Quite sim- ply: there's no rea- son to be- come so of-
p

FIORD.
cezza_ al_fin son galant _uo_mini e sono a_mi_ci mie_i. Co_me! e u_ di_re do.
fen- sive. They are not on- ly gen- tle- men, but al- so friends of mine. Real- ly! And why should we
GUGL.
vrei? Le nostre pe_ne e sen _ tir_ne pie_tà! La ce _ le_ ste bel_tà degli occhi
lis- ten? Be- cause we're suf- f'ring and de- serve to be heard. The heav- en- ly ra- diance of your
vostri la piaga aprì nei nostri cui ri_me_diar può so_lo il balsa_mo d'a.
beau- ty has thrown us in- to mis- er- y for which there is no rem- e- dy ex- cept the balm of
mo_re: un so_lo i_stante il core a_prite o bella a sue dol_ci fa_cel_le, a voi da.
love. Just for one mo- ment be- stow on the fa- vor of your mer- ci- ful pit- y! You see us
van_ti spi_rar ve _ dre_te i più fe_ de_li a_man_ti.
ly- ing ab- ject- ly be- fore you. Our pas- sion is un- dy- ing!

No. 15. Aria

Andantino

noi fe_li _ cis _ si_mi fa _ re_mo anche vo_i. Guar_da_te, toc_
life that is par- a- dise, all sun- shine and glad- ness! Have pa- tience, con-
ca_te, il tut _ to osser _ va_te: siam for_ ti e ben fat _ ti, e
sid- er our qual- i- fi- ca- tions: We're strong and ath- let- ic, ro-
co_ me ognun ve_ de, sia me_ ri_to, o ca_ so ab_ biamo, bel
man- tic, po- et- - ic, we're just o- ver twen- ty, with mon- ey a-
cresc.
p
pie_de, bell' occhio, bel na_so, bell' occhio, bel na_so, guar _
plen- ty, and so sym- pa- thet- ic, good- na- tured and health- y, well-
da_ te bel piede, os_ser_ va_te bell' occhio, toc _
bal- anced and wealth- y, and be- fore you fore- go us, we

ca_te bel na_so, il tut _ to os_ser_va_te: e que _ sti mu_
want you to know us—— two mod- - els of man- hood! And then these mus-
stac _ chi chia _ ma _ re si pos _ so_no tri _ on _ fi de _ gli uomi_ni, pen_
tach- - es, so right- - ly no- tor- - i-ous, what could be more glo- ri- ous a
cresc.
p
(The women leave.)
nac _ chi d'a _ mor, tri _ on _ fi de _ gli uo_mini, pen_nac _ chi d'a _
sym- - bol of love? They make us vic- tor- - i- ous and peer- less in
cresc.
p
f
(laughing)
mor, tri _ on _ fi, pen _ nacchi, mu _ stacchi!
love! What glo- rious, vic- to- rious mus- tach- es!
p

Nº 16. Terzetto

Allegro molto

va _ no, par _ la _ te in _ va _ no.
ny it, you can't de- ny it!
va _ no, par _ la _ te in _ va _ no.
ny it, you can't de- ny it!
Se vi sen _ tis _ se_ro, se vi sco _
How in- con- sid- - er-ate! Why not co-
D. ALF.
pris _ se_ro, si guaste _ reb _ be tut_to l'af _ far, si gua_ste _
op- - er- ate, try to be pa- tient an- oth- er day, try to be
FERR.
Ah che dal ri _ de_re,
This is hil- ar- - i- ous!
GUGL.
Ah che dal ri _ de_re,
This is hil- ar- - i- ous!
reb _ be tut_to l'af _ far. Mi fa da
pa- - tient an- oth- er day. It's too pre-

l'al_ma di_ vi_ de_re, ah,
I can't be ser- i- ous! Ha,
l'al_ma di_ vi_ de_re, ah,
I can't be ser- i- ous! Ha,
ri_ de_re que_sto lor ri_ de_re,
car- i- ous. You are de- lir- i- ous!
ah, ah, ah, ah, ah, ah, ah, ah, che le
ha, ha, ha, ha, ha, ha, ha, ha! What a
ah, ah, ah, ah, ah, ah, ah, ah, che le
ha, ha, ha, ha, ha, ha, ha, ha! What a
ma_ so che in pian_ ge_re dee ter_ mi_ nar, in
There'll be a trag- e- dy, sor- ry to say. Con-
cresc.
f
p
vi_ scere sen_ to scop_ piar. Ah che dal ri_ de_re,
com- e- dy, what a dis- play! It is ri- dic- u- lous,
vi_ scere sen_ to scop_ piar. Ah che dal ri_ de_re.
com- e- dy, what a dis- play! It is ri- dic- u- lous,
pian_ ge_re dee ter_ mi_ nar. Mi fa da
trol ___ your- self. Don't be so gay! You're too me-

l'al_ma di_vi_de_re, ah, ah,
it is ri- dic- u- lous! Ha, ha,
l'al_ma di_vi_de_re, ah, ah,
it is ri- dic- u- lous! Ha, ha,
ri_de_re que_sto lor ri_de_re, ma so che in
tic- u- lous, you're too me- tic- u- lous! There'll be a
cresc.
ah, ah, ah, ah, ah, ah, ah, che le vi - scere
ha, ha, ha, ha, ha, ha, ha! What a com- - e- dy!
ah, ah, ah, ah, ah, ah, ah, che le vi - scere
ha, ha, ha, ha, ha, ha, ha! What a com- - e- dy!
pian _ ge_re dee ter mi _ nar, in pian _ gere
trag- - e- dy, sor- ry to say. Con- trol — your- self!
f
p
sen_to scop _ piar, ah, che dal ri_de_re, l'al _
What a dis- - play! This is too much for me, past
sen_to scop _ piar, ah, che dal ri_de_re, l'al _
What a dis- - play! This is too much for me, past
dee ter _ mi _ nar, mi fa da ri _ de_re
Don't be so gay. Laugh, in your in- no- cence,
p

ma di_vi_de_re, ah, che le vi_scere sen_
my ca- pac- i- ty! Of all the laughs I had this
_ma di_vi_de_re, ah, che le vi_scere sen_
my ca- pac- i- ty! Of all the laughs I had this
que_sto lor ri_de_re, ma so che in pian _ge_re
hap- py in ig- no- rance, but he who laughs the last
_to scop_piar, sen_to scop_piar,
is the best, this is the best,
_to scop_piar, sen_to scop_piar,
is the best, this is the best,
dee ter _ mi_nar, dee ter _ mi_nar,
still laughs the best, still laughs the best,
sen_to scop_piar, sen_to scoppiar.
this is the best, this is the best!
sen_to scop_piar, sen_to scoppiar.
this is the best, this is the best!
dee ter _ mi_nar, dee ter _ mi_nar.
still laughs the best, still laughs the best!
cresc.
f

Recit.
D. ALF.
Si può sa_pe_re un po_co la ca_gion di quel
May I ask in all po- lite- ness, what's so ter- ri- bly
fp
GUGL.
ri_so? Oh cospettaccio, non vi pa_re che abbiam giusta ra_gione, il mio ca_ro pa_
fun_ny? How can you ask us? I should think we have more than am- ple rea- son, most re- vered ben- e-
FERR. (jokingly)
drone? Quanto pagar vo_le_te, e a monte è la scom_messa?
fac- tor. Pay us each fif- ty sov-'reigns and ad- mit that you are beat- en!
GUGL. (jokingly)
Pa_ga_te la me_
Or pay us at least one
FERR.
tà. Pa_ga_te so_lo ven_ti quattro zec_chi_ni.
half! I'll e- ven set- tle for a mere twen- ty sov-'reigns.
D. ALF.
Po_ve_ri in_no_cen_
Poor, in- ex- per- ienced
ti_ni! ve_ni_te quà, vi voglio porre il di_ti_no in boc_ca.
chil- dren! Just wait a bit and I will make you eat your words!
GUGL.
E a_ve_te an_
You want to
co_ra co_rag_gio di fia_tar?
tell us you still will not give up?
D. ALF.
A_van_ti se_ra ci par_le_
To- mor- row morn- ing we'll talk a-

FERR.
D. ALF.
rem. Quan_do vo_le_te. In _ tan_to si_lenzio e ubbi_dien_za
gain. I'll be de- light- ed. But mean- while, our bet is still val- id
GUGL.
fi_no a do_man mat_ti_na. Sia_mo sol _ da_ti, e a_miam la di_sci_
up to to- mor- row morn- ing. We are sol- diers and gave our word of
D. ALF.
pli_na. Or be_ne: an_da_te un po_co ad at_ten_der_mien_
hon- or. All right! I'll go a- head, then, and a- wait you be-
tram_bi in giar_di_net_to, co_là vi man_de_rò gli or_di_ni
hind the lit- tle gar- den, and there you shall re- ceive my fur- ther
GUGL.
FERR.
mie_i. Ed og_gi non si man_gia? Co_sa ser_ve:
or- ders. And what a- bout our din- ner? What's the dif- f'rence?
a bat_ta_glia fi_ni_ta fia la ce_na per noi più sa_po_ri_ta.
Once the bat- tle is o- ver, it will taste that much bet- ter to the win- ner!

Nº 17. Aria

Andante cantabile
FERR.
Un' au_ra a_mo_ro_sa del nostro te_so_ro un
My love is a flow- er, all fra- grant be- fore me, to
dol_ce ri_sto_ro al cor porge_rà, un' au_ra a_mo_ro_sa del
soothe and re- store me with won- der- ful art. Its charm and its pow- er, so
no_stro te_so_ro un dol_ce ri_sto_ro al cor por_ge_rà, un
sweet and al- lur- ing and al- ways en- dur- ing, will grow in my heart, and
dol_ce ri_sto_ro al cor por_ge_rà. Al
al- ways en- dur- ing, will grow in my heart. A
f
p
cresc.
tr

cor che nu_dri_to da spe_me d'a_mo_re, da
spir- it I nour- ish with ten- der de- vo- tion, with
spe_me d'a_more, d'un e_sca mi_glio_re bi_so _ gno non ha, d'un
ten- der de- vo- tion, for- ev- er will flour- ish in glo- ry a- part, for-
e_sca mi_glio_re bi_so_gno non ha, bi_sogno non ha, bi_
ev- er will flour- ish in glo- ry a- part, in glo- ry a- part, in
cresc.
mf
p
sogno non ha. Un' au_ra a_mo_ro_sa del nostro te_so_ro un
glo- ry a- part. My love is a flow- er, all fra- grant be- fore me, to

dol_ce ri_sto_ro al cor porge_rà, un' au_ra a_mo_ro_sa del
soothe and re- store me with won- der- ful art. Its charm and its pow- er, so
no_stro te_so_ro un dol_ce ri_sto_ro al cor por_ge_rà, un
sweet and al- lur- ing and al- ways en- dur- ing, will grow in my heart, and
f
p
dol - ce ri_sto - ro al— cor porge_rà, al—
al- - ways en- dur- - ing, will— grow in my heart, will—
cresc.
f
p
cor por_ge - rà, al— cor por_ge - rà, un dol_ce ri_sto -
grow in my— heart, will— grow in my— heart, and al- ways en- dur- -
mf
p

SCENA XIII SCENE XIII

Recit.

DESP.
drone? Le po-ve-re buf-fo-ne stanno nel giardi-net-to a la-gnar-si coll'
prog- ress? Those sim- ple- mind- ed crea- tures, they're in the lit- tle gar- den, and are tell- ing the
D. ALF.
a-ria e col-le mo-scke d'a-ver per-so gli a-man-ti. E co-me
birds and the bees of the loss of their lov- ers. What's your o-
cre-di che l'af-far fi-ni-rà? vo-gliam spe-ra-re che fa-
pin- ion on just how this will end? What can we do to a-
DESP.
ran-no giu-di-zio? Io lo fa-re-i; e do-ve piangon es-se io ri-de-
chieve our ob- jec- tive? Don't you wor- ry! The more they will la- ment, the more I'll
re-i, di-spe-rar-si, strozzarsi per-chè parte un a-man-te: guar-
cheer them. All this rant- ing and rav- ing for their for- mer two lov- ers — I
da-te che paz-zi-a. Se ne pi-glia-no due, s'u-no va
call that down- right fool- ish. For each man who is gone, two more are

D. ALF.
DESP.
vi_a. Brava! questa è pru_den_za. (Bisogna impunti_gliar_la.) E legge di na_
wait- ng. Splen- did! You are a wiz- ard! (It nev- er hurts to flat- ter.) It does- n't take much
tu_ra, e non prudenza so_la: a_mor cos' è? pia_cer, co_mo_do,
wis- dom, it's fe- male in- tu- i- tion. For what is love?, It's fun, pleas- an- try,
gusto, gio_ja, di_ver_ti_mento, passatempo, al_le_gria: non è più amo_re se in_
gai- e- ty, laugh- ter, en- ter- tain- ment, mere- ly pas- time, or a whim: once it gets ser- ious, it
co_mo_do di_ven_ta, se in_ve_ce di pia_cer nuo_ce e tor_
is no long- er love. be- cause it is a bur- den and a
D. ALF.
DESP.
men_ta. Ma in_tan_to que_ste paz_ze. Quel_le paz_ze? fa_
nui- sance. Let's think a- bout our la- dies. That is sim- ple. They'll
ran_no a mo_do nostro. E buon che sap_pia_no d'esser a_ma_te da co_
do what we tell them. But do they re- al- ize how much they mean to our

D. ALF.
DESP.
lor. Lo san_no. Dun_que ri_a_me_ran_no.
friends? They do. Then let's pre- pare the ground- work. Ex-
D. ALF.
Di_glie_lo si suol di_re e las_cia fa_re il dia_vo_lo. E
pose them to temp- ta- tion and leave the rest to na- ture. And
co_me far vuoi per_chè ri_tor_ni_no or che par_ti_ti
tell me, your two in- dig- nant mis- tress- es, now that they are so
so_no, e che li sen_ta_no e ten_ta_re si la_sciano
an- gry, how will you man- age to calm them suf- fi- cient- ly,
DESP.
que_ste tue be_stio_li_ne? A me la_scia_te la bri_ga di con-
make them re- con- sid- er? Leave it to me. In such mat- ters there is
f

dur tut_ta la mac_ chi_na. Quando Des_pi_na mac_chi_na u _ na
no- one who can e- qual me. When Des- pi- na man-ag- es a ro-
f
co_sa, non può mancar d'ef _ fet_to: ho già me_na_ti mill'
mance, she does not miss a chance. I have suc- ceed- ed in
p
uo_ mi_ni pel na _ so, sa _ prò me_nar due fem _ mi_ne. Son
fool- ing a thou- sand men — I can fool two fool- ish wo- men. You
fp
D. ALF.
DESP.
ric_chi i due mon _ sieurs mu _ stac_chi? Son ricchis_ si _ mi. Do_ve
said your friends are ver- y wealth- y? Lots of mon- ey! Where
D. ALF.
DESP.
son? Sulla strada at_ ten_dan_domi stanno. I _ te, e sul fatto per la
are they? They are wait- ing to re- ceive fur- ther or- ders. Splen- did! Then I ask you to

SCENA XIV

SCENE XIV

Nº 18. Finale

sfp
FIORD.
Ah! che tut_ta in un mo_mento si cangiò la sor_te
Ah, how sad and un- re- lent- ing is the fate that I must
DORAB.
Ah! che tut_ta in un mo_mento si cangiò la sor_te
Ah, how sad and un- re- lent- ing is the fate that I must
p
mi_a, ah,che un mar pien di tor_men_to, ah,che un
suf- fer, end- less grief, cruel- ly tor- ment- ing, end- less
mi_a, ah,che un
suf- fer, end- less
mar pien di tor_men_to, è la vi_ta o_mai per me, è la
grief, cruel- ly tor- ment- ing, makes my life too hard to bear, makes my
mar pien di tor_men_to, è la vi_ta o_mai per me, è la
grief, cruel- ly tor- ment- ing, makes my life too hard to bear, makes my

vi _ ta o _ mai per me.
life too___ hard to bear.
Finchè
All was
vi _ ta omai per me.
life_______ too hard to bear.
Finchè
All was
me_co il ca_ro be _ ne
hap- pi- ness and glad- ness
mi la_sciar le ingra_te
till the mo- ment we were
me_co il ca_ro be _ ne
hap- pi- ness and glad- ness
mi la_sciar le ingra_te
till the mo- ment we were
stel_le, non sa _ pea cos' e _ ran pe _ ne, non sa _
part- ed. Not a thought of pain and sad- ness, not a
stel_le, non sa _ pea cos' e _ ran pe _ ne, non sa _
part- ed. Not a thought of pain and sad- ness, not a
mf
p

pea lan-guir cos' è, non sa-pea cos' e-ran pe-ne, non sa-
troub-le, not a care, not a thought of pain and sad-ness, life was
pea lan-guir cos' è, non sa-pea cos' e-ran pe-ne, non sa-
troub-le, not a care, not a thought of pain and sad-ness, life was
pea languir cos' è no! Ah! che tutta in un mo-
sweet and life was fair. Ah! Now the love-ly dream is
pea languir cos' è no! Ah! che tutta in un mo-
sweet and life was fair. Ah! Now the love-ly dream is
mento si can-giò la sor-te mi-a, ah, che un
end-ed and my joy de-stroyed for-ev-er. All a-
mento si can-giò la sor-te mi-a,
end-ed and my joy de-stroyed for-ev-er.

SCENA XV SCENE XV

FIORD.
gra_te. Stel-
lu- tion! Heav-
DORAB.
gra_te. Stel-
lu- tion! Heav-
D. ALF.
C'è u_na speranza an_co_ra, non fate,oh dei,non fa_te.
I beg you re- con- sid- er so grim a res- o- lu- tion!
f p f p f p f p f
FERR.
-le, che grida or_ri_bi_li! Lasciatemi, la-
-ens, that noise is hor- ri- ble! Don't hin- der me! Don't
GUGL. D. ALF. GUGL.
-le, che grida or_ri_bi_li! Lasciatemi! Aspetta_te! La-
ens, that noise is hor- ri- ble! Don't hin- der me! Not so hast- y! Don't
sfp f p f p f p f p f p f p
(Ferrando and Guglielmo enter, each carrying a little flask, followed by Don Alfonso.)
sciate_mi! L'ar_se_ni_co mi
hin- der me! With ar- sen- ic up-
D.ALF. GUGL.
sciate_mi! A_spet_ta_te! L'ar_se_ni_co mi
hin- der me! Not so hast- y! With ar- sen- ic up-
f p f f p f sf p

FIORD.
li_be_ri di tan_ta cru_del_tà. Stel_le un ve_
on our lips, we leave the world be- hind. Good- - ness, they've
DORAB.
li_be_ri di tan_ta cru_del_tà. Stel_le un ve_
on our lips, we leave the world be- hind. Good- - ness, they've
sf p
cresc.
f p
(They drink, then throw their flasks to the ground; turning, they see the two women.)
len fu quel_lo?
tak- en poi- son?
D.ALF.
len fu quel_lo? Ve_le_no buo_no e bel_lo, che ad
tak- en poi- son? The strong- est kind of poi- son, some
Il
O
DORAB.
es_si in poc_chi i_stan_ti la vi_ta to_glie_rà. Il
ar- sen- ic and hen- - bane and strych- nine all com- bined. O

tra - gi - co spet - ta - colo ge - la - re il cor mi
trag- - ic woe- ful spec- ta- cle, — it makes my blood run
p
tra - gi - co spet - ta - colo ge - la - re il cor mi
trag- - ic woe- ful spec- ta- cle, — it makes my blood run
cresc.
p
FERR.
fa! Bar_bare av_vi - ci - na_te_vi, bar_bare av_vi - ci -
cold! Heart- less, un- feel- ing wo- man- kind, our will to live is
GUGL.
fa! Bar_bare av_vi - ci - na_te_vi, bar_bare av_vi - ci -
cold! Heart- less, un- feel- ing wo- man- kind, our will to live is
f
p
f
p
nate_vi: d'un di_spera_to af - fet - to mi - rate il tristo ef - fet - to e ab -
un- der- mined. You have dis- dained our woo- ing, brought on our sad un- do- ing, we
nate_vi: d'un di_spera_to af fet_to mi - rate il tristo ef_fetto e ab -
un- der- mined. You have dis- dained our woo- ing, brought on our sad un- do- ing, we
f
p

FIORD.
bia _ te al_men pie _ tà. Il tra _ _ gi _
can- not be con- soled! I'm ter- - ri-
DORAB.
bia te al_men pie _ tà. Il tra _ _ gi _
can- not be con- soled! I'm ter- - ri-
co spet _ ta _ colo ge_la _ re il cor mi fa
fied by su- i- cide — it fright- ens me to death!
co spet _ ta _ colo ge_la _ re il cor mi fa.
fied by su- i- cide — it fright- ens me to death!
cresc.
p
FIORD.
sotto voce
Ah, che del so_le il raggio fosco per me di_
All I can see is black- ness, hor- ror has stunned my
DORAB.
sotto voce
Ah, che del so le il raggio fosco per me di_
All I can see is black- ness, hor- ror has stunned my
FERR.
sotto voce
Ah, che del so_le il raggio fosco per me di
All I can see is black- ness, hor- ror has stunned my
D. ALF.
sotto voce
Ah, che del so_le il raggio fosco per me di_
All I can see is black- ness, hor- ror has stunned my
GUGL.
sotto voce
Ah, che del so_le il raggio fosco per me di_
All I can see is black- ness, hor- ror has stunned my
p

sotto voce
venta. Tre_mo, le fi_bre e l'a_nima par che man_
feel- ing! Trem- bling and shak- ing and shiv- er-ing, gid- dy and
sotto voce
venta. Tre_mo, le fi_bre e l'a_nima par che man_
feel- ing! Trem- bling and shak- ing and shiv- er-ing, gid- dy and
sotto voce
venta. Tre_mo, le fi_bre e l'a_nima par che man_
feel- ing! Trem- bling and shak- ing and shiv- er-ing, gid- dy and
sotto voce
venta. Tre_mo, le fi_bre e l'a_nima par che man_
feel- ing! Trem- bling and shak- ing and shiv- er-ing, gid- dy and
sotto voce
venta. Tre_mo, le fi_bre e l'a_nima par che man_
feel- ing! Trem- bling and shak- ing and shiv- er-ing, gid- dy and
car si senta, nè può la lingua o il labbro ac_
faint and reel- ing, I can- not ut- ter a whis- per, I
car si senta, nè può la lingua o il labbro ac-
faint and reel- ing, I can- not ut- ter a whis- per, I
car si senta, nè può la lingua o il labbro ac_
faint and reel- ing, I can- not ut- ter a whis- per, I
car si senta, nè può la lingua o il labbro ac-
faint and reel- ing, I can- not ut- ter a whis- per, I
car si senta, nè può la lingua o il labbro ac_
faint and reel- ing, I can- not ut- ter a whis- per, I

cen_ti ar _ ti _ co _ lar, nè può la lingua o il labbro
can- not draw a breath, I can- not ut- ter a whis- per,
cen_ti ar _ ti _ co _ lar, nè può la lingua o il labbro
can- not draw a breath, I can- not ut- ter a whis- per,
cen_ti ar _ ti _ co _ lar, nè può la lingua o il labbro
can- not draw a breath, I can- not ut- ter a whis- per,
cen_ti ar _ ti _ co _ lar, nè può la lingua o il labbro
can- not draw a breath, I can- not ut- ter a whis- per,
cen_ti ar _ ti _ co _ lar, nè può la lingua o il labbro
can- not draw a breath, I can- not ut- ter a whis- per,
ac _ cen _ ti ar _ ti _ co _ lar.
I can- not draw a breath.
ac _ cen _ ti ar _ ti _ co _ lar.
I can- not draw a breath.
ac _ cen _ ti ar _ ti _ co _ lar.
I can- not draw a breath.
ac _ cen _ ti ar _ ti _ co _ lar.
I can- not draw a breath.
(Ferrando and Guglielmo fall down on the grass.)
ac _ cen _ ti ar _ ti _ co _ lar.
I can- not draw a breath.

D. ALF.
Giacchè a morir vi - ci - ni so - no quei me - schi - nel - li pie -
Fro- zen in rig- or mor- tis, see how their mus- cles tight- en! Their
tade al - me - no a quelli cer - ca - te di mo - strar.
hand- some fac- es whit - en up- on the brink of death.
FIORD.
Gen - te, gente accor - re - te, gente! Nes -
Help us, some- bod- y come and help us! We're
DORAB.
Gen - te, gente accor - re - te, gente! Nes -
Help us, some- bod - y come and help us! We're
cresc.
f
p
su - no, o dio, ci sen - te! De - spi - na! De - spi - na!
pow- er- less to save them! Des- pi- - na! Des- pi- - na!
su - no, o dio, ci sen - te! De - spi - na! De - spi - na!
pow- er- less to save them! Des- pi- - na! Des- pi- - na!
f
fp
f p
f p

DESP. (backstage)
FIORD.
Chi mi chiama?
Did you call me?
De_spi _ na! De_spi _ na!
Des- pi- - na! Des- pi- - na!
De_spi _ na! De_spi _ na!
Des- pi- - na! Des- pi- - na!
DESP. (entering)
Co_sa ve_do! morti i meschini io credo, o prossimi a spi_rar.
What has hap-pened? How did they come to lie here in such a help- less state?
D. ALF.
Ah che pur troppo è ve_ro: fu_ren_ti, di_spe _ ra_ti si
Driv- en by hope- less pas- sion, des- pon- dent, mel- an- chol- ic, they
so_no av_ve _ le _ na_ti, oh a _ mo _ re sin _ go _
swal- lowed pure car- bol- ic! All help might come too

DESP.
lar. Abbandonar i mi_se_ri sa_ria per voi vergo_gna, soc_
late. How can you see them ly- ing there, with no at- ten- tion paid them? We
FIORD.
Co_sa possiam mai far?
Tell us what you sug- gest!
DORAB.
Co_sa possiam mai far?
Tell us what you sug- gest!
DESP.
cor_rerli bi_so_gna. Soc_cor rerli bi_
all must try to aid them. We all must try to
D.ALF.
Co_sa possiam mai far?
Tell us what you sug- gest!
Co_sa possiam mai far?
Tell us what you sug- gest!
DESP.
so_gna.
aid them.
DORAB.
Co_sa possiam mai far?
Tell us what you sug- gest!
DESP.
Di vi_ta an_cor dan
There still are signs of
Co_sa possiam mai far?
Tell us what you sug- gest!

se_gno, col_le pieto_se ma_ni fate un po lor so_ste_gno.
life left. Raise their heads just slight- ly, stroke their fore-heads light- ly,
(to Don Alfonso)
E voi con me cor_re_te: un me_dico un an_ti_do_to vo_liamo a ri_cer_
Let's run and get a doc- tor. I know of one who's mar-vel-ous with peo- ple who are
tr
p
car, un me_dico un an_ti_do_to vo_liamo a ri_cer_car, vo_liamo a ri_cer_
ill. He's known for work-ing mir-a-cles with-out a knife or pill. He's fa-mous for his
cresc.
FIORD.
Dei! che ci_men_to è
What can we do, I
DORAB.
Dei! che ci_men_to è
What can we do, I
car, vo_liamo a ri_cer_car.
skill. Per- haps he'll save them still.
(Exeunt Despina and Don Alfonso.)
f
p

que_sto! Dei! che ci_men_to è
won- der! What can we do, I
que_sto! Dei! che ci_men_to è
won- der! What can we do, I
FERR. (aside)
Più bel_la co_me_dio_la
This is so ver- y fun- ny!
GUGL. (aside)
Più bel_la co_me_dio_la
This is so ver- y fun- ny!
que_sto! e_ven_to più fu_ne_sto non
won- der! We made a fa- tal blun- der and
que_sto! e_ven_to più fu_ne_sto non
won- der! We made a fa- tal blun- der and
non si po_tea tro_var, più bel_la co_me-
I'll laugh my- self to death, This is so ver- y
non si po_tea tro_var, più bel_la co_me-
I'll laugh my- self to death, This is so ver- y
f p

si po_tea tro_var, non si po_tea tro_var, no,
brought a- bout their death, and brought a- bout their death, yes,
si po_tea tro_var, non si po_tea tro_var, no,
brought a- bout their death, and brought a- bout their death, yes,
dio_la non si po_tea tro_var, non si po_tea tro-
fun- ny, I'll laugh my- self to death, I'll laugh my- self to
dio_la non si po_tea tro_var, non si po_tea tro_
fun- ny, I'll laugh my- self to death, I'll laugh my- self to
f p f p
no, no, no, non si po_tea tro_var, no,
yes, it's true, we brought a- bout their death, it's
no, no, no, non si po_tea tro_var, no,
yes, it's true, we brought a- bout their death, it's
var, non si po_tea tro_var,
death, I'll laugh my- self to death,
var, non si po_tea tro_var,
death, I'll laugh my- self to death,

no, non si po - tea tro - var!
true, we brought a - bout their death!
no, non si po - tea tro - var!
true, we brought a - bout their death!
— non si po - tea tro - var!
— I'll laugh my - self to death!
non si po_tea tro_var!
I'll laugh my- self to death!
FERR.
Ah!
Ah!
FIORD.
So_spirang l'in_fe _ li_ci!
Poor fel- lows, they are sigh- ing!
GUGL.
Ah!
Ah!
DORAB.
So_spirang l'in_fe _ li_ci!
Poor fel- lows, they are sigh- ing!
FIORD.
(standing at quite a distance from the two lovers)
Che fac _ cia_mo?
Are they suf- f'ring?
DORAB.
Tu che di _ ci?
What do you think?
FIORD.
In mo_men _ ti
Hear them moan- ing,
— si do - len - ti chi po - tria li abban _ do_nar?
— loud- ly groan- - ing! Who could dis- - re- gard such pain!

DORAB. (coming a little closer)
Che fi - gure in-ter-es - santi!
They have quite dis- tin- guished fac- es.
(also coming closer)
FIORD.
Possiam
Let's ad-
farci un po-co a-vanti.
vance a few more pac- es.
DORAB.
Ha fre- dis - si-ma la
This one's head is sim- ply
te-sta.
frig- id.
FIORD.
Fredda, fredda è anco - ra que-sta.
This one's arms are ver- y rig- id.
DORAB.
Ed il pol-so?
Is he breath- ing?
FIORD.
Io non gliel' sen-to.
He is, but rare- ly.
DORAB.
Que - sto
This one's
bat - te len - to, len - to.
pulse is beat- - ing bare- ly.
FIORD.
Ah se tar-da an-cor l'a -
Help must come this ver- y

FIORD.
i _ ta, ah se tar _ da ancor l'a _ i _ ta, spe _ me più non v'è di
min- ute! Help must come this ver- y min- ute! Their en- dur- ance reached the
DORAB.
Ah se tar _ da ancor l'a _ i _ ta, spe _ me più non v'è di
Help must come this ver- y min- ute! Their en- dur- ance reached the
cresc.
FERR.
sotto voce
vi _ ta. Più do _ me_stiche e trat _ ta_bi_li sono en _ trambe di _ ven _
lim- - it! They have lost their proud re- lent- less-ness, get- ting tam- er by the
GUGL.
sotto voce
vi _ ta. Più do _ me _ stiche e trat _
lim- - it! They have lost their pride and re-
f
p
FIORD.
sotto voce
Po _ ve _ ri _ ni, po _ ve _ ri _ ni!
Oh, so help- less, so pa- thet- ic!
DORAB.
sotto voce
Po _ ve _ ri _ ni, po _ ve _ ri _ ni!
Oh, so help- less, so pa- thet- ic!
FERR.
ta _ te: sta a ve _ der che lor pie _
min- ute. I'm a- fraid that they may
GUGL.
ta _ bi _ li so _ no en _ trambe di _ ven _ ta _ te: sta a ve _ der
lent- less-ness, get- ting tam- er by the min- ute. I'm a- fraid
p

f
sotto voce
la lor mor - te mi fa - reb - be la - gri -
If they die now, I am sure that I will
f
sotto voce
la lor mor - te mi fa - reb - be la - gri -
If they die now, I am sure that I will
ta - de va in a - more a termi - nar,
weak- en, that's a thought I can't de- ny,
che lor pie - ta - de va in a - more a termi - nar,
that they may weak- en, that's a thought I can't de- ny,
f
p
mar, si, mi fa - reb - be la - gri -
cry, yes, I am sure that I will
mar, mi fa - reb - be la - gri -
cry, I am sure that I will
va in a - mo - re a ter - mi - nar, a ter - mi -
that's a thought I can't de- ny, a dread- ful
va in a - mo - re a ter - mi - nar, a ter - mi -
that's a thought I can't de- ny, a dread- ful

SCENA XVI SCENE XVI

Allegro (Enter Despina, disguised as a doctor.)

FERR.
pel-le!
planned it!
FIORD.
Parla un linguaggio che non sap-
That may be so, but we don't un-der-
GUGL.
pel_le!
planned it!
DOR.
Parla un linguaggio che non sap_
That may be so, but we don't un-der-
DESP.
Salvete a_ma_biles bones pu_el_les.
Sal- ve ad li- bi- tum cum gra- no sa- lis.
pia_mo.
stand it.
pia_mo.
stand it.
Co_me co_man_da_no dun_que par_lia_mo, so il gre_co e
If you in- sist on it, I will trans- late it, but the ver-
fp
l'a_ra_bo, so il turco e il van_da_lo, lo sveco e il tar_ta_ro so ancor par_
nac- u- lar sounds less spec- tac- u- lar, com- plete- ly fla- vor- less, not re- cher-
fp
fp
fp
D.ALF.
lar. Tanti lin_guaggi per se con_ser_vi, per se con_ser_vi,
ché. Who cares for fla- vor? Do us a fa- vor, make a sug- ges- tion.
fp
cresc.
f

quei mi_se_ra_bi_li per o_ra os_ser_vi: preso hanno il tos_si_co; che si può
These fran- tic gen- tle- men have tak- en poi- son, they swal- lowed ar- sen- ic. What do you
FIORD.
DESP.
Si_gnor Dot_to_re che si può far? Saper bi_sognami
What are their chanc- es? What do you say? That will ne- ces- si- tate
DORAB.
far? Si_gnor Dot_to_re che si può far?
say? What are their chanc- es? What do you say?
(Despina feels their pulses, and puts her hand to their foreheads.)
pria la ca_gio_ne e quinci l'in_do_le del_la po_zio_ne; se
know- ing the his- t'ry, I must in- ves- ti- gate, stu- dy this mys- t'ry. For
cal_da, o fri_gida, se po_co, o molta, se in u_na vol_ta,
in- stance, this su- i- cide, what caused it? The po- tion, have you a no- tion

FIORD.
ov - ve - ro in più. Preso han l'ar - se - nico, si - gnor Dot-
if it was brown? They both took ar- sen- ic, a doub- le
DORAB.
Preso han l'ar - se - nico, si - gnor Dot-
They both took ar- sen- ic, a doub- le
D. ALF.
Preso han l'ar - se - nico, si - gnor Dot-
They both took ar- sen- ic, a doub- le
mf
to - re, qui den - tro il beb - bero. La cau - sa è a - mo - re ed in un
por- tion. Love caused their su- i- cide. They had a bot- tle and with a
to - re, qui den - tro il beb - bero. La cau - sa è a - mo - re ed in un
por- tion. Love caused their su- i- cide. They had a bot- tle and with a
to - re, qui den - tro il beb - bero. La cau - sa è a - mo - re ed in un
por- tion. Love caused their su- i- cide. They had a bot- tle and with a
p mf p mf p
DESP.
sor - so sel mandar giù. Non vi affan - na - te, non vi tur - ba - te, non vi tur-
swal- low they gulped it down. I am de- light- ed, I am de- light- ed! Don't get ex-
sor - so sel mandar giù.
swal- low they gulped it down.
sor - so sel mandar giù.
swal- low they gulped it down.

ba - te, non vi affan - na - te, non vi affan - na - te, non vi tur - ba - te,
cit- ed, don't get ex- cit- ed! I'll make them well a-gain, as good as new.
FIORD.
ecco una pro - va di mia vir - tù
Just let me show you what I can do.
Egli ha di un
He is pro-
DORAB.
Egli ha di un
He is pro-
D. ALF.
Egli ha di un
He is pro-
ferro la man for - ni - ta.
duc- ing a gi- ant mag- net!
ferro la man for - ni - ta.
duc- ing a gi- ant mag- net!
ferro la man for - ni - ta.
duc- ing a gi- ant mag- net!
cresc.
f

(Touches the foreheads of the two imaginary invalids with the magnet, then gently strokes the whole length of their bodies.)

cra _ nio presto per_cuo _ to _ no.
vul- sions are real- ly des- per- ate!
DESP.
cra _ nio presto per_cuo _ to _ no. Ah lor la fron_te te _ ne _ te
vul- sions are real- ly des- per- ate! Help me sup- port them. They still are
cra _ nio presto per_cuo _ to _ no.
vul- sions are real- ly des- per- ate!
f
p
cresc.
p
FIORD.
(The two women put their hands to the foreheads of the two lovers.)
Ec_co_ci pron _ te, ec_co_ci pron_te.
We'll do it glad- - ly, we'll do it glad- - ly.
DORAB.
DESP.
sù. Ec_co_ci pron _ te, ec_co_ci pron_te. Te_ne_te for_te,
weak. We'll do it glad- - ly, we'll do it glad- - ly. You're do- ing nice- ly,
cresc.
f p
cresc.
te_ne_te for _ te, for _ te, for _ te, cor_
you're do- ing nice- ly. That's it, that's it pre-
p
cresc.
p
cresc.
rag _ gio! or li _ be_ri sie _ te ___ da morte.
cise- - ly! They soon ___ will be ful- - ly ___ re- cov- ered.
f
p

FIORD.
At_tor_no guar_da_no: for_ze ri_pren_do_no: ah que_sto
DORAB. See them re- vive a- gain, ful- ly a- live a- gain, thanks to the
At_tor_no guar_da_no: for_ze ri_pren_do_no: ah que_sto
See them re- vive a- gain, ful- ly a- live a- gain, thanks to the
D. ALF.
At_tor_no guar_da_no: for_ze ri_pren_do_no: ah que_sto
See them re- vive a- gain, ful- ly a- live a- gain, thanks to the
me_di_co va_le un Pe_rù, ah que_sto me_di_co va_le un Pe_
doc- tor's a- maz- ing tech- nique, thanks to the doc- tor's a- maz- ing tech-
rù.
nique.
Andante
(slowly raising themselves)
FERR.
Do_ve
Am I
GUGL.
Do_ve
Am I
fp

son!
che lo_co è questo?
dead?
Or am I dream-ing?
son!
che lo_co è questo?
dead?
Or am I dream-ing?
f p
Chi è co_lui? co_lor chi so_no? son di Giove innanzi al
Is this E- den or Val- hal- la? Or the gar- den realm of
Chi è co_lui? co_lor chi so_no? son di Giove innanzi al
Is this E- den or Val- hal- la? Or the gar- den realm of
trono? sei tu Pal_la, o Ci_te_re_a?
Al- lah? Are you Ve- nus? Or Cle- o- pat- ra?
trono? sei tu Pal_la, o Ci_te _ re_a?
Al- lah? Are you Ve- nus? Or Cle- o- pat- ra?
cresc.

(to Fiordiligi)
No, tu sei l'alma mia de_a; ti rav_vi_so al dol_ce
No, you are my dear be- lov- ed! E- ven death can't come be-
(to Dorabella)
No, tu sei l'alma mia de_a; ti rav_vi_so al dol_ce
No, you are my dear be- lov- ed! E- ven death can't come be-
f p
(They embrace the women tenderly and kiss their hands.)
vi_so: e al_la man ch'or ben co_no_sco e che
tween us. Here's the hand I love so dear- ly and would
vi_so: e al_la man ch'or ben co_no_sco e che
tween us. Here's the hand I love so dear- ly and would
DESP.
so_la è il mio te_sor. Son ef_fet_ti ancor del to_sco, non ab_bia_te al_cun ti_
kiss with all re- spect. If they talk a lit- tle queer- ly, it's the mag- net's strong ef-
D. ALF.
so_la è il mio te_sor. Son ef_fet_ti ancor del to_sco, non ab_bia_te al_cun ti_
kiss with all re- spect. If they talk a lit- tle queer- ly, it's the mag- net's strong ef-

FIORD.
Sa - rà ver, ma tan - te smorfie fan - no torto al nostro o -
That may be, but such ef- fu- sions mar the hon- or of my
DORAB.
mor. Sa - rà ver, ma tan - te smor-fie fan - no torto al nostro o -
fect. That may be, but such ef- fu- sions mar the hon- or of my
mor.
fect.
FIORD.
nor, sa - rà ver, ma tan - te
name. Make them see that these de-
DORAB.
nor, sa - rà ver, ma tan - te
name. Make them see that these de-
DESP.
Son ef - fet - ti an - cor del to - sco,
Please for- give them for their ef- fu- - sions,
FERR. (to himself)
(Dal - la voglia ch'ho di ri - de - re il pol - mon mi scoppia or -
Though it's real- ly too ri- dic- u- lous, I en- joy it just the
D.ALF.
Son ef - fet - ti an - cor del to - sco,
Please for- give them for their ef- fu- - sions,
GUGL. (to himself)
(Dal - la voglia ch'ho di ri - de - re il pol - mon mi scoppia or -
Though it's real- ly too ri- dic- u- lous, I en- joy it just the

smor_fie fan_no tor_to al no_stro o_nor.
lu- sions are a scan- dal and a shame.
smor_fie fan_no tor_to al no_stro o_nor.
lu- sions are a scan- dal and a shame.
non ab_bia_te alcun ti_mor, non ab_bia_te al_cun ti_mor.
their con- di- tion is to blame, their con- di- tion is to blame.
or, dalla vogliach'ho di ri_de_re il pol_mon mi scoppia or_or.)
same, though it's real- ly too ri- dic- u- lous, I en- joy it just the same.
non ab_bia_te alcun ti_mor, non ab_bia_te al_cun ti mor.
their con- di- tion is to blame, their con- di- tion is to blame.
or, dalla vogliach'ho di ri_de_re il pol_mon mi scoppia or_or.)
same, though it's real- ly too ri- dic- u- lous, I en- joy it just the same.
cresc.
FIORD.
Più re_si_ster non poss'
Who could hear with- out e-
DORAB.
Più re_si_ster non poss'
Who could hear with- out e-
FERR. (to Fiordiligi)
Per pie_tà, bell'i_dol mi_o!
Take my heart and my de- vo- tion!
GUGL.
(to Dorabella)
Per pie_tà, bell'i_dol mi_o!
Take my heart and my de- vo- tion!
f p

i _ o,
mo- tion?
DESP.
i _ o,
mo- tion?
Son ef _ fet _ ti ancor del tosco.
Please for- give them their ef- fu- sions!
vol _ gi a me le lu _ ci lie _ te.
Do not spurn my burn- ing ar- - dor!
D. ALF.
Son ef _ fet _ ti ancor del tosco.
Please for- give them their ef- fu- sions!
vol _ gi a me le lu _ ci lie _ te.
Do not spurn my burn- ing ar- - dor!
FIORD.
più re _ si _ ster non poss' i _ o,
Who could hear with- out e- mo- tion?
DORAB.
più re _ si _ ster non poss' i _ o,
Who could hear with- out e- mo- tion?
DESP.
In poch' o _ re lo ve _ dre _ te per vir _ tù del mag _ ne _
We are cer- tain they'll re- cov- er. On- ly wait a lit- tle
D. ALF.
In poch' o _ re lo ve _ dre _ te per vir _ tù del mag _ ne _
We are cer- tain they'll re- cov- er. On- ly wait a lit- tle

tis_mo fi _ ni _ re quel pa _ ros _ sis_mo, tor _ ne _ ran_no al pri_mo u _
long- er, till they feel a tri- fle strong- er. It is too much to ex-
tis_mo fi _ ni _ re quel pa _ ros _ sis_mo, tor _ ne _ ran_no al pri_mo u _
long- er, till they feel a tri- fle strong- er. It is too much to ex-
FERR. (aside)
FIORD.
mor. (Dal _ la vo _ glia ch'ho di ri_de_re più re _ si _ ster non poss'
pect. Though it's real- ly too ri- dic- u- lous! Who could hear with- out e-
GUGL. (aside)
DORAB.
mor. (Dal _ la vo _ glia ch'ho di ri_de_re più re _ si _ ster non poss'
pect. Though it's real- ly too ri- dic- u- lous! Who could hear with- out e-
FERR.
DESP.
i _ o! il pol_mon mi scop _ pia or_ or.) Son ef _ fet _ ti an_cor del
mo- tion? I en- joy it just the same. Please for- give them their ef-
GUGL.
D. ALF.
i _ o! il pol_mon mi scop _ pia or_ or.) Son ef _ fet _ ti an_cor del
mo- tion? I en- joy it just the same. Please for- give them their ef-

DESP.
tos_co, non ab_bia_te al_cun ti_mor,
fu- sions, it's the mag- net's strong ef- fect.
FERR. (to Fiordiligi)
Ah tu sei l'al_ma mia de_ a; ti rav-
Yes, you are my dear be- lov- ed! Take my
D. ALF.
tos_co, non ab_bia_te al_cun ti_mor,
fu- sions, it's the mag- net's strong ef- fect.
GUGL. (to Dorabella)
Ah tu sei l'al_ma mia de_ a; ti rav-
Yes, you are my dear be- lov- ed! Take my
FIORD.
più re_si_ster non poss' i_ o. Sa_ rà
Who could hear with- out e- mo- tion? Make them
DORAB.
più re_si_ster non poss' i_ o. Sa_ rà
Who could hear with- out e- mo- tion? Make them
DESP.
son ef_fet_ti
Please for- give them
FERR.
vi_so al dol_ce vi_ so. (Dal_la voglia ch'ho di
heart and my de- vo- tion. Though it's real- ly too ri-
(aside)
D. ALF.
son ef_fet_ti
Please for- give them
GUGL.
vi_so al dol_ce vi_ so. (Dal_la voglia ch'ho di
heart and my de- vo- tion. Though it's real- ly too ri-
(aside)

ver, ma tan - te smor - fie fan - no
see that such ef - fu - sions mar the
ver, ma tan - te smor - fie fan - no
see that such ef - fu - sions mar the
an - cor del to - sco, non ab.bia - te alcun ti -
for their ef - fu - sions, their con - di - tion is to
ri - de - re il pol - mon mi scoppia or - or, dal - la vo - glia ch'ho di
dic - u - lous, I en - joy it just the same, though it's real - ly too ri -
an - cor del to - sco, non ab - bia - te alcun ti -
for their ef - fu - sions, their con - di - tion is to
ri - de - re il pol - mon mi scoppia or - or, dal - la vo - glia ch'ho di
dic - u - lous, I en - joy it just the same, though it's real - ly too ri -
tor - to il no - stro o - nor, al no - stro o -
hon - or of my name, of my good
tor - to il no - stro o - nor, al no - stro o -
hon - or of my name, of my good
mor, non ab - bia - te al - cun ti - mor, non ab - bia - te alcun ti -
blame, their con - di - tion is to blame, their con - di - tion is to
ri - de - re il pol - mon mi scoppia or - or, dal - la vo - glia ch'ho di
dic - u - lous, I en - joy it just the same, though it's real - ly too ri -
mor, non ab - bia - te al - cun ti - mor, non ab - bia - te alcun ti -
blame, their con - di - tion is to blame, their con - di - tion is to
ri - de - re il pol - mon mi scoppia or - or, dal - la vo - glia ch'ho di
dic - u - lous, I en - joy it just the same, though it's real - ly too ri -

nor, al no - stro o - nor.
name, of my good name.
nor, al no - stro o - nor.
name, of my good name.
mor, non ab - bia - te alcun ti - mor.
blame, their con- di- tion is to blame.
ri - de - re, il pol - mon mi scoppia or - or.)
dic- u- lous, I en- joy it just the same.
mor, non ab - bia - te alcun ti - mor.
blame, their con- di- tion is to blame.
ri - de - re, il pol - mon mi scoppia or - or.)
dic- u- lous, I en- joy it just the same.
Allegro
p
FERR.
Dam - mi un ba - cio, o mio te - so - ro,
Kiss me, dar- - ling, I im- - plore you,
GUGL.
Dam - mi un ba - cio, o mio te - so - ro,
Kiss me, dar- - ling, I im- - plore you,

un sol ba - cio, o qui mi mo ro!
or I'll die right here be- fore you!
un sol ba - cio, o qui mi mo - ro!
or I'll die right here be- fore you!
FIORD.
DESP.
Stelle, un ba_cio? Se_con_da_te per ef_
Kiss you? Good heav- ens! Bet- ter do it out of
DORAB.
D. ALF.
Stelle, un ba_cio? Se_con_da_te per ef_
Kiss you? Good heav- ens! Bet- ter do it out of
FIORD.
Ah, che trop_po si ri_chie_de da u_na
What a shame- less im- po- si- tion on good
DORAB.
Ah, che trop_po si ri_chie_de da u_na
What a shame- less im- po- si- tion on good
DESP.
fet _ to di bon_ta_te.
kind- ness! Noth- ing to it.
D. ALF.
fet_to di bon_ta_te.
kind- ness! Noth- ing to it.
fp
fp

fi - da o - ne - sta a - man - te ol - trag - gia - ta è la mia fe - de, ol - trag-
faith and true de- vo- - tion, forc- ing us to give per- mis- sion for an
fi - da o - ne - sta a - man - te ol - trag - gia - ta è la mia fe - de, ol - trag-
faith and true de- vo- - tion, forc- ing us to give per- mis- sion for an
fp
fp
gia - to è que - sto cor, ol - trag - gia - to è que - sto cor.
out- rage we ab- hor, for an out- rage we ab- hor!
gia - to è que - sto cor, ol - trag - gia - to è que - sto cor.
out- rage we ab- hor, for an out- rage we ab- hor!
sf
p
fp
fp
fp
fp
f
DESP.
sotto voce
Un qua - dret - to più gio - con - do
Since the dawn- ing of Cre- - a- tion
FERR.
sotto voce
Un qua - dret - to più gio - con - do
Since the dawn- ing of Cre- - a- tion
D. ALF.
sotto voce
Un qua - dret - to più gio - con - do
Since the dawn- ing of Cre- - a- tion
GUGL.
sotto voce
Un qua - dret - to più gio - con - do
Since the dawn- ing of Cre- - a- tion
sf
p
sf
p
p

non si vi - de in tut - to il mondo,
was there ev- er a like flir- - ta- tion!
non si vi - de in tut - to il mondo,
was there ev- er a like flir- - ta- tion!
non si vi - de in tut - to il mondo,
was there ev- er a like flir- - ta- tion!
non si vi - de in tut - to il mondo,
was there ev- er a like flir- - ta- tion!
quel che più mi fu da ri - - de - re è quell' i - ra e
This has been the gay- est com- - e- dy I have ev- - er
ma non so se finta o ve - ra sia quell' i - ra e
This has been the gay- est frol- - ic I have ev- - er
quel che più mi fu da ri - - de - re è quell' i - ra e
This has been the gay- est com- - e- dy I have ev- - er
ma non so se finta o ve - ra sia quell' i - ra e
This has been the gay- est frol- - ic I have ev- - er

FIORD.
quel fu_ror. Dispe_ra_ti, attos_si_ca_ti i_te al diavol quan_ti
seen be- fore. Go a- way, you wick- ed mad- men, with your kiss- es and em-
DORAB.
quel fu_ror. Dispe_ra_ti, attos_si_ca_ti i_te al diavol quan_ti
seen be- fore. Go a- way, you wick- ed mad- men, with your kiss- es and em-
quel fu_ror.
seen be- fore.
quel fu_ror.
seen be- fore.
f p f p
sie_te; tar_di in ver vi pen_ti_re_te
brac- es! Shame- less, e- vil- mind- ed bad- men,
sie_te; tar_di in ver vi pen_ti_re_te
brac- es! Shame- less, e- vil- mind- ed bad- men.
cresc. f p
se più cre_sce, se più cre_sce il mio fu_
nev- er dare to show your fac- es an- y-
se più cre_sce, se più cre_sce il mio fu_
nev- er dare to show your fac- es an- y-
f p f p f cresc.

FIORD.
ror.
more!
Di_spe_ra_ti, at_tos_si_ca_ti i_te al
Go a- way, you wick- ed mad- men, with your
DORAB.
ror.
more!
Di_ _spe_ra_ti, at_
You are wick- ed and
DESP. sotto voce
Un qua_dretto più gio_con_do non si vi_de in tut_to il mon_do, quel che
Since the dawn- ing of Cre- a- tion, has there been a like flir- ta- tion? This has
FERR. sotto voce
Un qua_dretto più gio_con_do non s'è vi_sto in que_sto mon_do, ma non
Since the dawn- ing of Cre- a- tion, has there been a like flir- ta- tion? This has
D. ALF. sotto voce
Un qua_dretto più gio_con_do non si vi_de in tut_to il mon_do, quel che
Since the dawn- ing of Cre- a- tion, has there been a like flir- ta- tion? This has
GUGL. sotto voce
Un qua_dretto più gio_con_do non s'è vi_sto in que_sto mon_do, ma non
Since the dawn- ing of Cre- a- tion, has there been a like flir- ta- tion? This has
f p
dia_vol quanti sie_te: tar_di in_ver vi pen_ti_re_te se più cre_sce il mio fu_
kiss- es and em- brac- es! Nev- er dare to show your fac- es! Don't come back here an- y
tos_ _si_ca_ti: tar_ di in_ver vi pen_ _ti_
poi- -soned mad-men! Nev- - er you dare to show— your
più mi fa da ri_dere, da ri_dere, da ri_dere, è quell'
been the gay- est frol- - ic, the gay- - est, the gay- est that has
so se finta o ve_ra, se fin_ta o ve_ra, sia quell'
been the gay- est frol- ic, the gay- est, the gay- est, that has
più mi fa da ri_dere, da ri_dere, da ri_dere, è quell'
been the gay- est frol- - ic, the gay- - est, the gay- est that has
so se finta o ve_ra, se fin_ta o ve_ra, sia quell'
been the gay- est frol- ic, the gay- est, the gay- est that has

ror, il mio fu - ror.
more! There is the door.
re - te se più cre - sce il mio fu - ror, il mio fu - ror.
fac - - es! Don't come back here an - y more! There is the door
i - ra e quel fu - ror, e quel fu - ror.
ev - er been played be - fore, been played be - fore!
i - ra e quel fu - ror, e quel fu - ror. Dam - mi un
ev - er been played be - fore, been played be - fore! Kiss me
i - ra e quel fu - ror, e quel fu - ror.
ev - er been played be - fore, been played be - fore!
i - ra e quel fu - ror, e quel fu - ror. Dam - mi un
ev - er been played be - fore, been played be - fore! Kiss me
fp
FIORD.
Di - spe - ra - ti, at - tos - si - ca - ti i - te al diavol quan - ti
Go a - way, you wick - ed mad - men, with your kiss - es and em -
DORAB.
Di - spe - ra - ti, at - tos - si - ca - ti i - te al diavol quan - ti
Go a - way, you wick - ed mad - men, with your kiss - es and em -
FERR.
bacio, o mio te - so - ro,
dar - ling, I im - plore you,
GUGL.
bacio, o mio te - so - ro,
dar - ling, I im - plore you,
f

sie_te; tar_di in_ver vi pen_ti_
brac- es, we don't want to see your
sie_te; tar_di in_ver vi pen_ti_
brac- es, we don't want to see your
un sol ba_cio, o qui mi mo_ro!
or I'll die right here be- fore you!
un sol ba_cio, o qui mi mo_ro!
or I'll die right here be- fore you!
fp
f
re_te se più cresce il mio fu_ror. Stelle, un
fac- es for a sin- gle min- ute more! Nev- er! How
re_te se più cresce il mio fu_ror. Stelle, un
fac- es for a sin- gle min- ute more! Nev- er! How
un sol ba_cio!
Dar- ling, kiss me!
un sol ba_cio!
Dar- ling, kiss me!

FIORD.
DESP.
ba_cio? Se _ con _ da _ te per ef _ fet _ to di bon _
dare you? Bet- ter do it out of kind- ness! Noth- ing
DORAB.
D. ALF.
ba_cio? Se _ con _ da_te per ef _ fet_to di bon _
dare you? Bet- ter do it out of kind- ness! Noth- ing
p
FIORD.
Ah, che trop_po si ri _ chie _ de da u _ na fi _ da o _ ne_sta a_
Ah, how dare you stand and face us, af- - ter such a bold pro-
DORAB.
Ah, che trop_po si ri _ chie _ de da u _ na fi _ da o _ ne_sta a_
Ah, how dare you stand and face us, af- - ter such a bold pro-
DESP.
ta _ te, se _ con _ da _ te, se _ con_
to it. Bet- - ter do it out of
FERR.
(to himself)
(Dal _ la vo _ glia
This is real- - ly
D. ALF.
ta _ te, se _ con_da _ te, se _ con_
to it. Bet- - ter do it out of
GUGL.
(to himself)
(Dal _ la vo _ glia
This is real- - ly
fp
fp

man - te ol - trag - gia - ta è la mia fe - de, ol - trag - gia - to è que - sto
po - sal? Are you try - ing to dis - grace us? Nev - er dare to show your
man - te ol - trag - gia - ta è la mia fe - de, ol - trag - gia - to è que - sto
po - sal? Are you try - ing to dis - grace us? Nev - er dare to show your
da - te, se - con - da - te per ef - fet - to di bon -
kind - ness, bet - ter do it out of kind - ness, bet - ter
ch'ho di ri - de - re il pol - mon mi scop - pia or -
so ri - dic - u - lous, I en - joy it all the
da - te per ef - fet - to di bon -
kind - ness, bet - ter do it bet - ter
ch'ho di ri - de - re il pol - mon mi scop - pia or -
so ri - dic - u - lous, I en - joy it all the
fp
fp
cor, ol - trag - gia - to è que - sto cor.
face! Don't come back here an - y more!
cor, ol - trag - gia - to è que - sto cor.
face! Don't come back here an - y more!
sotto voce
ta - te.
do it!
Un qua -
Since the
or, mi scop - pia or - or.)
more, yes, all the more!
sotto voce
Un qua -
Since the
sotto voce
ta - te.
do it!
Un qua -
Since the
sotto voce
or, mi scop - pia or - or.)
more, yes, all the more!
Un qua -
Since the
fp fp fp fp
sf p
f
p

Di_spe_ra_ti, at_tos_si _ ca _ ti i_te al dia_vol quan_ti
Go a- way, you wick- ed mad- men, with your kiss- es and em-
Di_spe_ra_ti, at_tos_si _ ca _ ti i_te al dia_vol quan_ti
Go a- way, you wick- ed mad- men, with your kiss- es and em-
dret _ to più gio _ con_do
dawn- ing of Cre- - a- tion
dret _ to più gio _ con_do
dawn- ing of Cre- - a- tion
dret _ to più gio _ con_do
dawn- ing of Cre- - a- tion
dret _ to più gio _ con_do
dawn- ing of Cre- - a- tion
sf p sf p
sie _ te, i_te al dia_vol quan_ti sie _ te,
brac- es! You are e- vil- mind- ed bad- men!
sie _ te, i_te al dia_vol quan_ti sie _ te,
brac- es! You are e- vil- mind- ed bad- men!
non si vi_de in tut _ to il
was there ev- er a like flir-
non s'è vi_sto in que _ sto
was there ev- er a like flir-
non si vi_de in tut _ to il
was there ev- er a like flir-
non s'è vi_sto in que _ sto
was there ev- er a like flir-
sf p

di_spe_ra_ti, at_tos - si - ca_ti, tar_di in_ver vi pen_ti -
You are try- ing to dis- grace us! We don't want to see your
di_spe_ra_ti, at_tos - si - ca_ti, tar_di in_ver vi pen_ti -
You are try- ing to dis- grace us! We don't want to see your
mondo, quel che più mi fa da ri - de-
ta- tion? This has been the gay- est com- e-
mondo, ma non so se fin_ta o ve - ra
ta- tion? This has been the gay- est frol- ic
mondo, quel che più mi fa da ri - de-
ta- tion? This has been the gay- est com- e-
mondo, ma non so se fin_ta o ve - ra
ta- tion? This has been the gay- est frol- ic
re_te se più cre - sce il mio fu - ror. Di_spe-
fac- es ev- er dark- en- ing our door! Go a-
re_te se più cre - sce il mio fu - ror. Di_spe-
fac- es ev- er dark- en- ing our door! Go a-
re è quell' i - ra e quel fu - ror.
dy I have ev- er seen be- fore.
sia quell' i - ra e quel fu - ror.
I have ev- er seen be- fore.
re è quell' i - ra e quel fu - ror.
dy I have ev- er seen be- fore.
sia quell' i - ra e quel fu - ror.
I have ev- er seen be- fore.

FIORD.
ra_ti, at_tos _ si _ ca _ ti i_te al dia_vol quan_ti sie_te;
way, you wick- ed mad- men, with your kiss- es and em- brac- es!
DORAB.
ra_ti, at_tos _ si _ ca _ ti i_te al dia_vol quan_ti sie_te;
way, you wick- ed mad- men, with your kiss- es and em- brac- es!
p
f
p
cresc.
tar_di in_ver vi pen_ti _ re _ te se più
Shame- less, e- vil- mind- ed bad- men, nev- er
tar_di in_ver vi pen_ti _ re _ te se più
Shame- less, e- vil- mind- ed bad- men, nev- er
f
p
f
cre _ sce, se più cre _ sce il mio fu _
dare to show your fac- es an- y
cre _ sce, se più cre _ sce il mio fu _
dare to show your fac- es an- y
p
f
p
f
p
cresc.

FIORD.
ror. Di_spe_ra_ti, at_tos_si_ca_ti i_te al
more! Go a- way, you wick- ed mad- men, with your
DORAB.
ror. Di - spe_ra_ti, at-
more! You are wick- ed and
DESP. sotto voce
Un quadret_to più gio_con_do non si vi_de in tut_to il mon_do, quel che
Since the dawn-ing of Cre- a- tion has there been a like flir- ta- tion? This has
FERR. sotto voce
Un quadret_to più gio_con_do non s'è vi_sto in que_sto mon_do, ma non
Since the dawn-ing of Cre- a- tion has there been a like flir- ta- tion? This has
DALF. sotto voce
Un quadret_to più gio_con_do non si vi_de in tut_to il mon_do, quel che
Since the dawn-ing of Cre- a- tion has there been a like flir- ta- tion? This has
GUGL. sotto voce
Un quadret_to più gio_con_do non s'è vi_sto in que_sto mon_do, ma non
Since the dawn-ing of Cre- a- tion has there been a like flir- ta- tion? This has
p
di_vol quan_ti sie_te; tar_di in_ver vi pen_ti_re_te se più cre_sce il mio fu_
kiss- es and em- brac- es! Nev- er dare to show your fac- es! Don't come back here an- y
tos - si_ca_ti; tar - di in_ver vi pen - ti-
poi- soned mad- men! Nev- er you dare to show your
più mi fa da ri_dere, da ri_dere, da ri_dere, è quell'
been the gay- est frol- ic, the gay- est, the gay- est that has
so se fin_ta o ve_ra, se fin_ta o ve_ra sia quell'
been the gay- est frol- ic, the gay- est, the gay- est that has
più mi fa da ri_dere, da ri_dere, da ri_dere è quell'
been the gay- est frol- ic, the gay- est, the gay- est that has
so se fin_ta o ve_ra, se fin_ta o ve_ra sia quell'
been the gay- est frol- ic, the gay- est, the gay- est that has

ror, il mio fu - ror,
more! There is the door!
re - te se più cre - sce il mio fu - ror, il mio fu - ror, tar - di in -
fac- es! Don't come back here an- y more! There is the door! Do not
f
i - ra e quel fu - ror, e quel fu - ror. Ch'io ben
ev- er been played be- fore, been played be- fore. I'm con-
i - ra e quel fu - ror, e quel fu - ror. Nè vor -
ev- er been played be- fore, been played be- - fore. Yet I
i - ra e quel fu - ror, e quel fu - ror. Ch'io ben
ev- er been played be- fore, been played be- fore. I'm con-
i - ra e quel fu - ror, e quel fu - ror. Nè vor -
ev- er been played be- fore, been played be- - fore. Yet I
f
se più cre - - - - - - - - -
We dis- dain
ver vi pen - ti - re - te se più cre - sce, se più cre - - -
make our an- ger great- er, we dis- dain you, we dis- dain
so che tan - to fo - co can - ge - ras - si in quel d'a - mor, can - ge -
vinced that soon or lat- er their dis- dain will turn to love, their dis-
rei che tan - to fo - co ter - mi - nas - se in quel d'a - mor.
fear that soon or lat- er their dis- dain will turn to love.
so che tan - to fo - co can - ge - ras - si in quel d'a - mor, can - ge - ras - si in quel d'a -
vinced that soon or lat- er their dis- dain will turn to love, their dis- dain will turn to
rei che tan - to fo - co ter - mi - nas - se in quel d'a - mor, ter - mi - nas - se in quel d'a -
fear that soon or lat- er their dis- dain may turn to love, their dis- dain may turn to
cresc.
f

sotto voce
- sce il mio fu - ror, se ___ più cre - - sce,
and spurn your love, we ___ dis- dain ___ you,
sotto voce
- sce il mio fu - ror, se cre - sce il mio fu -
and spurn your love, we both dis- dain your
sotto voce
ras - si in quel d'a - mor, si can - ge - rà, si
dain will turn to love. I am con- vinced that
sotto voce
nè vor- rei che tan - to fo - co ter - mi - nas - -
Yet I fear that soon or la- ter their dis- dain ___
sotto voce
mor. ch'io ben so che tan - to
love. I'm con- vinced that now or
sotto voce
mor, nè vor - rei che tan - to
love. Yet I fear that soon or
fp fp fp fp
se più cre - sce il mio fu - ror, se più
we dis- dain and spurn your love. We dis-
f
ror, se cre - sce il mio fu - ror, tar - di in - ver vi pen - ti -
love, dis- dain and spurn your love Do not make our an- ger
f
can - ge - rà in quel d'a - mor, ch'io ben so che tan - to
their dis- dain will turn to love. I'm con- vinced that soon or
f
- - - se in quel d'a - mor, nè vor - rei che tan - to
___ may ___ turn ___ to ___ love. Yet I fear that soon or
f
fo - co can - ge - ras - si in quel d'a - mor, ch'io ben so che tan - to
lat- er their dis- dain will turn to love. I'm con- vinced that soon or
f
fo - co ter - mi - nas - se in quel d'a - mor, nè vor - rei che tan - to.
lat- er their dis- dain may turn to love. Yet I fear that soon or
cresc.

cre - - - - - - - - - - - sce il
dain and
re_te se più cre_sce, se più cre - - - - - sce il
greater, we dis- - dain you, we dis- dain and
fo_co can_ge - rassi in quel d'a_mor, can_ge_ras_si in
later their dis- dain will turn to love, their dis- dain will
fo_co ter - mi - nasse in quel d'a_mor,
later their dis- - dain may turn to love.
fo_co can - ge - rassi in quel d'a_mor, can_ge_ras_si in quel d'amor,
later their dis- - dain will turn to love, their dis- dain will turn to love.
fo_co ter - mi - nasse in quel d'a_mor, ter - mi_nas_se in quel d'amor,
later their dis- - dain may turn to love, their dis- dain may turn to love.
fp fp
sotto voce
mio fu - ror, se più cre - sce, se più
spurn your love, we dis- dain you, we dis-
sotto voce
mio fu - ror, se cre - sce il mio fu_ror, se
spurn your love, we both dis- dain your love, dis-
sotto voce
quel d'a - mor, si can - ge - rà, si can - ge -
turn to love. I am con- vinced that their dis-
sotto voce
nè vor_rei che tan_to fo_co ter_mi_nas - - - -
Yet I fear that soon or later their dis- dain
sotto voce
ch'io ben so, che tan - to fo_co can_ge -
I'm con- vinced that now or later their dis-
sotto voce
nè vor_rei che tan - to fo_co ter_mi -
Yet I fear that soon or later their dis-
fp fp

Presto
cre - sce il mio fu - ror, tar_di in_
dain and spurn your love. Do not
cre - sce il mio fu - ror, tar_di in_
dain and spurn your love. Do not
rà in quel d'a - mor, ch'io ben so che tan_to fo - co
dain will turn to love. I'm con- vinced that soon or lat- er
- se in quel d'a - mor, nè vor-
may turn to love. I'm a-
ras - si in quel d'a - mor, ch'io ben so che tan_to fo - co
dain will turn to love. I'm con- vinced that soon or lat- er
nas - se in quel d'a - mor, nè vor - rei che tan_to fo - co
dain may turn to love. I'm a- fraid that soon or lat- er
Presto
ver - vi pen - ti - re_te, se più cresce il mio fu - ror, il mio fu -
make our an- ger great- er, we dis- dain and spurn your love, we spurn your
ver - vi pen - ti - re_te, se più cresce il mio fu - ror, il mio fu -
make our an- ger great- er, we dis- dain and spurn your love. we spurn your
can - ge - ras - si in quel d'a - mor, in quel d'a -
their dis- dain will turn to love, will turn to
rei che tan - to fo - co ter - mi - nas_se in quel d'a - mor, in quel d'a -
fraid that soon or lat- er their dis- dain may turn to love, may turn to
can - ge - ras_si in quel d'a - mor, in quel d'a -
their dis- dain will turn to love, will turn to
ter - mi - nas_se in quel d'a - mor, in quel d'a -
their dis- dain may turn to love, may turn to

ror, tar-di in-ver vi pen-ti-re-te se più
love. Do not make our an-ger great-er, we dis-
ror, tar-di in-ver vi pen-ti-re-te se più
love. Do not make our an-ger great-er, we dis-
mor, ch'io ben so che tan-to fo-co can-ge-
love, I'm con-vinced that soon or lat-er their dis-
mor, nè vor-rei che tan-to fo-co ter-mi-
love. I'm a-fraid that soon or lat-er their dis-
mor, ch'io ben so che tan-to fo-co can-ge-
love. I'm con-vinced that soon or lat-er their dis-
mor, nè vor-rei che tan-to fo-co ter-mi-
love. I'm a-fraid that soon or lat-er their dis-
cresce il mio fu-ror, il mio fu-ror,
dain and spurn your love, we spurn your love.
cresce il mio fu-ror, il mio fu-ror,
dain and spurn your love, we spurn your love.
rassi in quel d'a-mor, in quel d'a-mor,
dain will turn to love, will turn to love.
nasse in quel d'a-mor, in quel d'a-mor,
dain may turn to love, may turn to love.
rassi in quel d'a-mor, in quel d'a-mor,
dain will turn to love, will turn to love.
nasse in quel d'a-mor, in quel d'a-mor,
dain may turn to love, may turn to love.
p

cresc.
se più cre - sce il mio
We dis- dain and spurn
se più cre - sce il mio
We dis- dain and spurn
ch'io ben so che tan -
their dis- dain will turn
nè vor- rei che tan -
their dis- dain will turn
ch'io ben so che tan -
their dis- dain will turn
nè vor- rei che tan -
their dis- dain will turn
cresc.
fu - ror, il mio fu - ror, il mio fu -
your love, we spurn your love, we spurn your
fu - ror, il mio fu - ror, il mio fu -
your love, we spurn your love, we spurn your
to fo - co can - ge - ras - si in quel d'a - mor, in quel d'a -
to love, will soon or lat- er turn to love, will turn to
to fo - co ter - mi - nas - se in quel d'a - mor, in quel d'a -
to love, may soon or lat- er turn to love, may turn to
to fo - co can - ge - ras - si in quel d'a - mor, in quel d'a -
to love, will soon or lat- er turn to love, will turn to
to fo - co ter - mi - nas - se in quel d'a - mor, in quel d'a -
to love, may soon or lat- er turn to love, may turn to

ror, il mio fu - ror, il mio fu - ror.
love, we spurn your love, we spurn your love!
ror, il mio fu - ror, il mio fu - ror.
love, we spurn your love, we spurn your love!
mor, in quel d'a - mor, in quel d'a - mor.
love, will turn to love, will turn to love!
mor, in quel d'a - mor, in quel d'a - mor.
love, may turn to love, may turn to love!
mor, in quel d'a - mor, in quel d'a - mor.
love, will turn to love, will turn to love!
mor, in quel d'a - mor, in quel d'a - mor.
love, may turn to love, may turn to love!
End of Act One

ATTO SECONDO ACT II

(Curtain.)

SCENA I SCENE I

(A room in the sisters' home.)

Recit.

nir la dis-grazia sì co-mu-ne a chi si fi-da in uo-mo, mangiar il fi-co, e
pend- ing up- on the man in ques- tion. That way you're al- ways win- ner, and have your bread
FIORD.
DESP.
non git-ta-re il po-mo. (Che diavolo!) tai co-se fal-le tu, se n'hai vo-glia. Io già le
but- tered on both sides. (What dev- il- try!) You may do things like that, if you want to. I've al- ways
f
p
fac-cio. Ma vor-rei che an-che voi per gloria del bel ses - so fa-ce-ste un po' lo
done them. But I wish that you both, for the sake of all wo- man- hood, would fol- low my ex-
stes-so; per e-sempio: i vo-stri Ga-ni-me-di son an-da-ti al-la guerra; in-fin che
am- ple. Let me tell you, now that your two Rom- eos have be- come val- iant war- riors, do as
DORAB.
DESP.
tor-na-no fa-te al-la mi-li - ta-re: re-clu-ta-te. Il cie-lo ce ne guar-di. Eh!
they did, seek your own ad- ven- tures, and do it quick- ly. May Heav- en pre- serve me! Eh,
che noi siamo in terra, e non in cie-lo! Fi-da-te-vi al mio ze-lo. Giacchè que-sti fo-re-
be glad we are not yet in Heav- en, but ver- y much on earth. You have met two nice young

stie-ri v'a-do-ra-no la - scia-te-vi a-do-rar. Son ric-chi, bel-li,
suit- ors. They wor- ship you! Then why not let them do so? They're wealth- y, hand- some,
no - bi - li, ge - ne - ro - si co - me fe - de fe - ce a voi Don Al -
gen- er- ous, well- bred. Don Al- fon- so told you ev- 'ry thing a-
fon-so; a-ve-an corraggio de mo - ri - re per voi; que-sti son mer-ti che sprezzar non si
bout them. They had the cour- age to die for your sake—is that not proof that they mean what they're
den-no da gio-va-ni qual voi belle e ga-lan-ti, che pon star senza a-mor, non senza a -
say- ing? And aren't you both young, lov- a- ble wo- men who de- serve to be loved and a-
FIORD.
manti. (Par che ci tro-vin gusto!) Per Bac-co ci fa - re-sti far del-le bel-le
dored? (Seems I am mak- ing head- way!) I am in- clined to think you want to lead us in-to
co-se; cre-di tu che vo - gliamo fa-vo-la di-ven - tar degli o-zio-si? ai
mis- chief! Are you real- ly pro- pos- ing that we be- come the top- ic for gos- sip? And

DESP.
no_stri ca_ri spo_si cre_di tu che vogliam dar tal tor_men_to? E chi di_ce, che ab-
what a- bout our lov- ers — do you think that we would ev- er be- tray them? And who said that you
DORAB.
bia_te a far lo_ro alcun tor_to? Non ti pa_re, che sia tor_to bastan_te, se
should? Where would be the be- tray- al? In my o- pin- ion, it would be bad e- nough if
DESP.
no_to si fa_ces_se, che trat_tia_mo co_stor? An_che per que_sto c'è un mezzo si_cu-
an- y- bod- y heard that we met oth- er men. That is no prob- lem. Let me take care of
DORAB. DESP.
ris_si_mo, io vo_glio sparger fa_ma, che ven_go_no da me. Chi vuolche il cre_da? Oh
that for you. I'll sim- ply spread a ru- mor they came to vis- it me. Who would be- lieve it? Why
bel_la! non ha for_se merto u_na ca_me_rie_ra d'a_ver due ci_cis_be_i? di me fi-
not? An- y av- 'rage la- dy's-maid has a lov- er — why could- n't I have two? Don't let that
FIORD.
da_te_vi. No, no, son troppo au_da_ci que_sti tuoi fo_re_stie_ri, non eb_ber la bal-
wor- ry you! No, no! I could not do it! Those two men are so reck- less! They e- ven had the

DESP.
dan_za fin di chie_der dei ba_ci (Che dis_grazia!) io pos_so assi_cu_rar_vi che le
dar- ing to beg us for kiss- es! (Isn't that aw- ful!) I give you my as- sur- ance that your
f
co_se che han fat_to fu_ro ef_fet_ti del tos_si_co, che han pre_so, con_vul_sio_ni, de_
suit- ors' be- hav- ior was due to the in- flu- ence of poi- son — all their tan- trums, their
p
li_ri, fol_li_e, va_neggia_menti; ma or ve_dre_te, co_me son dis_cre_ti, ma_nie_ro_si, mo_
rav- ing, their fits, and all their an- tics. Get to know them as they real- ly are. They are mod- est and
DORAB. DESP.
de_sti, e man_sue_ti, la_scia_te_li ve_nir. E poi? E poi:
de- cent, ver- y pol- ished. You'll see it for your- selves. And then? And then:
FIORD.
ca_spi_ta! fa_te vo_i. (L'ho det_to che cad_reb_be_ro.) Co_sa dob_bia_mo
ask your- self! That's your bus- 'ness! (I knew that I could han- dle them.) What do you sug-
DESP.
far? Quel che vo_le_te. Sie_te d'os_sa, e di car_ne, o co_sa sie_te?
gest? Fol- low your heart. Are you made of flesh and blood, or just what are you?

Nº 19. Aria

Andante
DESP.
U_na don_na a quin_di_ci an_ni dee sa_per — o_gni gran
An-y girl fif-teen or o- - ver must pur-sue — a wo-man's
f
p
mo_da, dove il dia_vo_lo ha la co_da, co_sa è be_ne, e mal cos'
mis- - sion, and with fem- in- ine in- tu- i- tion be an ex-pert man-ag-ing
è, dee sa_per le ma_li_ziet_te, che in_na_mo_ra_no gli a_
men. She must know a thou- sand rus- - es to at- - tract the man she
man_ti, fin_ger ri_so, fin_ger pian_ti, in_ven_tar_i bei per_
choos- - es. Laugh or chat- ter, weep or flat- ter, know the mo- - ment where and

chè, fin_ger ri_so, fin_ger pian_ti, in_ven_tar i bei per_
when, laugh or chat- ter, weep or flat- ter, know the mo- - ment where and
Allegretto
p
chè. Dee in un mo_men_to dar ret_ta a
when. When to a- - muse them, when to con-
cen_to, col_le pu_pil_le par_lar con mil_le,
fuse them, when she should tease them, when she should please them.
dar spe_me a tut_ti, sien belli o brut_ti, sa_per na_scon_der_si, sen_za con_
She must act sly- ly, clev- er and wi- ly, in all the rit- u- al, new or hab-

fon_der_si, senza arros _ si _ re sa_per men _ ti _ re, sa_per men _
it- u- al, nev- er re- - veal- ing her in- ner feel- ing, her in- ner
f. p
ti _ re, e qual re _ gi _ na dall' al _ to so _ glio col posso e vo _ glio
feel- ing. Love is the king- dom she rules in splen- dor. Men must sur- ren- der,
farsi ub_bi _ dir, e qual re _ gi _ na col posso e
serve her and bow. Love is her king- dom, men must sur-
vo_glio farsi ubbi _ dir. Par ch'abbian gu _ sto
ren- der, serve her and bow. Life can be keen- er,

di tal dot - tri - na, vi - va De - spi - na, che sa ser - vir, — che sa ser -
love can be green - - er. Come to Des - pi - na, she'll tell you how, — she'll tell you
vir.
how!
Dee in un mo - men - to dar retta a
She'll an - swer ques - - tions, give you sug-
cen - to, col - le pu - pil - le par - lar con mil - le,
ges - tions how you can han - - dle gos - sip or scan - dal.
dar spe - me a tut - ti, sien bel - li o brut - ti, sa - per na -
She can di - - rect you, she can per - fect you in all for-

scon_der_si, sen_za con_fon_der_si, senza arros_si_re, sa_per men_
mal- i- ties and tech- ni- cal- i- ties, nev- er re- veal- ing her in- ner
ti_re, sa_per men_ti_re. E qual re_gi_na dall' al_to so_glio col posso e
feel- ing, her in- ner feel- ing. Love is the king- dom she rules in splen- dor. Men must sur-
f p
f p
f p
vo_glio farsi ubbi_dir, e qual re_gi_na col posso e
ren- der, serve her and bow! Love is her king- dom, men must sur-
fp
fp
fp
vo_glio farsi ub_bi_dir, e qual re_gi_na dall' al_to
ren- der, serve her and bow! Love is the king- dom she rules in

so-glio, col posso e vo - glio, col pos - so e vo-glio,
splen- dor. Men must sur- ren- - der and serve her, o- bey her!
sfp
col pos-so e vo - glio far - si ub-bi - dir, si far - si ub-bi - dir, si
Men must sur- ren- der, serve her and bow, yes, serve her and bow, yes,
fp
cresc.
f
far - si ub - bi - dir. Par ch'abbian gu - sto di tal dot -
serve her and bow! Life can be keen- er, love can be
p
tri - na, vi-va De - spi - na, che sa ser - vir, vi-va De - spi - na, che sa ser-
green- er. Come to Des- pi- - na, she'll tell you how! Come to Des- pi- - na, she'll tell you

SCENA II

SCENE II

Recit.

cre_di tu de_lit_to per due gio_va_ni o_mai pro_messe spo_se il far di que_ste
do you think it prop- er for two la- dies en- gaged to be mar- ried to har- bor such i-
DORAB.
co_se? El_la non di_ce che fac_cia - mo al_cun mal.
de- as? But she as- sured us we'd be do- - ing no harm.
FIORD.
E mal che
If peo- ple
ba_sta il far par_lar di noi.
gos- sip, that would be harm e- - nough!
DORAB.
Quan_do si di_ce che
But she has of- fered to
ven_gon per De_spi_na!
claim them as her suit- ors!
FIORD.
Oh, tu sei trop_po lar_ga di co_scien_za!
My, what a nice, con- ven- ient type of con- science!
e che di_ranno gli spo_si no_stri?
Think of our lov- ers! What would they say?
DORAB.
Nul_la: o non sa_pran l'af-
Noth- ing! Ei- ther they will not

fa_re ed è tut_to fi_ni_to: o sa_pran qual_che
know it — in that case it is sim-ple. Or if by chance they should
FIORD.
co_sa e al_lor di_re_mo che ven_ne_ro per lei. Ma i no_stri
hear it, then we will tell them they are Des- pi-na's friends. And our en-
DORAB.
co_ri? Re_sta_no quel che so_no; per di_ver_tirsi un
gage-ments? They will re-main un- bro-ken. An in- no-cent di-
po_co, e non mo_ri_re del_la ma_lin_co_ni_a non si man_ca di
ver- sion to pass a-way the te- di-ous time of wait-ing can't be called a breach of
FIORD. DORAB. FIORD.
fè, so_rel_la mi_a. Questo è ver. Dunque? Dunque fa un po tu: ma non
faith — don't you think so? That is true. Well, then? Do as you please. But re-

Nº 20. Duetto

Andante

FIORD.
set_ta ai dol_ci det_ti io di quel ri_spon_de_rò. So_spi_
light in his love- lorn phras- es with a most en- gag- - ing smile. If he
cresc.
p
DORAB.
ran_do i so_spi_ret_ti io dell' al_tro i_mi_te_rò. Mi di_
sighs and moons and gaz- - es, I will ech- - o him in style. Mine will
FIORD.
DORAB.
rà, ben mio, mi mo_ro. Mi di_rà, mio bel te_so_ro! Ed in_
say, "My soul is burn- ing!" Mine will say, "My heart is yearn- ing!" How ro-
FIORD.
tan_to che di_let_to, Ed in_tan_to che di_
man- - tic, how en- - chant- ing! How ro- man- - tic, how en-

FIORD.
let_to, che spas_setto io pro_ve_rò, che spas_setto io pro_ve_rò!
chant-ing, how a- mus-ing it will be, how a- - mus-ing it will be! Ah!
DORAB.
che spas_setto io pro_ve_rò, che spas_setto io pro_ve_rò!
How a- - mus-ing it will be, how a- - mus-ing it will be!
f
Ed in_tan_to io col bion_
I my- self pre- fer the
Pren_de_rò quel bru_net_ti_no, che più
I will choose the hand- some dark one if it's
p

di_no vo un po ri_de_re e bur_lar.
blond one. He is gay and win-ning too!
le_pi_do mi par. Scher_zo_set_ta ai dol_ci
all the same to you. I'll en-joy his love-lorn
DORAB.
FIORD.
DORAB.
det_ti So_spi_ran_do i so_spi_ret_ti io di quel ri_sponde_
phrases — If he sighs and moons and gaz-es — With the most en-chant-ing
mf
cresc.
FIORD.
DORAB.
rò. io dell' al_tro i_mi_te_rò. Mi di_
smile! I will ech-o him in style! Mine will
f
p
FIORD.
DORAB.
rà, ben mio, mi mo_ro. Mi di_rà, mio bel te_so_ro! Ed in_
say, "I love you on-ly!" Mine will say, "My heart is lone-ly!" How ro-

FIORD.
Ed in_tan_to che di_let_to, ed in_tan_to che di_
How ro- man- tic, how en- chant- ing! It may be a lit- tle
DORAB.
tan_to che di_let_to, ed in_tan_to che di_
man- tic, how en- chant- ing! It may be a lit- tle
mfp
let_to, che spas_set_to io pro_ve_rò, ed in_tan_to che di_
naugh- ty, but at least it will be fun, it may be a lit- tle
let_to, che spas_set_to io pro_ve_rò, ed in_tan_to che di_
naugh- ty, but at least it will be fun, it may be a lit- tle
mfp
let_to, che spas_setto io pro_ve_rò, io pro_ve_rò,
naugh- ty, but at least it will be fun, a lot of fun,
let_to, che spas_setto io pro_ve_rò, io pro_ve_rò,
naugh- ty, but at least it will be fun, a lot of fun,
mfp
mf
p

— io pro - ve - rò, ed in - tan - to che di - let - to, che spas - setto io pro - ve -
— a lot of fun, it may be a lit - tle naugh - ty, but we'll have a lot of
— io pro - ve - rò, ed in - tan - to che di - let - to, che spas - setto io pro - ve -
— a lot of fun, it may be a lit - tle naugh - ty, but we'll have a lot of
mf
p
mf
p
mf
p
rò, che spas - set - to io pro - ve - rò, che spas - setto io pro - ve -
fun, we will have a lot of fun, we will have a lot of
rò, che spas - set - to io pro - ve - rò, che spas - setto io pro - ve -
fun, we will have a lot of fun, we will have a lot of
cresc.
fp
rò, che spassetto io pro - ve - rò, — che spasset - to io pro - ve - rò!
fun, we will have a lot of fun, — yes, we'll have a lot of fun!
rò, che spassetto io pro - ve - rò, — che spasset - to io pro - ve - rò!
fun, we will have a lot of fun, — yes, we'll have a lot of fun!
cresc.
f
(They start to leave, and run into Don Alfonso.)
tr

SCENA III — SCENE III

Recit.

SCENA IV — SCENE IV

Nº 21. Duetto con Coro

Andante

(Curtain. A garden at the seashore, with grass seats and two little stone tables. A barge decorated with

flowers, and a band of musicians. Servants in elaborate costumes. Despina, Ferrando, and Guglielmo on-stage. Then Don Alfonso, Fiordiligi, and Dorabella.)

FERR.
Se - con - da - te, au - ret - te a - mi - che, se - con - da - te i
Friend- ly breez- es, bear my mes- sage to the one I
GUGL.
Se - con - da - te, au - ret - te a - mi - che, se - con - da - te i
Friend- ly breez- es, bear my mes- sage to the one I
f p
miei de - si - ri, e por - ta - te i miei so - spi - ri
love so dear- ly! Ask her fa - vor, beg her to hear me,
miei de - si - ri, e por - ta - te i miei so - spi - ri
love so dear- ly! Ask her fa - vor, beg her to hear me,
al - la de - a di que - sto cor, di que - sto cor.
love- - ly god- dess that I a- dore, that I a- dore!
al - la de - a di que - sto cor, di que - sto cor.
love- - ly god- dess that I a- dore, that I a- dore!

Voi, che u_di_ste mil_le vol_te il te_nor del_le mie
Go and tell her, friend- ly breez- es, how my lone- ly heart is
Voi, che u_di_ste mil_le vol_te il te_nor del_le mie
Go and tell her, friend- ly breez- es, how my lone- ly heart is
pe_ne; ri_pe_te_te al ca_ro be_ne, tut_to
break- ing, ev- er long- ing, ev- er ach- ing. Say I
pe_ne; ri_pe_te_te al ca_ro be_ne, tut_to
break- ing, ev- er long- ing, ev- er ach- ing. Say I
quel che u_di_ste al_lor, tut_to quel che u_di_ste al_lor.
love her more and more, say I love her more and more!
quel che u_di_ste al_lor, tut_to quel che u_di_ste al_lor.
love her more and more, say I love her more and more!
Sopr.
Alt.
CORO
Ten.
Bass
Se_con_
Friend- ly
Friend- ly

(During this Chorus, Ferrando and Guglielmo, decked with chains of flowers, rise. Don Alfonso and Despina lead them to the two women, who look at them astonished and speechless.)

FERR.
via, co_raggio: a_ve_te per_so l'u_so del_la fa_vel_la? Io tre_mo, e
chance. Don't miss it! Can't you speak up — or has the cat got your tongue? I'm will- ing, but
p
GUGL.
D.ALF.
pal_pi_to dal_la testa al_le piante. A_mor le_ga le membra a vero aman_te. Da
some- how I'm a vic- tim of stage- fright. It seems I have for- got- ten all my lines. Dear
FIORD.
(to the lovers)
DORAB.
FERR.
brave incorrag_gi_te_li. Par_la_te! Li_be_ri di_te pur quel che bra_ma_te! Ma_
la- dies, please en- cour- age them. We're lis- t'ning! Don't be a- fraid to say what's on your mind! My
GUGL.
FERR.
GUGL.
D. ALF.
da_ma_ An_zi ma_da_me_ Par_la pur tu. No, no, par_la pur tu. Oh! co_spet_to del
la- dy_ Say "Fair- est la- dies." You make the speech. No, you, you're so much bet- ter. Why, this is too ri-
dia_vo_lo! la_sciate ta_li smorfie del se_co_lo pas_sa_to: De_spi_net_ta, ter_mi_
dic- u- lous! The way you are be- hav- ing is hope- less- ly old- fash ioned. Des- pi- net- ta, if they
niam que_sta fe_sta, fa tu con lei, quel ch'io fa_rò con que_sta.
can't talk them- selves, I'll do it for them. You do it for the la- dies.
p

Nº 22 Quartetto

Allegretto grazioso

mante, v'of - fe - se, lo ve - de, ma so - lo un i -
ent it. If we have dis- turbed you, we deep- ly re-
FERR.
(The lovers repeat the last words always in the same tone of voice.)
ta - ce...
dore you ...
GUGL.
D. ALF.
stante; or pe - na, ma ta - ce... ta - ce... or
pent it. Two slaves who a- dore you, dore you ... have
in pa - ce...
im- plore you ...
GUGL.
la - scia - vi in pa - ce... in pa - ce...
come to im- plore you, im- plore you ...
D. ALF.
non può quel che vuo - le, vor - rà, quel che può,
What- ev- er you ask us, we glad- ly will do."

FERR. (in one big breath)
non può quel che vuo_le, vor_rà quel che può,
What- ev- er you ask us, we glad- ly will do,
GUGL. (in one big breath)
D. ALF.
non può quel che vuo_le, vor_rà quel che può, vor_rà quel che
What- ev- er you ask us, we glad- ly will do, we glad- ly will
mf p
vorrà quel che può, vor_rà quel che può.
we glad- ly will do, we glad- ly will do.
GUGL.
D. ALF.
GUGL.
D. ALF.
può, vorrà quel che può, vor_rà quel che può, vor_ra quel che può. Su!
do, we glad- ly will do, we glad- ly will do, we glad- ly will do. And
mf p
mf p
mf p
via! rispon_de_te! su! via! rispon_de_te! guar_
now you must an- swer, my la- dies, you must an- swer! You are
da_te, e ri_de_te?
si- lent? You are laugh- ing?

DESP. (Stands in front of the two women.)
Per voi la ri_spo_sta a lo_ro da_rò, per voi la ri_
Since they are so bash- ful, so mod- est and shy, I'll ven- ture to
mf p
spo_sta a lo_ro da_rò, per voi la ri_spo_sta a lo_ro da_
give you my la- dies' re- ply, I'll ven- ture to give you my la- dies' re-
mf p
Allegro
Recit.
rò. Quel_lo ch'è sta_to, è sta_to, scordiam_ci del pas_
ply. "Let us for- get what hap- pened and think a- bout the
f
a tempo (Despina takes Dorabella's hand, Don Alfonso Fiordiligi's; the two ladies break the flower-chains around the two lovers.)
sa_to. Rom_pasi o mai quel laccio, se_gno di ser_vi_
fu- ture. All for- mer ties are bro- ken. Now we shall be good
fp cresc. f p tr
Tempo I
tù. A me por_ge_te il brac_cio: nè so_spi_ra_te
friends. Let's join our hands in to- ken that all your suf- f'ring

più, nè so - spi - ra - te più, nè so - spi - ra - te
ends, that all your suf- - f'ring ends, that all your suf- - f'ring
Presto
più.
ends."
(aside) DESP. sotto voce
Per ca - ri - tà par - tia - mo, quel
And now that we have spo- ken, let's
(aside) D.ALF. sotto voce
Per ca - ri - tà par - tia - mo, quel
And now that we have spo- ken, let's
Presto
p
che san far veg-gia - mo, per ca - ri - tà par -
watch it from a dis- tance. I think the ice is
che san far veg-gia - mo, per ca - ri - tà par -
watch it from a dis- tance. I think the ice is
tia - mo, quel che san far veg - gia - mo, le sti - mo più del
bro- ken. They need no more as- sis- tance. I'm ab- - so- lute- ly
tia - mo, quel che san far veg - gia - mo, le sti - mo più del
bro- - ken. They need no more as- sis- tance. I'm ab- - so- lute- ly

dia_vo_lo, del dia_vo_lo, del dia_vo_lo s'o_ra non cas_can giù, non
pos- i- tive, I'm pos- i- tive, I'm pos- i- tive the bat- tle has been won, com-
dia_vo_lo, del dia_vo_lo, del dia_vo_lo s'o_ra non cas_can giù, non
pos- i- tive, I'm pos- i- tive, I'm pos- i- tive the bat- tle has been won, com-
cas_can giù, le sti_mo più del dia_vo_lo, del dia_vo_lo, del
plete- ly won! I'm ab- so- lute- ly pos- i- tive, I'm pos- i- tive, I'm
cas_can giù, le sti_mo più del dia_vo_lo, del dia_vo_lo, del
plete- ly won! I'm ab- so- lute- ly pos- i- tive, I'm pos- i- tive, I'm
dia_vo_lo, s'o_ra non cas_can giù, non cas_can giù, s'o ra non cas_can
pos- i- tive the bat- tle has been won, com- plete- ly won! The com- e- dy is
dia_vo_lo, s'o_ra non cas_can giù, non cas_can giù, s'o_ra non cas_can
pos- i- tive the bat- tle has been won, com- plete- ly won! The com- e- dy is

giù, s'o - ra non cascan giù, s'o - ra non cascan giù.
on, the com- e- dy is on, the com- e- dy is on!
(Exeunt Despina and Don Alfonso.)
giù, s'o - ra non cascan giù, s'o - ra non cascan giù.
on, the com- e- dy is on, the com- e- dy is on!
SCENA V
Recit.
(Guglielmo arm in arm with Dorabella. Ferrando and Fiordiligi more distant to each other. A short pantomimed scene, in which the four look at each other, sigh, giggle in embarrassment.)
SCENE V
FIORD.
FERR.
DORAB.
Oh che bel - la gior - na - ta! Cal - det - ta an - zi che no. Che vez -
What a beau- ti- ful morn- ing! I think it's a tri- fle too warm. Oh, what
fp
GUGL.
FIORD.
zo - si ar - boscel - li! Certo, cer - to: son bel - li: han più fo - glie che frutti. Quei vi -
beau- ti- ful flow- ers! That's what I say. How- ev- er they could smell a lit- tle strong- er. In the
FERR.
a - li co - me so - no leg - gia - dri; vo - le - te passeg - giar? Son pronto, o ca - ra ad
gar- den there are nice shad- y al- leys. Do you wish to prom- en- ade? With great- est plea- sure! It's
FIORD.
FERR. (passing by Guglielmo)
FIORD.
og - ni vostro cenno. Troppa grazia! (Ec - coci al - la gran cri - si.) Co - sa gli a - ve - te
good for your health. I a- gree with you. (Now we are at the cross-roads.) What was it that you
fp

FERR.
det_to? Eh gli rac_co_man_da_i di di_ver_tir_la
told him? Oh, I on- ly was say- ing there's moss on the
DORAB.
be_ne. Pas_seggiamo an_che
road. Shall we, too, take a
GUGL.
noi. Co_me vi pia_ce.
walk? I am all for it!
(They walk)
DORAB.
Ahi_mè! Che co_sa a_ve_te?
Good Lord! Is some- thing wrong?
GUGL.
Io mi
All at
sen_to sì ma_le, sì ma_le, a_ni_ma mi_a, che mi par di mo_ri_re.
once I feel dread- ful — per- haps it's some kind of fe- ver — I may e- ven be dy- ing.
DORAB.
(Non ot_ter_rà nien_tis_si_mo.) Sa_ran_no ri_ma_su_gli del ve_
(I don't be- lieve a word of it.) You still are feel- ing ef- fects from the
espr.
p
fp
GUGL. (passionately)
len che be_ve_ste. Ah che un ve_le_no assai più for_te io be_vo in que' cru_di e fo_
poi- son you've tak- en. There is a far more dead- ly poi- son, a far more fat- al dan- ger, in the
(Fiordiligi strolls off with Ferrando.)
co_si mongi_belli a_mo_ro_si!
flames of your two glo- ri- ous eyes.
DORAB.
Sa_rà ve_le_no ca_li_do; fa_te_vi un po_co
A flat- ter- ing com- pa- ri- son! You ought to write a
fp

GUGL.
fresco. In_grata, voi bur_la_te, ed in_tan _ to io mi moro! (Son spa_ri _ ti: do_ve
po- em! You real- ly should not tease me when you know how I'm suf- f'ring. (I can't see them. Are they
DORAB.
GUGL.
dia_min son i _ ti?) Eh via non fa_te. Io mi mo_ro, cru _ de_le, e voi bur_
hid- ing on pur- pose?) Don't be so sil- ly! You are heart- less and cru- el to go on
DORAB.
GUGL.
la_te? Io bur_lo? io bur_lo? Dunque da_te_mi qualche se_gno, a _ ni_ma
jok- ing! I'm jok- ing? You think so? Won't you show me a sign of pit- y, fair- est of
DORAB.
bella, del_la vo_stra pie_tà. Due, se vo_le_te; di_te quel che far deggio, e lo ve_
la- dies, to up- hold my mor- ale? On- ly too glad- ly. Mere- ly say what you wish and you shall
GUGL.
drete. (Scher_za, o di_ce dav_ve_ro?) Questa pic_cio_la of_fer_ta d'accet_ta _ re de_
have it! (She's fool- ing, or could she have meant it?) Will you do me one fa- vor? Let me give you this
DORAB.
GUGL.
gna _ te _ vi. Un co _ re? Un co _ re: è sim_bo _ lo di
lock- et. A heart? Yes, dar- ling! A most ap- pro- priate

DORAB.
GUGL.
quello ch'ar_de, languisce e spa_si_ma per voi. (Che do_no pre_zio_so!) L'ac_cet_
sym- bol to re- as- sure you of my ev- er- last- ing love. (Oh, dear, it is charm- ing!) You ac-
DORAB.
GUGL.
ta_te? Cru_de_le, di se_dur non ten_ta_te un cor fe_de_le. (La monta_gna va_
cept it? I'd like to, but my heart is not free, as you well know. (The ice- berg is
cil_la: mi spia_ce ma im_pe_gna_to è l'o_nor di sol_da_to.) V'a_
melt- ing. I'm sor- ry, but my sold- ier- ly word can't be bro- ken.) I
DORAB.
GUGL.
DORAB.
GUGL.
do_ro! Per pie_tà_ Son tut_to vo_stro! Oh De_i! Ce_de_te, o
love you! Please don't! I love you mad- ly! Don't say it! Do not re-
DORAB.
GUGL.
ca_ra! Mi fa_re_te mo_rir. Mor_re_mo in_sie_me, a_mo_ro_sa mia spe_me.
ject me! I in- sist that you go! If you re- ject me I'm de- ter- mined to per- ish!
fp
f
DORAB.
(after a short hesitation, with a sigh)
GUGL.
L'accet_ta_te? L'ac_cet_to. (In_fe_li_ce Fer_rando!) Oh che di_letto!
You'll ac- cept it? I will then! (What a blow for Fer- ran- do!) I am de- lir- ious!
fp
p
p

Nº 23. Duetto

Andante grazioso

GUGL.
DORAB.
da_i, che mai bal_za lì? Per_chè bat_te, bat_te, bat_te quì? Che mai
near then, if I have your own? What is beat- ing, beat- ing loud and clear? What is
DORAB.
bal_za, bal_za, bal za lì, che mai bal_za, bal_za, bal_za lì? E il
throb- bing, throb- bing in my ear? What is beat- ing, beat- ing loud and clear? It
GUGL.
per_chè bat_te, bat_te, bat_te quì? E il
What is beat- ing, beat- ing loud and clear? It
mf
mio co_ri - ci_no, che più non è me_co, che più non è
must be my own heart, my lov- ing and lone heart, a heart which is
mio co_ri - ci_no, che più non è me_co, che più non è
must be my own heart, my lov- ing and lone heart, a heart which is
cresc. p cresc. p
me_co, ei ven_ne a star te_co, ei bat_te co_
yours now for- ev- er and ev- er! A heart true as
me_co, ei ven_ne a star te_co, ei bat_te co_
yours now for- ev- er and ev- er! A heart true as
mf

sì, ei bat - te co - sì, ei bat - te co - sì, ei
gold, to have and to hold, a heart true as gold, to
sì, ei bat - te co - sì, ei bat - te co - sì, ei
gold, to have and to hold, a heart true as gold, to
mf p mf p mf p
bat - te co - sì.
have and to hold!
(Wants to put the heart where she keeps the portrait of her lover.)
Ei quì non può
I real - ly don't
bat - te co - sì. Quì la - scia ch'il met - ta.
have and to hold! And now you must wear it!
GUGL.
DORAB.
star. T'in - ten - do fur - bet - ta, t'in - ten - do fur - betta. Che
dare. You rascal, I know you! Just wait till I show you! What
mfp mfp
(He gently turns her face the other way, then takes away the portrait and puts the heart in its place.)
GUGL.
DORAB.
(to herself)
fa - i? Non guardar. Nel pet - to un Ve -
is it? Don't look yet. I feel so ex-
mfp mfp

DORAB.
su _ vio d'a _ ve _ re mi par, nel
cit- - ed, a- - glow and on fire, so
GUGL. (to himself)
(Fer _ ran _ do me _ schi _ no!
Fer- ran- - do, poor fel- - low!
pet _ to un Ve _ su _ vio d'a _ ve _ re mi par.
strange- ly de- light- ed and filled with de- sire.
pos _ si _ bil non par.)
His fu- ture looks dire.
cresc.
GUGL.
L'oc_chiet_to a me gi _ ra.
And now you may see it.
DORAB.
Che bra_mi?
Oh, may I?
GUGL.
Ri _ mi _ ra, ri _ mi _ ra, se me_glio può an_dar.
Look here, dear, look here, dear. Now what do you say?

DORAB.
Oh cam - bio fe - li - ce
How joy - ful a un - ion
GUGL.
Oh cam - bio fe - li - ce
How joy - ful a un - ion
di co - ri e d'af - fet - ti! che nuo - vi di - let - ti, che
of hearts and af - fec - tion, the no - blest per - fec - tion that
di co - ri e d'af - fet - ti! che nuo - vi di - let - ti, che
of hearts and af - fec - tion, the no - blest per - fec - tion that
dol - ce pe - nar, che nuo - vi di - let - ti, che dol - ce pe - nar!
love can at - tain, the no - blest per - fec - tion that love can at - tain!
dol - ce pe - nar, che nuo - vi di - let - ti, che dol - ce pe - nar!
love can at - tain, the no - blest per - fec - tion that love can at - tain!

Oh cam_bio fe_li_ce
How joy-ful a un-ion
Oh cam_bio fe_li_ce
How joy-ful a un-ion
p
mf
di co_ri e d'af_fet_ti! che
of thought and of feel-ing, so
di co_ri e d'af_fet_ti! che
of thought and of feel-ing, so
p
f p
nuo_vi di_let_ti, che dol_ce pe_nar, che nuo_vi di_let_ti, che
sweet-ly re-veal-ing the won-der of love, so sweet-ly re-veal-ing the
nuo_vi di_let_ti, che dol_ce pe_nar, che nuo_vi di_let_ti, che
sweet-ly re-veal-ing the won-der of love, so sweet-ly re-veal-ing the
mf
f p f p f p

SCENA VI **SCENE VI**

L'a_spide, l'i_dra, il ba_si_li_sco, e
All of them, the hy-dra, the writh-ing ser-pent, and
quanto i Li_bi_ci de_ser_ti han di più fie_ro, in me so_lo tu
all the hor-ri-fy-ing mon-sters you could im-ag-ine you have seen in my
FIORD.
ve_di. È ve_ro, è ve_ro. Tu vuoi tor_mi la
per- son. 'It's true, I ad-mit it. You have caused me such
Adagio
FERR.
FIORD.
pa_ce. Ma per far_ti fe_li_ce. Ces_sa di mo_le_
an- guish. For your hap- pi- ness on- ly. If you would on- ly
FERR.
FIORD.
FERR.
star_mi! Non ti chie_do ch'un guardo. Par_ti_ti! Non spe_
leave me! All I ask is one glance. Nev- er! You dis-

rar_lo, se pria gli occhi men fie_ri a me non gi _ ri. O
miss me, a- ban- don me to grief and des- per- a- - tion! Dear
ciel! ma tu mi guardi e poi so_spi_ri?
God! Is there no hope, no con- so- la- tion?
No. 24 Aria
Allegretto
FERR. (happily)
Ah! lo veggio quell'a _ ni_ma bel_la al mio pianto re_si _ sternon
Though you try to be deaf to my plead- ing, I am sure you will yield in the
sà: non è fat _ ta per es_ser ru_bel_la agli af_fet_ti di ami_ca pie_
end. You're not meant to be cold and un- heed- ing to the love of so faith- ful a

tà, non è fat_ta per es_ser ru_bel_la, ru_bel_la agli af_
friend, you're not made to be cold and un- heed- ing, un- heed- ing to the
mfp
mfp
fet_ _ti di a_mi_ _ca pie_tà. In quel
love of so faith- ful a friend. All your
guardo, in quei ca_ri so_spi_ri dol_ce raggio lampeggia al mio cor, lam_
glanc- es, so de- mure and ap- peal- ing, make my heart glow with soft, ra- diant light, with
peg- gia al mio cor: già ri_spondi a miei cal_di de_si_ ri, già tu
soft, ra- diant light. You will yield to the force of my feel- ing, to its
sf
p
sfp
sfp

ce_di al più te_nero a_mor. già tu ce_di, tu ce_di al più
bound- less en- dur- ance and might. You'll sur- ren- der, sur- ren- der, to its
sfp
sfp
te- ne- ro a- mor, già ri_spondi a miei cal_di de_
end- less de- light! You will yield to the force of my
sfp
si_ ri, già tu ce_di al più te_nero a_mor, già tu
feel- ing, to its bound- less en- dur- ance and might. You'll sur-
sfp
sfp
sfp
ce_di, tu ce_di al più te- ne- ro a- mor. Ah, lo
ren- der, sur- ren- der, to its end- less de- light. Though you
p

veggio, che l'a - ni - ma bel - la al mio pianto re - si - ster non sà: non è
try to be deaf to my plead- ing, I am sure you will yield in the end. You're not
fat - ta per es - ser ru - bel - la agli af - fet - ti di a - mi - ca pie - tà, non è
made to be cold and un- heed- ing to the love of so faith- ful a friend, you're not
fat - ta per es - ser ru - bel - la, ru - bel - la a - gli af - fet - -
made to be cold and un- heed- ing, un- heed- ing to the love
- - ti di a - mi - ca pie - tà. In quel guardo, in quei
of so faith- - ful a friend. All your glanc- es, so de-

ca_ri so_spi_ri dol_ce raggio lampeggia al mio cor, lam_peg_gia al mio
mure and ap- peal- ing, make my heart glow with soft, ra- diant light, with soft, ra- diant
cor: già ri_spondi a miei cal_di de_si_ri, già tu cedi al più te_nero a_
light. You will yield to the force of my feel- ing, to its bound-less en-dur-ance and
mor, già tu ce_di, tu ce_di al più te_
might. You'll sur- ren- der, sur- ren- der, to its end-
ne_ro a_mor, già ri_spondi a miei cal_di de_si_ri, già tu
less de- light. You will yield to the force of my feel- ing, to its
sf
p
sfp

cedi al più te_ne_ro a_mor, già ___ tu ce_di, tu ce_di al più
bound- less en- dur- ance and, might. You'll ___ sur- - ren- der, sur- ren- der, to its
sfp sfp
te - - ne - ro a - mor, al più
end- - - less de- - light, to its
cresc. fp
te - ne_ro a - mor, al più te - - ne_ro a_
end- - less de- light, to its end- - - less de-
cresc. fp
mor. Ma tu fug_gi, spie_ta - ta tu ta_ci, ed in_va_no mi
light. But you spurn me, dis- dain- ful, un- car- ing, cold- ly leave_ me to
sf p
sfp sfp sfp sfp sf p

Allegro
sen _ ti lan_guir? Ah, ces _ sa _ te spe _ ran _ ze fal _
lan- - guish and sigh! Ah, I'm hope- less, a- - ban- - doned, de-
sfp
sfp
la _ ci, spe _ ran _ ze fal _ la _ ci, la cru _ del mi condanna a mo _
spairing, a- - ban- - doned, de- spair- ing, for you cruel- ly con- demn me to
sfp
rir, mi con _ dan _ na a mo _ rir, la cru _ del! Ah, ces _
die, — you con- demn — mo to die, you a- lone! Ah, I'm
cresc.
f
sfp
sfp
sa _ te spe_ranze fal _ la _ ci, la cru _ del mi condan_na a mo_rir, — la cru _
hope- less, a- ban- doned, de- spair- ing, for you cruel- ly con- demn me to die, — for you
sfp

del — mi con_dan - - - na a mo_rir, la cru_del mi con_
cruel- - ly con- demn me to die, for you cruel- ly con-
cresc.
p
sfp
dan_na a mo_rir, la crudel mi con_dan_na a mo_rir, la cru_del mi con_
demn me to die, for you cruel- ly con- demn me to die, for you cruel- ly con-
sfp
sfp
dan_na, con_dan_na a mo_rir.
demn — me, con- demn me to die!
(Exit Ferrando.)
cresc.
f
sfp
sfp
f
Recit.
Allegretto
SCENA VII
SCENE VII
FIORD.
Ei par_te... senti... ah no! par_tir si la_sci, si
I hurt him! Should I? . . . ah, no! It's bet- ter this way. At
p
f
p

tol_ga ai sguardi mie_i l'in_fausto og_get_to del_la mia de_bo_
least I will not see him, the wretch- ed per- son who has caused me to
lez_za. A qual ci_mento il barba_ro mi po_se! un premio è
weak- en. What griev- ous an- guish the cru- el man has brought me! But I de-
que_sto ben do_vu_to a mie col_pe! In ta_le istante do_
serve it for my shame- less be- hav- ior! At such a mo- ment how
vea di nuovoaman_te, i so_spiri a_scol_tar? l'al_trui quere_le dovea
could I ev- er lis- ten to a new lov- er's plea? Should I have treat- ed his pro-
vol_ger in gio_co? Ah, que_sto co_re a ra_gio_ne condanni, o giusto a_
pos- al more light- ly? Yes, I am guilt- y. I am pun- ished quite just- ly. O dear Gu-
p
f
p
f
p
f
p
fp

Nº 25. Rondo

Adagio

FIORD.

mante fra quest' ombre, e que_ste piante sem_pre a_sco_so, oh Dio,_ sa_
bro- ken. May my er- ror re- main un- spo- ken, stay for- got- ten, un- known_ and
rà, sem_pre a - sco - so, a - sco - so,oh Dio,___ sa -
past, stay for- - got- - ten, re- - main___ un- - known ___ and___
rà! Sve_ne_rà quest'em_pia voglia l'ar_dir mio, la mia_ co...
past. May my hon- est, true de- vo- tion, glow- ing love, and deep_ re- - -
f
p
stanza, per - de_rà la ri_ membranza,
pen- tance purge my heart of all re- mem- brance,
dolce

che vergogna e or_ror mi fà, che vergogna, che ver_go - -
make me worth-y of you__ at last, make me worth-y, make me worth- - -
_gna e or_ror__ mi__ fà. Per pie_tà, ben mio, per_do_na
- - y of you__ at__ last. Dear- est love, I beg your par- don
all' er_ror d'un al_ma a_mante; fra__ quest'__
for the faith that I__ have bro- ken. May__ my__
ombre, e que_ste pian_te sem_pre a_
er- ror re- main un- spo- ken, stay for-
sco_so, oh Dio,__ sa_rà, sempre a_sco_ so, a_sco_so, oh Dio,__ sa_
got- ten, un- known__ and past, stay for- got- ten, re- main__ un- known__ and__
tr
p
f

Allegro moderato
rà. A chi mai mancò di
past. Why did I embrace temp-
p
fe-de que-sto va-no, ingra-to cor, si do-vea miglior mer-
ta-tion, break the ten-der vows I swore, when it was my as-pir-
ce-de, ca-ro be-ne, al tuo can-dor, ca-ro be-
a-tion to be faith-ful ev-er-more, to be faith-
cresc.
f
p
ne, al tuo can-dor. Per pie-
ful ev-er-more? Dear-est
dol.
tà, ben mio, per-do-na all'— er-
love, I beg your par-don for — the

ror d'un al _ ma a _ mante; sve_ne_rà quest'em _ pia
faith that I have bro- ken. May my hon- - est, true de-
vo_glia l'ar_dir mio, la mia co_stanza, per_de_rà la ri_mem_
vo- tion, glow- ing love, and deep re- pen- tance purge my heart of all re-
fp fp fp fp fp fp fp fp fp fp
branza, che ver_gogna e orror mi fà. Ah chi
mem- brance, make me worth- y of you at last. Why did
mai man_cò di fe_de que_sto va_no, ingra_to cor, si do_
I em- brace temp- ta- tion, break the ten- der vows I swore, when it
vea mi_glior mer_ce_de, ca_ro be_ne, al tuo can _
was my as- pir- a- tion to be faith- - ful ev- er- -
cresc.

dor, ca - ro be - ne, al tuo can - dor.
more, to be faith - ful ev - er - more?
A chi mai man - cò di
Heav - en grant me one kind
fe - de que - sto va - no, in - gra - to
fa - vor, let my se - cret re - main un -
cor, que - sto va - no, que - sto va - no, in -
known, let my se - cret, let my se - cret re -
p
f
fp

gra - to cor, si do - vea mi-glior mer-
main un- - known. With un-fail- - - - - - - ing en-
ce-de, ca-ro be-ne, al tuo can-dor, ca - ro
deav- or for my fault I shall a- - tone, for my
be-ne, al tuo can - dor, ca - ro
er- ror I shall a- - tone, for my
rallent.
be-ne, ca - ro be - ne, al tuo can - dor, ca-ro
er- ror, for my er- - ror I shall a- - tone, for my
fp
rallent.

a tempo
be - ne, al tuo can - dor, ca - ro be - ne, al tuo can - dor, ca - ro
er - - ror I shall a - tone, for my er - - ror I shall a - tone, for my
colla parte.
fp
tr
be - ne, ca - ro be
er - - ror, for my er -
ne, al
ror
(Exit Fiordiligi.)
tuo can - dor.
so a - tone.
cresc.
f

SCENA VIII

SCENE VIII

FERR.
van_ti. Fin_go lab_bra tre_man_ti, fin_go di pian_ger, fin_go di mo_
on, friend. I said all I could think of, swore that I loved her, threat- - ened to
GUGL.
rir al suo piè___ Bra_va as_sai per mia fè! Ed
die at her feet. My dear boy, you did well! And
FERR. GUGL. FERR.
el_la? El_la da pri_ma ri_de, scher_za, mi bur_la_ E poi? E poi fin_ge d'impie_to_
she? At the be- gin- ning she was laugh- ing and jok- ing. And then? For a mo- ment I thought she
GUGL. FERR.
sir_ si_ Oh co_spet_tac_cio! Al - fin scop_pia la bom_ba:
wa- vered. That lit- tle vix- en! But then, bang! went the bomb- shell.
"pu_ra co_me colomba al suo ca_ro Guglielmo el_la si ser_ba," mi dis_sac_cia su_
"Dare you ques- tion my vir- tue? I will al- ways be faith- ful to my Gu- gliel- mo." She be- gan to a-

per_ba, mi mal_trat_ta, mi fug_ge, te_sti_mo_nio ren_den_do_mi, e mes_
buse me, called me names and left me. So you see from her at- ti- tude there's no
GUGL.
sag_gio, che u_na fem _ mi_na ell' è sen_za pa_rag_gio. Bra_vo
doubt, Fior- di- li- gi is one wo-man in a mil- lion. Good for
f
tu, bravo io, brava la mia Pe _ ne_lope! lascia un po ch'io ti abbrac_ci
you, good for me, good for my faith- ful sweet-heart! You're a friend in a mil- lion,
f
(They embrace.)
FERR.
per sì fe_li_ce au_gu_rio, o mio fi _ do Mer_cu_rio. E la mia Do_ra_bel_la?
bring- er of hap- py tid- ings. I'm de- lir- ious- ly hap- py! And my dear Do- ra- bel- la?
p
f
(enthusiastically)
co_me s'è di_por_ta_ta? Oh non ci ho nep_pur dub_bio, as_sai co_
How did you fare with her? Why do I e- ven ask you! I know your
p

GUGL.
no_sco quel_la sen_si_bil al_ma. Ep_pur un dub_bio, par_
an_swer! How could I e- ven doubt it? A lit- tle doubt- ing, my
FERR.
lan_do_ti a quattr'oc_chi, non sa_ria mal, se tu l'a _ ves_si! Co_me?
dear un- doubt- ing Thom- as, might be ad- vis- a- ble at times. How so?
GUGL.
Di_co co_sì per dir. (A_vrei pia _ ce_re d'in_dol_rar _ gli la
Oh, it was just a thought. (I wish I knew how to sweet- en his cup of
FERR.
pil_lo_la.) Stel_le, ces_se el_la for_se al_le lu_sin_ghe tu_e?
bit- ter- ness!) Brag- gart! Are you im- ply- ing she yield- ed to your ad- vanc- es?
GUGL.
ah, s'io po_tes_si so_spet_tar _ lo sol_tan_to! E sem_pre
No, it can't be! I will nev- er sus- pect her! You would be

FERR.
be - ne il so_spet_ta_re un po_co in que_sto mon_do. E_ter_ni
wis- er to leave a lit- tle room for some sus- - pi- cion. What do you
De - i, fa_vel_la: a fo_co len_to non mi far qui mo-
mean? Speak up! If you must poi- son me, must it be drop by
f
fp
rir; ma no, tu vuo_i prender_ti me_co spasso: el_la non
drop? But no! It can't be! Tell me that you are jok- ing. I am her
GUGL.
a_ma, non a_do- ra che me. Cer- to! anzi in pro_va di suo a-
love and she loves on- ly me. Sure- ly! And to prove the fact be-
mor, di sua fe - de que_sto bel ri_trat_ti_no el_la mi
yond an- y ques- tion, she gave me this de- light- ful lit- tle

FERR. (raging)
(Starts to leave.)
diede. Il mio ri_tratto! ah per_fi_da!
por-trait. Gave you my por- trait? Ah, shame on her!
senza tempo
Allegro a tempo
p
cresc.
f
sf
GUGL.
FERR. (furiously)
O_ve va_i? A trarle il cor dal scel_le_ra_to pet_to, e a vendi -
Are you rav- ing? No, I am not, but she will pay me dear-ly for her mis-
p
GUGL.
FERR.
(determined)
car il mio tra_di_to af_fet_to. Fermati! No, mi
deed. How could she dare be- tray me? Calm your-self! No, I
f
GUGL.
la_scia. Sei tu pazzo, vuoi tu pre_ci_pi_tar_ti per u_na
can- not! This is mad- ness! Why do you want to wreck your- self for a
(aside)
don_na che non val due sol_di? (Non vor_rei che fa -
wo- man so com- plete- ly worth- less? (If I just could pre-

FERR.
ces_se qual_che cor_bel - le - ri_a!) Nu_mi, tan_te pro-
vent him from do-ing some- - thing fool-ish.) Think of it! Her deep de-
sp
mes_se, e la_gri_me, e so_spi_ri, e giu_ra_menti in si
vo-tion, her prom-is-es, her af-fec-tion and prot-es-ta-tions — all for-
Andante
p
GUGL.
FERR.
po_chi mo_menti co_me l'empia o_bliò! Per Bacco io non lo so! Che fare or
got-ten en-tire-ly in the wink of an eye! That seems to be the case. My life is
sp
deggio, a qual par_ti_to, a qual i_dea m'appi_glio?
ru-ined! What shall I do now? What use is there in liv-ing?
Allegro
f
GUGL.
Abbi di me pie_tà, dam_mi con_si_glio. A_mi_co, non sa-
I'm in a dread-ful state! Help me, I beg you! I wish I could ad-

№26. Aria
Allegretto

che, se il ver vi deggio dir, se si la_gna_no gli a_
I have some-thing on my mind. It's a bas- ic, hu- man
manti li com_mincio a compa_tir, li com_mincio a compa_tir.
prob- lem and it touch- es all man- kind, and it touch- es all man- kind.
Io vo bene al ses_so vo_stro lo sa_
Like my fel- low- men and broth- ers, I have
pe_te, ognun lo sà, o_gni giorno ve lo mostro, ve lo
wor- shiped be- fore your shrine. Like a hun- dred mil- lion oth- ers, like a
mostro, ve lo mostro, vi do se_gno d'a_mi_stà, ve lo
hun- dred mil- lion oth- ers, I be- lieved you were di- vine. I've re-
fp
f

mostro, ve lo mostro, vi do se_gno d'a_mi_stà, vi do
spect- ed and pro- tect- ed your good name in ev- 'ry way, yes, in
cresc.
se_gno d'a_mi_stà. Ma quel farla a tan_ti e tanti, a tanti e
each and ev- 'ry way. But you thank- less, love- ly, love- ly, love- ly
fp
tanti, m'avvi_lisce in ve_ri_tà, m'avvi_
wo- men fill my soul with deep dis- may, fill my
li_sce in ve_ri_tà. Mil_le volte il brando
soul with deep dis- may. With my sword I saved your
f
presi per sal_var il vostro o_nor, mil_le vol_te,
vir- tue, I have fought a fear- less fight. I've dis- cov- ered
f
f

mil_le vol_te, mil_le vol_te vi di_fe_si col_la
and un- cov- ered ev- 'ry plot de- signed to hurt you. I have
p
bocca e più col cor. Ma quel farla a tanti e tanti, a tanti e
been your peer- less knight. But you wicked, love- ly, love- ly, love- ly
tan_ti è un vi_ziet_to sec_ca_tor, è un vi_
wo- men put my chiv- al- ry to flight, put my
ziet_to sec_ca_tor. Sie_te vaghe, siete a_ma_bili,
chiv- al- ry to flight. You're de- light- ful, you're a- dor- a- ble,
più te_so_ri il ciel vi diè, e le
you are pre- cious, you are sweet, you are
mf

gra_zie vi cir_con_da_no dal_la te_sta si_no ai
gra- cious, fair, and lov- a- ble, and we men are at your
p
mf
p
piè, dal_la te_sta si_no ai piè. Ma, ma, ma, la
feet, and we men are at your feet. But, but. but, you
fa_te a tanti e tanti, a tanti e tanti che cre_di_bi_le non
thank- less, love- ly, love- ly, love- ly wo- men shock my heart with your de-
è, che cre_di_bi_le non è. Io vo bene al ses_so
ceit, shock my heart with your de- ceit. In the most po- et- ic
vostro, ve lo mostro, mil_le volte il brando presi,
phras- es I have sung your sex- -'s prais- es, I have laud- ed
fp

vi di - fe - si, gran te - sori il ciel vi diè, sino ai
and ap - plaud - ed and ex - tolled you to the sky, to the
piè, ma, ma, ma, la fate a tanti e tanti, a
sky. But, but, but, you wick - ed, love - ly wo - men, you
tanti e tanti, a tanti, la fate a tanti e tanti, a tanti e tanti
love - ly, love - ly wo - men, you wick - ed, love - ly, love - ly, love - ly, wo - men,
che se gri - da - no gli a - manti hanno certo un gran per -
when I see how you mis - treat us I be - gin to won - der
cresc.
chè, un gran per - chè, ah la fate a tanti e tan - ti che se
why, to won - der why, when I see how you mis - treat us and how
f

gri_da_no gli a_manti hanno certo un gran per_chè, un gran per -
cal- lous- ly you cheat us, I be- gin to won- der why, to won- der
cresc.
f
chè, per - chè, perchè, perchè han certo un gran per -
why, to won- - der why, I be- gin to won- der
p
chè, per - chè, per_chè, perchè han cer_to un gran per -
why, to won- - der why, I be- gin to won- der
chè, un gran per_chè, un gran per - chè, hanno certo un gran per -
why, to won- - der why, to won- der why, I be- gin to won- der
f p f p f
cresc.
(Exit Guglielmo.)
chè.
why.
f

SCENA IX — SCENE IX

Recit.

Al_fon_so, Al _ fonso, quanto ri_der vor_rai del_la mia stu_pi _
Al- - fon- so! Al- - fon- so! You were right, af- ter all! Now you will be tri-
dezza! Ma mi ven_di_che_
um- phant! But I shall be a-
fp
rò, sa_pro dal se_no can_cel_
venged! I'll tear her im- age from my
f
lar quell' i _ ni_qua... sa_prò can_cel _ lar_la_ cancel_
heart and my mem- 'ry, and shall not re- gret her! Not re-
Andante
p
lar_la? Troppo oh Dio! que_sto cor per lei mi par_la.
gret her? No, dear God, I can- not! I can't for- get her!

Nº 27. Cavatina

vo - ci d'a - mor, le vo - ci d'a - mor, le vo - -
love that I mourn, the love — that I mourn, the love —
ci d'a - mor Tra - di - to, scher - ni - to dal
that I mourn. Re - ject - ed, ne - glect - ed, my
per - fi - do cor, dal per - fi - - do cor,
heart grieved and sore, my heart grieved and sore!
(Don Alfonso enters with Guglielmo. They stay in the background, listening to Ferrando.)
dol.
io sen - to che an - co - ra quest'
I still love her aear - ly, tor -
al - ma l'a - do - ra, io sen - to per es - sa le vo - ci d'a -
ev - er sin - cere - ly. My love is as great — and as strong — as be -

mor; io sén - to per es - sa le vo - ci d'a - mor, le
fore, my love is as great and as strong as be - fore, as
vo - ci d'a - mor, d'a - mor, le vo - ci d'a -
strong as be - fore, my love as strong as be -
mor, le vo - ci d'a - mor.
fore, as strong as be - fore,
le vo - ci, le vo - ci d'a -
for - ev - er as strong as be -
(Don Alfonso and Guglielmo step forward.)
mor.
fore!
sfp
fp
f
p
cresc.

Recit.
D. ALF.
FERR.
Bra_vo! que_sta è co_stanza. An_da te, o bar_ba_ro, per voi mi _ se_ro
Bra- - vo! That's how it should be. Stay a- way from me! You have caused all my
fp
D. ALF.
so_no. Via se sa_re _ te buono vi tor_ne_rò l'anti_ca calma. U _dite: Fiordi_
mis- 'ry! Learn how to bear it calm- ly, and you will be so much the wis- er. The fact is, Fior- di-
li _ gi a Guglielmo si con_ser_va fe_del, e Do_ra_bel_la in_fe_del a voi
li- - gi was faith- ful, at least up to now, but Do- ra- bel- la was too weak to re-
FERR.
GUGL.
fù. Per mia ver_go_gna. Caro a_mi_co, bi_so_gna far del_le dif_fe_renze in o_gni
sist. Yes, to my shame. Dear Fer- ran- do, you must be a- ble to see a thing in its true
co_sa. Ti pa_re che u_na sposa man_car possa a un Gugliel_mo? un pic_ciol
as- pect. Where would you find a wo- man who'd fail a Gu- - gliel- - mo? If you com-

cal_co_lo, non par_lo per lo _ dar_mi, se fac_cia_mo tra noi...
pare us — I say it in all mod- es- ty — you will have to ad- mit,
D. ALF.
GUGL.
tu vedi a_mi_co che un po_co di più merto _Ehanch'io lo di_co! In_tan_to mi da_
if you are hon- est, I have a slight ad- van- tage. He's got a point there. And now, sup- pose you
D. ALF.
re_te cinquanta zecchi _ net_ti. Vo_lon_tie_ri: pria pe_rò di pa_gar vo che fac_
pay me my half of the wa- ger. I'll be glad to, but be- fore I shall do it, per-
GUGL. D. ALF.
ciamo qualche altra espe_rienza. Come? Ab_bia_te pa_zienza: In_fin do_ma_ni siete en_
mit me to try one more test. You mean? I'm not yet de- feat- ed. Un- til to- mor- row you are
trambi miei schiavi: a me voi deste pa_ro_la da sol_da_ti, di far quel ch'io di_
bound to our wa- ger, and just re- mem- ber, you gave your word of hon- or to o- bey my com-
rò. Ve_ni_te; o spe_ro mostrar_vi ben che fol_le è quel cer_vel_lo, che_
mand. Till then, I will not give up the ship, and I am still com- pet- ing, for —

(Exeunt.)
— sul_la fra_sca an_cor ven_de l'uc_cel_lo.
the proof of the pud-ding is in the eat-ing!
(Curtain)
Recit.
SCENA X
(Curtain)
SCENE X
(A room with several doors, a mirror, and a little table. Dorabella and Despina on-stage.)
DESP.
O_ra ve_do che sie_te u_na don_na di garbo.
Now at last you are act-ing like a wo-man of the world.
DORAB.
In_van De_spi_na, di re_si_ster ten_tai: quel de_mo_niet_to ha un ar_ti_fi_zio, un e_lo_quen_za, un trat_to, che ti fà ca_der giù se sei di sas_so.
I was not a-ble to re-sist the temp-ta-tion. That charm-ing dev-il is so per-sua-sive, he is so clev-er, so gen-tle, he would e-ven suc-ceed in melt-ing mill-stones.
DESP.
Cor_po di sa_ta_nasso, que_sto vuol dir sa_per, tan_to di ra_ro noi po_ve_re ra_gazze ab_biamo un po di be_ne, che bi_so_gna pi_gliar_lo all_or ch'ei
Now you are talk-ing log-ic and real-ly show-ing sense! On-ly too sel-dom are we poor girls per-mit-ted to snatch a bit of plea-sure, so it is up to us to make hay while the

FIORD. (entering)
vie_ne. Ma ec_co la so_rel_la, che cef_fo! Scia_gu_ra_te,
sun shines! Who's com- ing? It's your sis- ter! She's rav- ing! How dis- grace-ful!
f fp
DESP.
ec_co per colpa vostra in che sta _ to mi tro_vo! Cosa è na _ to, ca_ra Ma_da_mi_
It's on ac-count of you that I'm in this di- lem- ma. What has hap- pened? Why are you so ex-
DORAB.
FIORD.
gel_la? Hai qualche mal so _ rel _ la? Ho il diavo_lo, che por_ti me, te, le_i,
cit- ed? Is some- thing wrong, dear sis- - ter? I hope the dev- il takes you all, you, and her,
DORAB.
Don Alfonso, i fo_re_stie_ri e quanti pazzi ha il mon _ do. Hai per_du_to il giu_
Don Al- fon- so, those two in- trud- ers! And all the fools in this world! Are you out of your
f
FIORD.
di_zio? Peggio, peggio, in _ or_ri_disci: io a_mo! e l'amor mi_o non è
mind? Worse than that! Dare I ad- mit it? I love him! And worst of all is, I do
f p

DESP.
DORAB.
sol per Guglielmo. Meglio, meglio! E che si, che anche tu se' inna_mo_ra_ta
not mean Gu- gliel- mo! Sounds ex- cit- ing! Do you mean that you've al- so start- ed yield- ing,
FIORD. (sighing)
DESP.
del ga_lan_te bion_di_no? Ah pur trop_po per noi. Ma bra_va!
and you love your new suit- or? Ah, yes, on- ly too much! De- light- ful!
DORAB.
Tie_ni, set_tan_ta mil_le ba_ci: tu il biondi_no, io'l bru_net_to, ec_coci en_trambe
Sis- ter, I sim- ply have to kiss you! Then we both will be mar- ried! What could be more ro-
FIORD.
spo_se! Co_sa di_ci? non pen_si a_gli in_fe - li_ci che sta_ma_ne par_
man- tic! But how can we? Just think of our poor sol- diers who have gone to the
tir, ai lo_ro pianti, al_la lor fe_del_tà tu più non pen_si, co_sì
wars! Have you no feel- ing for those two faith- ful men, the grief we'd cause them? How
42735

bar_ba_ri sen_si, do_ve, dove apprendesti, sì di _ ver_ sa da te co_me ti
could we de- ceive them? What has come o- ver you, that you want to com- mit such a be-
DORAB.
fe_ sti? O_ di_ mi: sei tu cer_ta che non muo _ jano in guerra i
tray- al? Wait a bit! How do we know that the worst might not hap- pen? Sup-
no_stri vecchi a_ manti? E al_ lo_ ra, en_trambe re_ste_ rem col_le man pie_ ne di
pose they fell in bat- tle? In that case, what would be- come of us? Would- n't we be the
mosche: tra un ben cer_ to e un in _ cer_to c'è sempre un gran di _
los- ers? You know the say- - ing: A bird in the hand is worth two in the
FIORD.
DORAB.
va_ rio. E se poi tor_ ne _ ran_no? Se tor_ ne_ ran lor
bush! But if they should re- - turn? In that e- vent, it's

dan_no, noi sa_re - mo al_lor mo_gli, noi sa_re_mo lon -
their loss! By that time we'll be mar-ried, and what's more, we'll be
FIORD.
ta_ne mil_le miglia. Ma non so, co_me mai si può can_giar in un sol giorno un
liv-ing a-broad. I am still at a loss to un-der-stand this sud-den change of
DORAB.
co_re? Che do_man - da ri - di - co_la, siam don_ne, e poi tu com'hai
heart. That is down- -right ri- dic- -u-lous! We're wo-men! Af-ter all, what did
FIORD.
DESP.
FIORD.
fat_to? Io sa_prò vin_cer_mi. Voi non sa_pre_te nul_la. Fa -
you do? But I'm not sur-ren- -der-ing! There you are quite mis-tak-en! I
DORAB.
rò che tu lo ve_da. Credi so_rel_la, è me_glio che tu ce_da.
won't! I'll nev-er do it! Come, dear-est sis-ter, you must, or you will rue it.

Nº 28. Aria

Allegretto vivace

tà, che l'a_ni_ma in ca_te_na, e to_glie li_ber_tà.
heart, he ties his chain a- round you and rules your help- less heart.
cresc.
È a_more un la_dron_cel_lo, un ser_pen_tello e a_mor, ei
I know a naugh- ty fel- low, a wi- ly rogue called Love He
f
p
to_glie e dà la pa_ce, la pa_ce co_me gli piace ai cor.
sly- ly steals your calm- ness, your calm- ness, sweet as a tur- tle-dove.
Por_ta dol_cez_za, dol_cez_za e gu_sto, se
He can be charm- ing, di- vine, de- light- ful, if
tu lo la_sci far, ma t'em_pie di dis_gu_sto, ma
he's al- lowed his way, but al- so cru- el and spite- ful, ma-
fp

t'em_pie di dis_gu_sto se ten_ti di pu_gnar,
lev- - o- lent and spite- - ful, if you should dis- - o- - bey.
fp
fp
f
p
por_ta dol_cez_za e gu_sto se tu lo la_sci far, ma
He can be so de- light- - ful, if he's al- lowed his way, but
t'em_pie di dis_gu_sto se ten_ti di pu_
al- - - so cru- - el and spite- - - ful, if you should dis- - - o-
fp
fp
fp
fp
fp
g'nar. È a_mo_re un la_dron_cel_lo, un
bey. I know a naugh- ty fel- - low, a
fp

ser _ pen_tel _ lo è a _ mor, ______ ei to _ glie e dà __ la
wi- - ly thief called Love ______ He sly- - ly steals__ your
pa _ ce, la pa _ ce co_me gli piace ai cor. Se nel tuo petto ei
calm- - ness, your calm- - ness, sweet as a tur- tle- dove. Each time his fire___
sie _ de, s'e _ gli ti bec_ca qui, fa tut _ to quel ch'ei chie _ de che anch'
brands_ you, rag- ging in- side your breast, do all_ that he com- mands you and
io fa_rò co _ sì.__ Se nel tuo petto ei
bet- - ter not pro- test.__ If he should come_ and

sie _ de, s'e_gli ti bec_ca qui, qui, qui, qui, fa
seize — you, pull- - ing your heart- strings tight, tight, tight, tight. just
tut_to quel ch'ei chie_de che anch'io fa_rò co_sì, s'e_gli ti bec_ca, s'e_gli ti
let the ras- cal tease — you and do not try to fight, just let him seize you, tick- le and
bec_ca, s'e_gli ti bec_ca, ti bec_ca, ti bec_ca, ti bec_ca, ti
tease you, tick- - le and tease you and tick- - le and tease you and tick- le and
bec - ca, fa tut - to quel ch'ei chie - de, ch'ei
tease — you! Just let the ras- - cal seize — you and
chie _ de che anch' io fa_rò co_sì, co_sì, ch'anch' io fa_rò co_
tease — you, as I in- tend to do, I too, as I in- tend to

SCENA XI SCENE XI

pace, agliocchi mi_ei mai più non compa_ri_sca! a tutti i servi mi_na_cierò il con_
trol him. I must a- void him, not e- ven let him see me. I will give or- ders that an- y of my
ge_do, se lo la_scian pas_sar, ve_der nol vo_glio quel se_dut_
ser- vants will be dis- missed on the spot if they should dare to let him come
GUGL. (listening at the door, unseen by Fiordiligi)
tor (Bra_vis_si_ma! la mia ca_sta Ar_te_mi_sia la sen_
near me. (By Ju- pi- ter! What a mod- - el of vir- - tue! Let's hear
FIORD.
ti_te?) Ma po_tria Do_ra_bel_la sen_za sa_pu_ta mi_a_
more!) I'm a- fraid Dor- a- bel- - la can- not be per- suad- ed.
piano! un pen_sie_ro per la men_te mi pas_sa: in ca_sa mi_a re_
Wait! An i- de- a! Now I know what to do! By some good for- tune Gu-
star molte u_ni_for_mi di Guglielmo e di Ferrando, ar_dir! De_spi_na! De_
gliel- mo and Fer- ran- do left some u- ni- forms be- hind. That's luck- y! Des- pi- na! Des-

DESP. (Enters.) FIORD.
spi_na! Co_sa c'è? Tie_ni un po que_sta chia_ve, e sen_za re_pli_ca,
pi- na! My la- dy called? Go up to the at- tic, and with- out ques- tion- ing
sen_za re_pli_ca al_cu_na pren_di nel guar_da_ro_ba, e quì mi
and with- out con- tra- dic- tion, o- pen your mas- ters' trunks and
por_ta due spa_de, due cap_pel_li, e due ve_sti_ti de' no_stri
bring me two hel- mets, two sa- bers, and two com- plete u- ni- forms they
DESP. FIORD. DESP.
spo_si. E che vo_le_te fa_re? Van_ne, non re_pli_ca_re. (Co_
left there. What for, if I may ask you? Go, do as I told you! (What a
(Leaves.) FIORD.
manda in ab_re_gè donna Arro_gan_za.) Non c'è al_tro; ho spe_ranza che Dorabella
high and might- y tone! It is dis- gust- ing.) I'm de- ter- mined. Now my prob- lem is get- ting Dor- a-
stes_sa se_gui_rà il bell' e_sempio: al cam_po, al cam_po, altra stra_da non
bel- la to con- sent to go with me. The soon- er, the bet- ter. It's the on- ly so-

D. ALF.
(at the door to Despina who returns)
re_sta per serba_ci in_no_cen_ti. (Ho ca_pi_to ab_ba_stan_za: van_ne pur non te_
lu- tion to pre-serve our in- -teg-ri-ty. (I can see what she's up to. Bet- ter do what she
DESP. FIORD.
mer.) Ec_comi. Vanne. Sei ca_val_li di po_sta voli un servo ordi_nar, di a Dora_
says.) There you are. Thank you. Now or- -der us hors-es and a man we can trust. Tell Dor-a-
DESP.
bella che parlar le vor_rei. Sa_rà servi_ta. (Questa don _ na mi par di senno u_
bel-la that I want her at once. I'm at your ser-vice. (This to- do and com-mo-tion is be-
SCENA XII
SCENE XII
(Exit Despina)
FIORD.
sci_ta.) L'a_bi_to di Fer_ran_do sa_rà buo_no per me; può Do_ra_
yond me!) This u-ni-form of Fer- -ran-do should be just a-bout my size, and Dor-a-
f fp
bel_la prender quel di Guglielmo; in questi ar_ne_si raggiungerem gli spo_si
bel-la can wear one of Gu-gliel-mo's. Dis-guised as sol- diers, we two can go and find our

no_stri, a lo_ro fian_co pugnar po_tre_mo, e mo_rir se fa
sweet- hearts. If it must be, we shall fight be- side them. E- ven death shall not
(Throws off her headdress.)
d'uo_po: i_te in ma_lo_ra or_na_men_ti fa_ta_li, io vi de_
part us! Off with this head- gear, this in- ane dec- o- ra- tion! Oh, how I
f
fp
GUGL.
FIORD.
te_sto. (Si può dar un a_mor si_mi_le a questo?) Di tor_nar non spe_ra_te al_la mi_a
hate it! (Her de- vo- tion and cour- age are a- stound- ing!) Not un- til I re- turn with my be-
fron_te pria ch'io qui tor_ni col mio ben; in vo_stro lo_co por_
lov- ed shall it a- dorn my head a- gain! And, in its stead, this
rò que_sto cappel_lo; oh co_me ei mi tras_for_ma le sem_
hel- met will dis- guise me! Now off to war and ad- ven- ture! I'll be
bianze e il vi_so, come ap_pe_na io me_des_ma or mi rav_vi_so!
luck- y, I'm cer- tain! Not a soul will sus- pect that I am a wo- man!

No. 29. Duetto

Adagio
FIORD.
Fragli amplessi in pochi istanti giungerò del fido sposo; sconosciuta a lui davanti in quest' abito verrò, in quest' abito verrò.
By tomorrow we'll be united! I will join you, dear Guglielmo! Unexpected, your Fiordiligi will appear in her disguise. What a wonderful surprise!
f
p
tr
Con moto
Oh che gioja il suo bel core proverà nel ravvisarmi!
You'll be joyful and so delighted when you see your faithful sweetheart!
FERR.
Ed intanto di dolore meschinello io mi morrò, meschi-
And I'll die here, unrequited, right before your very eyes, right be-
(stepping forward)

FIORD.
nel - lo io mi mor - rò! Co - sa veg-gio! son tra -
fore your ver - - - y eyes! Why are you here? Oh, how
Allegretto
di - ta! Deh par - ti - te!
dread - ful! Spare my feel - ings!
FERR.
Ah no mia vi - ta: con quel
Be - - fore you leave me, take this
(Takes his sword from the table, and draws it from its sheath.)
fer - ro di tua ma - no que-sto
sword and plunge it through me, through this
cor tu fe - ri - ra - i, e se
lov - - ing heart you wound - - ed! Take this
sf
p
cresc.

for _ _ za oh Dio non hai,
sword and pierce my heart,
cresc.
f
io la man ti reg_ge_ro, ti reg_ge_
take this sword and pierce my heart, and pierce my
p
cresc.
f
FIORD.
Ta_ci ahi _ mè, son ab_ba_stan_za tor_men_ta_ta,ed in_fe_
Nev_er! Please go! I have en_dured too much un_hap_pi_ness al_
FERR.
rò.
heart!
p
li_ce!
read_y!
Ah che o_mai la mia co_
My re_sis_tance starts to
Ah che o_mai la sua co_stanza
Her re_sist_ance starts to weak_en.

stanza a quei sguardi, a quel che
weak- en. Now my cour- age is less
a quei sguardi, a quel che di- ce,
Now her cour- age is less stead- y,
di- ce, in- co- min- cia a va- cil- lar, in- co- min- cia a va- cil- lar, in- co-
stead- y, and my will is fail- ing fast, and my will is fail- ing fast, and my
in- co- min- cia a va- cil- lar, in- co- min- cia a va- cil- lar, in- co-
and her will is fail- ing fast, and her will is fail- ing fast, and her
cresc.
p
cresc.
min- cia a vacil- lar. Sor- gi, sor- gi- Per pie-
will is fail- ing fast. Do not tempt me! Why on
min- cia a vacil- lar. In- van lo cre- di.
will is fail- ing fast. I beg you, hear me!
p

tù, da me che chie - di?
earth must you pur- sue— me?
Ah non son, non son più
He is strong and so ap-
Il tuo cor, o la mia morte.
Take my life or say you love me!
(He takes her hand and covers it with kisses.)
Ce - di
Dear- est
p cresc.
f
p
for - te, ah non son, non son più for - te, Dei con - si - glio,
peal- ing! I will yield, I have a feel- ing. God a- bove me!
ca - ra — ce - di ca - ra — ce - di
an- gel, say you love me! Don't re-
ah! non son più for te, Dei con - siglio!
I re- sist no long- er! God a- bove me!
ca - ra — ce - di ca - ra —
sist me an- - y long- er!
f
fp
Larghetto
FERR. (with great tenderness)
Vol - gi a me pie - to - so il ci - glio, in me
Al- ways o- bey— your heart's true feel- ing, yield to
p

sol tro_var tu puo_i spo_so, a_mante, e più se
love_ sin- cere and ten- der. Dear- est, I beg you, you must_ sur-
cresc.
vuo_i, i_dol mio_ più non tar_dar, spo_so,
ren- der! Do not let_ me plead in vain!_ Dear- est,
p
FIORD. (trembling)
Giusto ciel, giu_sto
Gra- cious Lord! Gra- cious
ciel, giu_sto ciel, cru_del
Lord! I am frail! I fail!
a_man_te, e più se_ vuo_i i_dol
be- lov- ed, you must sur- ren- der! Let my
cresc.
f
hai vin_to, Fa di me quel che ti
Have pit- y! I have fought my love in
mi_o più non tar_dar.
plead- ing not be in vain!_
p

(Guglielmo wants to rush in, but Don Alfonso holds him back.)

ciam _ ci o ca _ ro be_ne e un con _ for_to a tan_te pe_ne sia lan_
hap- - py past be- - liev- ing! All our tor- tured hours of griev- ing are for-
be _ ne, o ca _ ro be_ne e un con_ for_to a tan_te pe_ne sia lan_
hap- py past be- liev- ing! All our tor- tured hours of griev- ing are for-
guir di dol _ ce af_fet to, di di_let_to so_spi_rar, so_spi_rar, so_spi_
got- ten now for- ev- er! We shall nev- er part a- - gain! Dear- est heart, dear est
guir di dol _ ce af_fet to, di di_let_to so_spi_rar, so_spi_rar,
got- ten now for- - ev- er! We shall nev- er part a- - gain! Dear- est heart,
rar, di di_let _ _ to so_spi _ rar, so_spirar,
heart, we shall nev- - er part a- gain, dear- est heart,
so_spirar, di di_let to so_spi _ rar, so_spi_rar, so _ spi _
dear- est heart, we shall nev- er part a- - gain, dear- est heart, dear- est

so - spi - rar, di di - let - to so - spi -
dear- - est heart, we shall nev- - er part a- -
rar, di di - let - to so - spi -
heart, we shall nev- - - er part a-
rar, di di - let - to so - spi - rar, di di - let - to so - spi -
gain, we shall nev- er part a- - gain, we shall nev- er part a- -
rar, di di - let - to so - spi - rar, di di - let - to so - spi -
gain, we shall nev- er part a- - gain, we shall nev- er part a-
mfp
mfp
(Exeunt Flordiligi and Ferrando.)
rar, di di - let - to so - - spi - rar.
gain, we shall nev- - er part a- - gain!
rar, di di - let - to so - - spi - rar.
gain, we shall nev- - er part a- - gain!
fp
fp
cresc.
f
sf
sf
sf
sf

SCENA XIII — SCENE XIII

Recit.

FERR.
GUGL.
è! Chi? la tua Fiordi_li_gi? La mia Fior, Fior di dia - vo_lo, che
is she? Who? Your good Fior- di- li- gi? My good Fior — good for noth- - ing! The
p
FERR.
strozzi lei prima e do_po me! Tu ve_di be_ne, v'han del_le dif_fe_renze in ogni
dev- il may take her, and me with her! Do you re- mem- ber? I say it with- out the least bit of con-
f
(ironically)
GUGL.
co_sa, un po_co di più mer_to_ Ah ces_sa, ces_sa di tor_men_tar_mi, ed
ceit, "I have a slight ad- - van- tage!"? Keep qui- et! This is no time for jok- ing. We'd
fp
DON ALF.
u_na via piut_to_sto stu_diam di ca_sti_gar_le so_no_ra_mente. Io so, qual è: spo-
bet- ter think of some way to pun- ish those two hus- sies most se- vere- ly. I'll tell you how: You
GUGL.
FERR.
sar_le. Vor_rei spo_sar piut_to_sto la barca di Ca_ron_te. La grot_ta di Vul_
mar- ry them! I'd much rath- er mar- ry the dev- il's own grand- moth- er! And I an ug- ly
GUGL.
DON ALF.
ca_no. La por_ta dell' In _ fer_no. Dun _ que re_sta_te ce_li_bi in e_
o- gress! Or an- y fe- male drag- on! Then you will end your days as lone- ly

FERR.
DON ALF.
ter_no. Mancheran for_se donne ad uo_min co_me no_i? Non c'è abbondan_za
bach'lors! For men of your kind there are wo- - men a- plen- ty! I do not ac-
d'al_tro. Ma l'al_tre, che fa_ran se ciò fer que_ste? In
ny that. How- ev- er, do you think they would be dif- f'rent? You
GUGL.
FERR.
fon_do voi le u_ma_te queste vo_stre cornacchie spennac_chiate. Ah pur troppo! Pur
might as well ad- mit it, you love your un- faith- ful lit- tle sweet- hearts. Yes, we love them! We
DON ALF.
trop_po! Eh ben piglia_te_le com' el_le son, na_tu_ra non po_
love them! Why don't you mar- ry them just as they are? What gives you the
tea fa_re l'eccezzio_ne, il pri_vi_le_gio di cre_a_re due donne d'al_tra pa_sta per i
right to de- mand of na- ture to make ex- cep- tions and cre- ate two su- per- hu- man wo- men, just be-
vo_stri bei mu_si; in ogni co_sa ci vuol fi_lo_so_fi_a. Ve_ni_te me_co; di
cause you would like it? We can- not al- ter what has al- read- y hap- pened. There's on- ly one way to

Nº 30.

Andante

uso, ed a me par ne_ces_si_tà del co_re. L'a_man_te che si
take them as they are, as Moth- er Na- ture made them. You lov- ers, there is
f p cresc. p
tro_va al fin de_luso, non con_dan_ni l'al_trui, ma il proprio er_ro_re: giacchè
on- ly one con- clu-sion: they are al- ways un- true, it's no il- lu- sion. All your
cresc. f
gio_va_ni, vecchie, e bel_le, e brut_te, ri_pe_te_te con
an- ces- tors, fa- thers, and broth- ers went through it. Wom- en al- ways be-
p cresc. f
FERR.
Co_sì fan tut_te!
"Co- sì fan tut- te."
me: Co_sì fan tut_te! Co_sì fan tut_te!
tray, that's how they do it. "Co- sì fan tut- te."
GUGL.
Co_sì fan tut_te!
"Co- sì fan tut- te."
p f

SCENA XIV — SCENE XIV

Recit. (Enter Despina.)

SCENA XV

SCENE XV

(Curtain)

(A hall, richly decorated and illuminated. An orchestra at the back. Table set for four people, with silver candlesticks. Four servants in rich costumes. Despina, the Servants and Musicians.)

Nº 31. Finale

Allegro assai

(to the musicians)
nei son già di _ spo _ sti: e voi gi _ te ai vo stri
wed- - ding cel- - - e- - bra- - tion. Let us plan a great o-
po _ sti fin _ chè i spo _ si ven _ gon quà, fin _ chè i
va- - tion when the brides and grooms ap- - pear, when the
spo _ si ven _ gon quà.
brides and grooms ap- - - pear.
Sopr.
Alt.
Ten.
Bass
(Chorus of servants and musicians)
Facciam pre _ sto, o ca _ ri a _
Go a- head and light the
mi _ ci, al _ le fa _ ci il fo _ co dia _ mo,
can- - dles and com- plete the dec- - - o- - ra- - tions.

e la men_sa pre_pa_ra_te con ric_
Make the fi- nal prep- a- ra- tions. Soon the
chez_za e no_bil_tà, con ric_chez_za e no_bil_
coup- les will be here, soon the coup- les will be
tà, con ric_chez_za e no_bil_tà.
here, soon the coup- les will be here.
DON ALF.
Bravi!
This is
(While Don Alfonso sings, the musicians tune their instruments.)
bra_vi! ot_ti_ma_men_te! che abbon_dan_za, che e_le_
per- -fect! I am de- light- ed! This is splen- did, sim- ply

gan _ za! u _ na man _ cia con _ ve _ nien _ te l'un e
splen- - did! I shall see that you're com- - mend- - ed in a
l'al _ tro a voi da _ rà, l'un e l'al _ tro a voi da _
most sub- - stan- - tial way, in a most sub- - stan- - tial
rà. Le due cop _ pie o _ mai si av _ van _ za _ no fa _ te
way. When the coup- - - les make their en- - tranc- es, at my
plau _ so al lo _ ro ar _ ri _ vo, lie _ to
sig- - - nal gath- - - er near them. Wish them
f
p
tr
can _ to e suon giu _ li _ vo em _ pia il ciel d'i _ la _ ri _
luck and loud- - - ly cheer them. Clap your hands and shout hur-
tr
tr
tr
tr

DESP. (softly)
La più bel_la co_me_
I am ab- so- lute- ly
(softly)
tà, em_pia il ciel d'i_la_ri_tà. La più bel_la co_me_
ray, clap your hands and shout hur- - ray. I am ab- so- lute- ly
cresc.
f
pp
tr
dio_la non s'è vista, o si ve_drà, la più bel_la co_me_
cer- tain that the eve- ning will be gay! Ver- - y soon we'll raise the
dio_la non s'è vista, o si ve_drà, la più bel_la co_me_
cer- tain that the eve- ning will be gay! Ver- - y soon we'll raise the
dio_la non s'è vista, o si ve_drà, non s'è vi_sta o si ve_
cur- tain on the play with- in the play, on the play with- in the
dio_la non s'è vista, o si ve_drà, non s'è vi_sta o si ve_
cur- tain on the play with- in the play, on the play with- in the

(Exeunt Despina and Don Alfonso through different doors.)

(As the two sets of lovers enter, the Chorus sings and the orchestra begins a march.)

CORO

SCENA XVI SCENE XVI

lor il ciel be _ ne_fi_co, ed a
live in per- fect har- mon- y, care- - free,
gui _ sa di gal _ li _ ne sien di fi_ gli o _ _
peace- - ful, and un- - troub- - led, and at- - tain re- -
gnor pro _ li_fi_che che le ag_ gua _ gli_no in bel _
doub- - led hap- pi- ness with your chil- - dren at your

f
tà, — che le ag-gua - gli-no in bel - tà.
side, — with your chil- - - dren at your side.
FIORD.
Come par che qui pro-met-ta — tutto gioja e tut-to a - mo - re!
For- tune show- ers us with fa- vor! — Life can hold no great- er prom- ise!
DORAB.
Come par che qui pro-metta tutto gioja e tut-to a-mo - re!
For- tune show- ers us with fa- vor! Life can hold no great- er prom- ise!
FERR.
Come par che qui pro-metta tutto gioja e tut-to a-mo - re!
For- tune show- ers us with fa- vor! Life can hold no great- er prom- ise!
GUGL.
Come par che qui pro-metta tutto gioja e tut-to a-mo - re!
For- tune show- ers us with fa- vor! Life can hold no great- er prom- ise!
p
mf
p

Del - la ca-ra De - spi - net-ta certo il
Thank you, dear-est Des- pi- net- ta, for our
Del - la ca-ra De - spi - net-ta
Thank you, dear-est Des- pi- - net- ta,
Cer - to il me-ri-to sa-rà,
for our hap- pi- ness to- - night.
Cer - to il me-ri-to sa-rà,
for our hap- pi- ness to- - night,
me - - - - - - - - - ri-to, cer-to,
hap- - - - - - - - - - pi- ness, thank you,
del-la ca-ra De-spi-net-ta cer - to,
thank you, dear- est Des- pi- - net- ta, thank you
del-la ca-ra De-spi-net-ta cer - to,
thank you, dear- est Des- - pi- - net- ta, thank you
del-la ca-ra De-spi-net-ta cer - to,
thank you, dear- est Des- - pi- - net- ta, thank you

cer_to, certo il me_ri_to sa_rà, del_la ca_ra De_spi_
thank you for our hap- pi- -ness to- -night, thank you, dear- est Des- pi-
cer_to il me_ri_to sa_rà, del_la ca_ra De_spi_
for our hap- pi- ness to- -night, thank you, dear- est Des- pi-
cer_to il me_ri_to sa_rà, certo il me - - - -
for our hap- -pi- ness to- night, for our hap- - - - -
cer_to il me_ri_to sa_rà, del_la ca_ra De_spi_
for our hap- -pi- ness to- night, thank you, dear- est Des- pi-
net_ta cer_to, cer_to il me_ri_to sa_
net- ta, thank you for our hap- pi - ness to-
net_ta cer_to, cer_to il me_ri_to sa_
net- ta, thank you for our hap- pi - ness to-
- - - - - ri_to, cer_to, cer_to, certo il me_ri_to sa_
- - - - pi- ness, thank you, thank you for our hap- - pi- ness to-
net_ta cer_to, cer_to il me_ri_to sa_
net- ta, thank you for our hap- - pi- ness to-

rà.
Rad_dop_piate il lie_to suo_no,
night!
Dear- est friends, con- tin- ue sing- ing
rà.
Rad_dop_piate il lie_to suo_no,
night!
Dear- est friends, con- tin- ue sing- ing
rà.
Rad_dop_piate il lie_to suo_no,
night!
Dear- est friends, con- tin- ue sing- ing
rà.
Rad_dop_piate il lie_to suo_no,
night!
Dear- est friends, con- tin- ue sing- ing
re_pli_cate il dol_ce can_to, e noi qui seg_gia_mo in_tan_to in mag-
in your bright and mer- ry cho- rus! Sing to hap- py days be- fore us and a
re_pli_cate il dol_ce can_to, e noi qui seg_gia_mo in_tan_to in mag-
in your bright and mer- ry cho- rus! Sing to hap- py days be- fore us and a
re_pli_cate il dol_ce can_to, e noi qui seg_gia_mo in_tan_to in mag-
in your bright and mer- ry cho- rus! Sing to hap- py days be- fore us and a
re_pli_cate il dol_ce can_to, e noi qui seg_gia_mo in_tan_to in mag-
in your bright and mer- ry cho- rus! Sing to hap- py days be- fore us and a

gior gio-via-li - tà, in mag-gior gio-via - li - tà, in mag-
life of new de- - light, and a life of new de- light, and a
gior gio-via-li - tà, in mag-gior gio-via-li - tà, in mag-
life of new de- - light, and a life of new de- light, and a
gior gio-via-li - tà, in mag-gior gio - via-li - tà, in mag-
life of new de- - light, and a life of new de- light, and a
gior gio - via - li - tà, in mag-gior gio-via - li - tà, in mag-
life of new de- -light, and a life of new de- light, and a
CORO (The betrothed couples eat.)
gior gio - via-li - tà.
life of new de- light!
Be - ne-detti i doppi conju gi, e le a - ma-bi - li spo-
gior gio - via-li - tà.
life of new de- light!
Hea- ven bless you with pros- per- i- ty and suc- cess in each en-
gior gio- via - li - tà.
life of new de- light!
Hea- ven bless you with pros- per- i- ty!
gior gio- via - li - tà.
life of new de- light!
Hea- ven bless you with pros- per- i- ty!

si _ ne, be_ne_detti i doppi conjugi, splen _ da
deav- -or.
e le a_ma_bi_li spo_si_ne:
With our heart-felt, true sin- cer- i- ty may we wish you joy for- - ev- - er. May you
lor il ciel be _ ne_fi_co, ed a
live in per- fect har- mon- y, care- - free,
gui _ sa di gal _ li _ ne sien di fi_gli o _ gnor pro -
peace- ful, and un- - troub- - led, and at- - tain re- - doub- - led

li_fi_che che le ag_gua_glino in bel_tà, che le ag_
hap-pi-ness with your chil- - dren at your side, with your
gua_gli_no in bel_tà, che le agguaglino in bel_tà, che l'ag_
chil- - dren at your side. Hail the bride-groom and the bride! Hail the
gua_glino in bel_tà.
bride-groom and the bride!

FERR.
Tut_to, tut_to o vi_ta mi_a
Hap-py, hap-py end of sor-row,
GUGL.
Tut_to, tut_to o vi_ta mi_a
Hap-py, hap-py end of sor-row,
mfp mfp mfp mfp
al mio fo_co or ben ri_spon_de!
bright new prom-ise of joy here-af-ter!
FIORD.
Pel mio san_gue l'al_le_gri_a
Glow-ing hope for life to-mor-row,
al mio fo_co or ben ri_spon_de!
bright new prom-ise of joy here-af-ter!
DORAB.
Pel mio san_gue l'al_le_gri_a
Glow-ing hope for life to-mor-row,
cre_sce, cre_sce e si dif_fon_de!
filled with ten-der love and laugh-ter!
cre_sce e si dif_fon_de!
filled with love and laugh-ter!
cresc.
fp

FERR.
Sei pur bel - la!
You're my an- gel!
FIORD.
Sei pur
You're my
GUGL.
Sei pur bel - la!
You're my an- gel!
DORAB.
Sei pur
You're my
tr
va_go!
he- ro!
FERR.
Che bei ra - i!
Say you love me!
va_go!
he- ro!
GUGL.
Che bei ra - i!
Say you love me!
FIORD.
Che bel_la boc_co!
I'll al- ways love you!
FERR.
Toc_ca e be_vi,
Here's to glad- ness!
DORAB.
Che bel_la boc_co!
I'll al- ways love you!
GUGL.
Toc_ca e be_vi,
Here's to glad- ness!

(They clink their glasses.)
FIORD.
Be_vi e toc_ca, be_vi, toc_ca, toc_ca, be_vi, be_vi, toc_ca!
Let's be hap- py, hap- py, drink a toast to hap- py days to- geth- er!
DORAB.
Be_vi e toc_ca, be_vi, toc_ca, toc_ca, be_vi, be_vi, toc_ca!
Let's be hap- py, hap- py, drink a toast to hap- py days to- geth- er!
toc_ca, be_vi, be_vi, toc_ca, toc_ca, be_vi!
Hap- py, hap- py, drink to hap- py aays to- geth- er!
toc_ca, be_vi, be_vi, toc_ca, toc_ca, be_vi!
Hap- py, hap- py, drink to hap- py days to- geth- er!
Larghetto
FIORD.
E nel__ tuo, nel mio bic_chiero si____ som_mer_ga
May the___ glow__ of wine's__ con- tent- ment heal____ our woe___ and
p
o_gni pen_sie_ro, e non re_sti,____ e non re_sti più me_
drown__ all___ re- sent- ment. May our___ sor- row_______ and our sad- ness switt- ly
PERR.
E nel__ tuo, nel mio bic_chiero
May the___ glow__ of wine's__ con- tent- ment

mo - ria del pas - sa - to ai no - - stri cor, ah no, non
van - ish from our mem - 'ry for - ev - - - er - - more, may all our
si som - mer - ga o - gni pen - sie - ro,
heal our woe and drown all re - - sent - ment.
FIORD.
re - - sti, non re - sti più me - mo - ria, no,
sor - - rows and sad - - ness swift - - - ly van - ish far
DORAB.
E nel tuo, nel mio bic - chie - ro
May the glow of wine's con - - tent - - ment
FERR.
e non re - sti, e non re - sti più me -
May our sor - row and our sad - - ness swift - ly
del pas - sa - to ai no - stri cor,
from our mem - - - 'ry for - ev - - er - - more.
si som - mer - ga o - gni pen - sie - ro,
heal our woe and drown all re - sent - ment.
mo - ria, del pas - sa - to ai no - - - stri cor, ah no, non
van - - ish from our mem - 'ry for - ev - - - - - er - - more, may all our

e nel tuo, nel mio bic-
May the glow of wine's con-
e non re-sti, e non
May our sor-row and all
re-sti, non re-sti più me-
sor-rows and sad-ness swift-ly
GUGL. sotto voce (to himself)
(Ah, ah be-ves-se-ro del tos-si-co,
(Ah! Just to think of their dis-hon-es-ty,
chie-ro si som-
tent-ment heal our
re-sti più me-mo-ria del pas-
sad-ness swift-ly van-ish from our
mo-ria, nò, del pas-
van-ish far from our
ah be-ves-se-ro, be-ves-se-ro del tos-si-co, del
just to think of these two Jez-e-bels' dis-hon-es-ty, dis-

mer - gu o - gni pen -
woe and drown all re-
sa - to ai no - - - - stri
mem- - 'ry for- ev- - - - er-
sa - - to ai no - - stri
mem- - - 'ry for- - ev- - - - er- -
tos - si - co, que - ste vol - pi, queste vol - pi senza o -
hon- - es- - ty, makes me wish there had been poi- son in their
SCENA XVII
SCENE XVII
Allegro
sie - ro.
sent- ment.
cor.
more.
cor.
more. (Enter Don Alfonso.)
D. ALF.
nor.)
wine!)
Miei Si - gno - ri, tut - to è
Now it's time that we pro-
Allegro
fat - to; col con - trat - to nu - zi - a - le il no - tajo è sul - le scale e ip - so
ceed- ed with the sign- ing of the con- tract. We have ev- 'ry- thing that's need- ed, and the
cresc.

Bra_vo, bra_vo, pas_si su_bi_to.
We are read- y, call the no- - ta- ry!
Bra_vo, bra_vo, pas_si su_bi_to.
We are read- y, call the no- - ta- ry!
Bra_vo, bra_vo, pas_si su_bi_to.
We are read- y, call the no- - ta- ry!
GUGL.
D. ALF.
fat_to qui ver_rà. Bra_vo, bra_vo, pas_si su_bi_to. Vò a chia_
coup- les both are here. We are read- y, call the no- - ta- ry! Hon- - ored
f
p
(Enter Despina, disguised as a notary.)
marlo, vò a chia_marlo: ec_co_lo quà.
Coun- s'lor Il- - le- gal- is, kind- ly come in.
f
p
cresc.
f
DESP.
Au_gu_ran_do_vi og_ni be_ne il no_ta_jo Bec_ca_
"Cor- nu- co- pi- - a ver- - bo- rum," as we al- ways say in
tr
p
vi_vi coll'u_sa_ta a voi sen vie_ne no_ta_ri_le di_gni_
Lat- in. Since we have a le- gal quo- rum, I sug- gest that we pro-
tr

tà! È il con_trat_to sti_pu_
ceed. Here's the bo- na fide a-
cresc.
la_to col_le re_go_le or_di_na_rie nel_le for_me giu_di_
gree- ment with the state- ment of the caus- es and the mod- i- fy- ing
zia_rie, pria tos_sen_do, poi se_den_do cla _ ra
claus- es. With de- co- rum, ha- rum, ho- rum, I shall
FIORD.
Bravo, bravo in ve_ri_tà!
Ver- y well, pro- ceed, pro- ceed!
DORAB.
Bravo, bravo in ve_ri_tà!
Ver- y well, pro- ceed, pro- ceed!
DESP.
FERR.
DESP. (with a nasal tone)
vo- ce leg_ge_rà. Bravo, bravo in ve_ri_tà! Per con_trat_to
now be- gin to read. Ver- y well, pro- ceed, pro- ceed! Mar- riage is the
GUGL.
Bravo, bravo in ve_ri_tà!
Ver- y well, pro- ceed, pro- ceed!

da me fatto si con_giun_ge in ma_tri_monio Fior_di_
sworn in- ten- tion of the par- ties I now men- tion. Fior- di-
li_gi con Sem_pronio e con Ti_zio Do_ra_
li- gi and Sem- pro- nio, Dor- a- bel- la and An-
bel_la sua le_gi_ti_ma so_rel_la, quel_le da_me
to- nio, la- dies here- by called "the sis- ters", to the des- ig-
fer_ra_re_si, que_sti no_bili al_ba_ne_si
nat- ed mis- ters, lat- ter no- bles of Al- ban- ia,
e per do_te, e con_tra_
dow- ry, gifts, and mis- cel-
tr 3

FIORD.
Co _ se no _ te, co _ se no _ te, vi cre _ diamo,
Nev- - er mind it, nev- - er mind it, we will read it
DORAB.
Co _ se no _ te, co _ se no _ te, vi cre _ diamo,
Nev- - er mind it, nev- - er mind it, we will read it
DESP. FERR.
do _ te... Co _ se no _ te, co _ se no _ te, vi cre _ diamo,
la- nea... Nev- - er mind it, nev- - er mind it, we will read it
GUGL.
Co _ se no _ te, co _ se no _ te, vi cre _ diamo,
Nev- - er mind it, nev- - er mind it, we will read it
cresc.
f
ci fi _ dia _ mo so _ scri _ viam, da _ te pur quà.
when we've signed it lat- - er on! Hand us a pen!
ci fi _ dia _ mo so _ scri _ viam, da _ te pur quà.
when we've signed it lat- - er on! Hand us a pen!
DESP.
ci fi _ dia _ mo so _ scri _ viam, da _ te pur quà. Bravi,
when we've signed it lat- - er on! Hand us a pen! Hap- py
D. ALF.
ci fi _ dia _ mo so _ scri _ viam, da _ te pur quà. Bravi,
when we've signed it lat- - er on! Hand us a pen! Hap- py
p

(Only the two women sign the contract. Don Alfonso takes the contract.)
(The sound of drums and singing is heard.)
Maestoso
Sopr.
Alt.
CORO
Ten.
Bas.
bravi in ve_ri _ tà!
la- dies! Luck-y men!
bravi in ve_ri _ tà!
la- dies! Luck- y men!
Bel_la vi _ ta mi_li_
On to glo- ry, on to
Maestoso
f
sf
pp
tar, bel_la vi_ta mi_li_ tar, o_gni dì si cangia lo_co og_gi
war, on to glo - ry, on to war! We are free of care and sor- row, here to-
molto e do_man po_co, ora in terra ed or sul mar, ora in terra ed or sul
day and there to- mor- row, o- ver land and o- ver sea, o- ver land and o- ver

FIORD.
Che ru_mor, che can _ to è que _ sto!
Hear that song! It sounds fa- mil- iar!
DORAB.
Che ru_mor, che can _ to è que _ sto!
Hear that song! It sounds fa- mil- iar!
DESP.
Che ru_mor, che can _ to è que _ sto!
mar.
sea!
Hear that song! It sounds fa- mil- iar!
FERR.
Che ru_mor, che can _ to è que _ sto!
sea!
Hear that song! It sounds fa- mil- iar!
GUGL.
Che ru_mor, che can _ to è que _ sto!
Hear that song! It sounds fa- mil- iar!
D. ALF.
Sta_te
Wait a
(He goes to me window.)
cheti, io vò a guar_dar, sta_te cheti, io vò guar_dar.
mo- ment, let me look — wait a mo- ment, let me look!
Allegro
Mi_se_ri_cor_di_a, Nu_mi del
Oh, bound- less mis- er- y! Heav- en pre-
sf
f
p cresc.

cie_lo, che ca_so or_ri_bi_le, io tre_mo, io ge_lo: gli spo_si
serve us! What a ca- tas- tro- phe! How aw- ful! How dread- ful! Your for- mer
FIORD.
Lo spo_so mi_ó_
Our for- mer sweet- hearts!
DORAB.
Lo spo_so mi_o_
Our for- mer sweet- hearts!
vo_stri_ in questo i_stan_te tor_naro, o Di_o, ed al_la
sweet- hearts! I see them land- ing down at the moor- ing. I hate to
FIORD.
Co_sa mai sento, bar_ba_re stel_le,
Oh, this is shock- ing! How can we stay them?
DORAB.
Co_sa mai sento, bar_ba_re stel_le,
Oh, this is shock- ing! How can we stay them?
FERR.
Co_sa mai sento, bar_ba_re stel_le,
Oh, this is shock- ing! How can we stay them?
GUGL.
Co_sa mai sento, bar_ba_re stel_le,
Oh, this is shock- ing! How can we stay them?
ri_va sbarca_no già!
say so, but it is true!
p
fp
f

in tal mo_men_to che si fa_rà? Pres_to par_
At least de-lay them! What can we do? You can- not
in tal mo_men_to che si fa_rà? Pres_to par_
At least de-lay them! What can we do? You can- not
in tal mo_men_to che si fa_rà?
At least de-lay them! What can we do?
in tal mo_men_to che si fa_rà?
At least de-lay them! What can we do?
sfp
(The servants take the table away, and the musicians hurry off.)
ti_te! Pre_sto fug_gi_te! Là, là ce_
stay here! You can- not stay here! Ei- ther you
ti_te! Pre_sto fug_gi_te! Là, là ce_
stay here! You can- not stay here! Ei- ther you
DESP.
Ma se li veg_go_no? ma se li in_contra_no?
If they dis- cov- er you what will they do to you?
FERR.
Ma se ci veg_go_no? ma se ci in_contra_no?
If they dis- cov- er us what will they do to us?
D.ALF.
Ma se li veg_go_no? ma se li in_contra_no?
If they dis- cov- er you what will they do to you?
GUGL.
Ma se ci veg_go_no? ma se ci in_contra_no?
If they dis- cov- er us what will they do to us?
fp fp fp fp

(They hide their lovers in one room.
Don Alfonso leads Despina to another room.)
la_te_vi per ca_ri_tà, per ca_ri_tà!
hide your- self or run a- way, or run a- way!
la_te_vi per ca_ri_tà, per ca_ri_tà!
hide your- self or run a- way, or run a- way!
f
p
(frantically)
Nu_mi, soc_cor_so, Nu_mi, con_si_glio! Chi dal pe_
Heav- en pro- tect us! Heav- en pre- serve us! Who will ad-
(frantically)
Nu_mi, soc_cor_so, Nu_mi, con_si_glio! Chi dal pe_
Heav- en pro- tect us! Heav- en pre- serve us! Who will ad-
D.ALF.
Ras_se_re_na_te_vi, ri_tranquil_la_te_vi!
Do not get pan- ick- y! My la- dies, calm your- selves!
fp
ri_glio ci sal_ve_rà, chi?
vise us in our dis- may? Who?
D.ALF.
ri_glio ci sal_ve_rà, chi? In me fi_da_te_vi
vise us in our dis- may? Who? Just put your trust in me!
cresc.
f
p

Allegro
FIORD.
sotto voce
Mil_le bar_ba_ri pen_sie_ri tormen_tan_do il cor mi
I have nev- -er been so fright-ened, so up- set and so be-
DORAB.
sotto voce
ben tutto an_drà. Mil_le bar_ba_ri pen_sie_ri tormen_tan_do il cor mi
I'll save the day! I have nev- -er been so fright-ened, so up- set and so be-
Allegro
f
p
van_no, se di_sco_pro - no l'in - ganno,
wil- dered. If they learn how we de- ceived them,
van_no, se di_sco_pro - no l'in - ganno,
wil- dered. If they learn how we de- ceived them,
ah di noi che mai sa_rà, ah di noi che mai sa_rà!
Heav- en knows what we can say, Heav- en knows what we can say!
ah di noi che mai sa_rà, ah di noi che mai sa_rà!
Heav- en knows what we can say, Heav- en knows what we can say!
fp
fp
fp
fp

SCENA ULTIMA LAST SCENE

tà.
end!
D.ALF.
tà. Giusti Numi, Guglielmo, Fer_ran_do, oh che giu_bi_lo, qui,
end! Well, I nev-er! Gu-gliel-mo! Fer-ran-do! This is mar-vel-ous! You!
co_me, e quan_do? Ri_chia_ma_ti da re_gio con_
Back here? So quick-ly! Our com-man-der has al-tered his
GUGL.
Ri_chia_ma_ti da re_gio con_
Our com-man-der has al-tered his
cresc.
p
tror_di_ne, da re_gio con_tror_di_ne, pieni il cor di con_ten_to e di
strat-e-gy, his strat-e-gy, strat-e-gy. To our joy we were called back to
tror_di_ne, da re_gio con_tror_di_ne, pieni il cor di con_ten_to e di
strat-e-gy, his strat-e-gy, strat-e-gy. To our joy we were called back to

gau_dio, ritor_niamo al_le spose ado_ra_bi_li, al_le spose ado_ra_bi li,
Na- -ples. With our hearts full of won- der-ful hap- pi- ness, of won- der- ful hap- pi- ness,
gau_dio, ritor_niamo al_le spose ado_ra_bi_li, al_le spose ado_ra_bi_li,
Na- -ples. With our hearts full of won- der-ful hap- pi- ness, of won- der- ful hap- pi- ness,
ri_tor_niamo al_la vostra a_mi_stà, ri_tor_niamo al_la vostra ami_stà.
we re- turn to our sweet- hearts and friend, we re- turn to our sweet- hearts and friend.
ri_tor niamo al_la vostra a_mi_stà, ri_tor_niamo al_la vostra ami_stà.
we re- turn to our sweet- hearts and friend, we re- turn to our sweet- hearts and friend.
GUGL. (to Fiordiligi)
Ma cos' è quel pal_lor, quel si_len_zio?
Dear- est love, why so pale and so si- lent?
FERR. (to Dorabella)
L'i_dol mio per_chè me_sto si stà?
Dear- est heart, why this sor- row- ful air?
D.ALF.
Dal di_let_to, con_fu_se ed at_
They are to- tal- ly speech- less from

FIORD.
Ah che al lab_bro le vo_ci mi man_ca_no, se non
I am speech- less with ter- ror and mis- er- y! I am
DORAB.
Ah che al lab_bro le vo_ci mi man_ca_no, se non
I am speech- less with ter- ror and mis- er- y! I am
to_ni_te, con_fu_se ed at_to_ni_te mu_te,
hap- pi- ness. You took them so un- a- -ware. That should
mo_ro un pro_di_gio sa_rà.
read- y to die of de- spair!
mo_ro un pro_di_gio sa_rà.
read- y to die of de- spair!
GUGL.
mu_te si re_sta_no là. Per_me_tet_te che sia po_sto quel ba-
show you how deep- -ly they care! If you la- -dies will per- mit us, we will
ul in quel_la stanza. Dei che veggio, un uom na_sco_sto, un no_
put a- way our bag- gage. What does this mean? Is some- one hid- ing? An at-
f

Con più moto
DESP.
(Enters, without wearing her notary's hat.)
ta - jo, qui che fa? Non Signor non è un No-ta-jo, è De-spi-na ma-sche-
tor- ney? Who is this? I am nei- ther man nor law- yer but Des- pi- na, pure and
p
ra - ta, che dal bal-lo or è tor - na-ta e a spogliar-si ven - ne
sim- ple. I was try- ing on my cos- tume for to- mor- row's mas- quer-
FIORD.
La Despina, la De - spina,
How she fooled us so com- plete- ly
DORAB.
La Despina, la De - spina,
How she fooled us so com- plete- ly
DESP.
quà. U-na fur - ba che m'ag - gua - gli do-ve
ade. There is no- -one like Des- - pi- - na, there is
FERR.
U-na furba uguale a que - sta do - ve mai si tro-ve-
There is no- one like Des- pi- - na, that is plain e- nough to
GUGL.
U-na furba uguale a que - sta do - ve mai si tro-ve-
There is no- one like Des- pi- - na, that is plain e- nough to

(Don Alfonso discreetly lets the contract signed by the ladies fall to the floor.)

FERR.
GUGL.
sotto voce
Ma che car - te so - po que-ste? Un con-trat - to nu-zi -
May I ask what's in this pa- per? Are you will- ing to ex-
f
p
FERR.
Allegro
Giu-sto ciel,
What a crime!
a piacere
a - le, un con-trat - to nu - zi - a - le? Giu-sto ciel,
plain it? Can it be a mar- riage con- tract? What a crime!
Allegro
tr
tr
voi qui scri-ve-ste! con-tra-dir - ci o-mai non va-le, tra-di -
And you have signed it! To de- ny your guilt is use- less! To my
voi qui scri-ve-ste! con-tra-dir - ci o-mai non va-le, tra-di -
And you have signed it! To de- ny your guilt is use- less! To my
p
cresc.
f
p
men - to, tra - di-men - - - - to, ah si
hor- - ror I dis- cov- - - - er you be-
men - to, tra - di-men - - - - to, ah si
hor- - ror I dis- cov- - - - er you be-
cresc.
f

fac - cia il sco - pri - men - - - - to; e a tor-
trayed your faith- - ful lov- - - - er! You will
fac - cia il sco - pri - men - - - - to; e a tor-
trayed your faith- - ful lov- - - - er! You will
p
cresc.
f
ren - ti, a fiu - mi, a ma - ri in - - - di il
not es- - cape my ven- geance! Streams of
ren - ti, a fiu - mi, a ma - ri in - - - di il
not es- - cape my ven- geance! Streams of
san - gue scor - re - rà, si, e a tor - ren - ti, a fiu - mi, a
guilt- - y blood will flow! Yes, you will not es- - cape our
san - gue scor - re - rà, si, e a tor - ren - ti, a fiu - mi, a
guilt- - y blood will flow! Yes, you will not es- - cape our

ma_ri in - di il san - gue, in_di il
ven- geance! We have caught you! Streams of
ma_ri in - di il san - gue, in_di il
ven- geance! We have caught you! Streams of
Andante
FIORD.
(They try to go into the other room, but the ladies hold them back.)
san_guescorre_rà! Ah! Si_gnor son rea di mor_te e la
guilt- y blood will flow! Ah! I beg of you to kill me! I am
DORAB.
san_guescorre_rà! Ah! Si_gnor son rea di mor_te e la
guilt- y blood will flow! Ah! I beg of you to kill me! I am
Andante
p
mor - te io sol vi chie_do; il mio fal_lo tar_di
guilt- y, as you de- clare me. Show no pit- y, do not
mor - te io sol vi chie_do; il mio fal_lo tar_di
guilt- - y, as you de- clare me. Show no pit- y, do not

ve - do, tar - di ve - do, con quel ferro un sen fe - ri - te che non
spare me, do not spare — me! Take your sa- ber and do your du- ty. I will
ve - do, tar - di ve - do, con quel ferro un sen fe - ri - te che non
spare me, do not spare. me! Take your sa- ber and do your du- ty. I will
FERR.
me - ri - ta, non me - ri - ta pie - tà! Co - sa
wel- come it, for I de- serve it so! Tell the
GUGL.
me - ri - ta, non me - ri - ta pie - tà! Co - sa
wel- - come it, for I de- serve it so! Tell the
FIORD. (Points to Despina and Don Alfonso.)
fù? Per noi fa - vel - li il cru -
truth! These are the trai- - tors! All we
DORAB (Points to Despina and Don Alfonso.)
fù? Per noi fa - vel - li il cru -
truth! These are the trai- - tors! All we

del, la se - dut - tri - ce.
did was their sug- ges- - tion.
D. ALF.
del, la se - dut - tri - ce. Trop - po
did was their sug- ges- - tion. That is
ve - ro è quel che di - ce, e la pro - va è
true with- out a ques- - tion. I can prove it
(Shows them the room where the lovers had gone to hide. Ferrando and Guglielmo go into the room for a moment,
chiu - sa lì, e la pro - va è chiu - sa
ver- - y well. I can prove it ver- - y
then come out, without the hats, coats, and beards, but with the outer clothing of their former disguise, in the comic manner they had formerly affected.)
FIORD.
Dal ti - mor io ge - lo, io
What a dread- - ful trick to
DORAB.
lì. Dal ti - mor io ge - lo, io
well. What a dread- - - ful trick to

pal - pi - to: per - chè mai li di - - sco -
play on us! Oh, why did he have to
pal - pi - to: per - chè mai li di - - sco -
play on us! Oh, why did he have to
prì, per - chè mai li di - sco - prì!
tell? Oh, why did he have to tell?
prì, per - chè mai li di - sco - prì!
tell? Oh, why did he have to tell?
Allegretto
FERR. (with an exaggerated bow to Fiordiligi)
A voi s'in - chi - na bel - la da - mi - na il Ca - va -
You are my god- dess! I kneel be- fore you! I am your
lie - re dell' Al - ba - ni - a.
he- ro who wants to a- dore you!
Andante
GUGL. (to Dorabella)
Il ri - trat - ti - no pel co - ri -
Here is a por- trait I know you

Allegretto
FERR. (to Despina)
Ed al magne_ti_co
Let us con- grat- u- late
ci _ no ec_co io le ren_do Si_gno_ra mi_a.
treasure. Give me my heart now, measure for measure!
(to Despina)
Ed al magne_ti_co
Let us con- grat- u- late
Allegretto
mf
p
Si_gnor Dot_to_re ren_do l'o_no _ re che me _ ri_tò.
Doc- tor Fa- tal- is, mas- ter of mag- nets, the par- a- gon!
Si_gnor Dot_to_re ren_do l'o_no _ re che me _ ri_tò.
Doc- tor Fa- tal- is, mas- ter of mag- nets, the par- a- gon!
f
sf
p
FIORD.
Stel_le che veggo! Al duol non reggo!
Gra- cious! A- maz- ing! Stun- ning and daz- ing!
DORAB.
FERR.
Stel_le che veggo! Son stu _ pe_fat_te! Al duol non reggo!
Gra- cious! A- maz- ing! They're struck by thun- der! Stun- ning and daz- ing!
DESP.
D.ALF.
Stel_le che veggo! Son stu _ pe_fat_te! Al duol non reggo!
Gra- cious! A- maz- ing! They're struck by thun- der! Stun- ning and daz- ing!
GUGL.
Son stu _ pe_fat_te!
They're struck by thun- der!

FIORD. (pointing to Don Alfonso)
Ec_co là il bar_ba_ro che c'in_gan_
He is the guilt-y one who led us
FERR.
DORAB. (pointing to Don Alfonso)
Son mez_ze mat_te! Ec_co là il bar_ba_ro che c'in_gan_
Speech-less with won-der! He is the guilt-y one who led us
D. ALF.
Son mez_ze mat_te!
Speech-less with won-der!
GUGL.
Son mez_ze mat_te!
Speech-less with won-der!
f
sfp
Andante con moto
nò.
on!
D. ALF.
nò. V'in_gan_nai, ma fu l'in_gan_no dis_in_gan_no ai vo_stri a_
on! Yes, I did, but my de-cep-tion was to un-de-ceive your
Andante con moto
p
man_ti, che più sag_gi o_mai sa_ran_no, che fa_ran quel ch'io vor_
lov-ers and to prove there's no ex-cep-tion to a rule that's al-ways

rò. Quà le de_stre, sie_te spo_si, ab_brac_
true. Learn your les- -son, heed the mor- -al! Let's be
cia_te_vi e ta_ce_te. Tut_ti quat_tro ora ri_de_te ch'io già risi e ri_de_
friends a-gain! End your quar-rel! Laugh a- bout what's past and o- ver and I'll laugh a-long with
FIORD.
I_dol mio se que_sto è ve_ro, i_dol
Dear be- lov- ed, please for- give me, dear be-
DORAB.
I_dol mio se que_sto è ve_ro, i_dol
Dear be- lov- ed, please for- give me, dear be-
rò.
you.
fp
mio se que_sto è ve_ro, col_la fe_de e coll'a_mo_re compen_
lov-ed, please for- give me! Oh, my sweet-heart, I hope to show you all the
mio se que_sto è ve_ro, col_la fe_de e coll'a_mo_re compen_
lov- ed, please for- give me! Oh, my sweet- heart, I hope to show you all the

sar sa.prò il tuo co _ re, a _ do _ rar _ ti o _ gnor sa _
lov- ing faith I owe _ you. I will prove my worth to
sar sa.prò il tuo co _ re, a _ do _ rar _ ti o _ gnor sa _
lov- ing faith I owe _ you. I will prove my worth to
FERR.
Te lo
You don't
GUGL.
Te lo
You don't
cresc.
fp
cresc.
p
(They embrace each other.)
prò, col _ la fe _ de e coll' a _
you. Oh, my sweet- heart, I hope to
prò, col _ la fe _ de e coll' a _
you. Oh, my sweet- heart, I hope to
cre _ do, gio _ ja bel _ la, ma la pro _ va io far non vò,
have to, my be- lov- ed, I shall ask no proof from you.
cre _ do, gio _ ja bel _ la, ma la pro _ va io far non vò, te lo
have to, my be- lov- ed, I shall ask no proof from you. You don't

FIORD.
mo - re, compen - sar sa - prò il tuo co - - - - re,
show you all the lov - ing faith I owe you.
DORAB.
mo - re, compen - sar sa - prò il tuo co - - - - re,
show you all the lov - ing faith I owe you.
DESP.
Io non so se que - sto è so - gno, mi con - fon - do, mi ver - go - gno:
I who was the mas - ter schem - er find my - self a baf - fled dream - er.
man - co mal se a me l'han fat - ta che a molt' al - tri anch'io la
I have learned a use - ful les - son, some - thing that I nev - er
FERR.
te lo cre - do gio - ja bel - la,
You don't have to, my be - lov - ed,
ma la pro - va io far non
I shall ask no proof from
GUGL.
cre - do gio - ja bel - la,
have to, my be - lov - ed,
ma la pro - va io far non
I shall ask no proof from
cresc.
fp

a - do - rar - ti o - gnor sa - prò, o -
I will prove my worth to you, my
a - do - rar - ti o - gnor sa - prò, o -
I will prove my worth to you, my
fò, man_co mal se a mel'han
knew. Tricks you play on oth- er
vò, no, ma la prova io far non vò, ma la
you, no, I shall ask no proof from you, my be-
vò, no, ma la pro_va io far non vò,
you, no, I shall ask no proof from you,
cresc.
p
gnor - sa - prò, o -
worth to you, my
gnor sa - prò, o -
worth to you, my
fat ta che a molt' al - tri an_ch'io la fò, man_co mal se a me l'han
peo- - ple, oth- - er peo- - ple play on you, tricks you play on oth- - er
pro - va no, ma la
lov- - - ed, no, I shall
io far non vò, no, la
I'll ask no proof, no, I'll

Allegro molto
gnor sa - prò.
worth to you.
gnor sa - prò.
worth to you.
fat_ta che a molt'al_tri anch'io la fo.
peo- ple, oth- er peo- ple play on you!
pro _ va io far non vò.
ask no proof from you.
pro _ va io far non vò.
ask no proof from you.
Allegro molto
p
FIORD.
sotto voce
For_ tu _ na_ to
Hap- py is the
DORAB.
sotto voce
For_ tu _ na_ to
Hap- py is the
DESP.
sotto voce
For_ tu _ na_ to
Hap- py is the
FERR.
sotto voce
For_ tu _ na_ to
Hap- py is the
D. ALF.
sotto voce
For_ tu _ na_ to
Hap- py is the
GUGL.
sotto voce
For_ tu _ na_ to
Hap- py is the

f
l'uom, che pren - de o - gni co - sa pel buon ver - so, e tra i
man of — rea - son who can face the world in sea - son. Firm and
f
l'uom, che pren - de o - gni co - sa pel buon ver - so, e tra i
man of — rea - son who can face the world in sea - son. Firm and
f
l'uom, che pren - de o - gni co - sa pel buon ver - so, e tra i
man of rea - son who can face the world in sea - son. Firm and
f
l'uom, che pren - de o - gni co - sa pel buon ver - so, e tra i
man of — rea - son — who can face the world in sea - son. Firm and
f
l'uom, che pren - de o - gni co - sa pel buon ver - so, e tra i
man of rea - son who can face the world in sea - son. Firm and
f
l'uom, che pren - de o - gni co - sa pel buon ver - so, e tra i
man of rea - son who can face the world in sea - son. Firm and
f
ca - si, e le vi - cen - de da ra - gion gui -
stead - fast and un - com - plain - ing, he will go his —
ca - si, e le vi - cen - de da ra - gion gui -
stead - fast and un - com - plain - ing, he will go his —
ca - si, e le vi - cen - de da ra - gion gui -
stead - fast and un - com - plain - ing, he will go his —
ca - si, e le vi - cen - de da ra - gion gui -
stead - fast and un - com - plain - ing, he will go his —
ca - si, e le vi - cen - de da ra - gion gui -
stead - fast and un - com - plain - ing, he will go his
ca - si, e le vi - cen - de da ra - gion gui -
stead - fast and un - com - plain - ing, he will go his

sotto voce
dar si fà, da ra - gion gui - dar si fà. Quel che
cheer - ful way, he will go his — cheer - ful way. Things that
sotto voce
dar si fà, da ra - gion gui - dar si fà. Quel che
cheer - ful way, he will go his — cheer - ful way. Things that
sotto voce
dar si fà, da ra - gion gui - dar si fà. Quel che
cheer - ful way, he will go his — cheer - ful way. Things that
sotto voce
dar si fà, da ra - gion gui - dar si fà. Quel che
cheer - ful way, he will go his — cheer - ful way. Things that
sotto voce
dar si fà, da ra - gion gui - dar si fà. Quel che
cheer - ful way, he will go his cheer - ful way. Things that
sotto voce
dar si fà, da ra - gion gui - dar si fà. Quel che
cheer - ful way, he will go his cheer - ful way. Things that
p
suo - le altrui far pian - - - - - - - ge - re
make his broth - ers sor - - - - - - - row - ful,
suo - le altrui far pian - - - - - - - ge - re
make his broth - ers sor - - - - - - - row - ful,
suo - le altrui far pian - - - - - - - ge - re
make his broth - ers sor - - - - - - - row - ful,
suo - le altrui far pian - - - - - - - ge - re
make his broth - ers sor - - - - - - - row - ful,
suo - le altrui far pian - - - - - - - ge - re
make his broth - ers sor - - - - - - - row - ful,
suo - le altrui far pian - - - - - - - ge - re
make his broth - ers sor - - - - - - - row - ful,

fia per lu_i ca_gion di ri_so, di ri_so,
he will an- swer with know- ing laugh- - ter, with laugh- ter,
fia per lu_i ca_gion di ri_so, di ri_so,
he will an- swer with know- ing laugh- - ter, with laugh- ter,
fia per lu_i ca_gion di ri_so, di ri_so, di
he will an- swer with know- ing laugh- - ter, with laugh- ter, with
fia per lu_i ca_gion di ri_so, di ri_so,
he will an- swer with know- ing laugh- - ter, with laugh- ter,
fia per lu_i ca_gion di ri_so, di ri_so,
he will an- swer with know- ing laugh- ter, with laugh- ter,
fia per lu_i ca_gion di ri_so, di ri_so, di ri_so, di
he will an- swer with know- ing laugh- - ter, with laugh- - ter, with laugh- ter, with
di ri_so, e del mon_do in mez_zo i tur_
with laugh- ter. He has learned that life's ad- ver- -
di ri_so, e del mon_do in mez_zo i tur_
with laugh- ter. He has learned that life's ad- ver- -
ri_so, di ri_so, e del mon_do in mez_zo i tur_
laugh- ter, with laugh- ter. He has learned that life's ad- ver- -
di ri_so, e del mon_do in mez_zo i tur_
with laugh- ter. He has learned that life's ad- ver- -
di ri_so, e del mon_do in mez_zo i tur_
with laugh- ter. He has learned that life's ad- ver- -
ri_so, di ri_so, e del mon_do in mez_zo i tur_
laugh- ter, with laugh- ter. He has learned that life's ad- ver- -

bi_ni, e del mon_do in mez_zo i tur
si- ties, he has learned that life's ad- ver-
bi_ni, e del mon_do in mez_zo i tur
si- ties, he has learned that life's ad- ver-
bi_ni, e del mon_do in mez_zo i tur
si- ties, he has learned that life's ad- ver-
bi_ni, e del mon_do in mez_zo i tur
si- ties, he has learned that life's ad- ver-
bi_ni, e del mon_do in mez_zo i tur
si- ties, he has learned that life's ad- ver-
bi_ni, e del mon_do in mez_zo i tur
si- ties, he has learned that life's ad- ver-
bi_ni,
si- ties
bi_ni,
si- ties
bi_ni,
si- ties
bi_ni,
si- ties
bi_ni,
si- ties
bi_ni,
si- ties

sotto voce
bel_ la cal_ma tro_ve_rà,
turn_ to_ joy an- - oth- er day,_
sotto voce
bel_ la cal_ma tro_ve_rà,
turn_ to_ joy an- - oth- er day,_
sotto voce
bel_ la cal_ma tro_ve_rà,
turn to joy an- - oth- er day,_
sotto voce
bel_ la cal_ma tro_ve_rà,
turn to joy an- - oth- er day,_
sotto voce
bel_ la cal_ma tro_ve_rà,
turn to joy an- - oth- er day,_
sotto voce
bel_ la cal_ma tro_ve_rà,
turn to joy an- - oth- er day,_
p
f
bel_ la_ cal_ma_ tro_ve_rà, bel la
turn_ to_ joy an- - oth- er day, turn to
f
bel_ la_ cal_ma_ tro_ve_rà, bel la
turn_ to_ joy an- - oth- er day, turn to
f
bel_ la cal_ma tro_ve_rà, bel la
turn to joy an- - oth- er day, turn to
f
bel_ la cal_ma_ tro_ve_rà, bel la cal_ -
turn to joy an- - oth- er day, turn to joy
f
bel_ la cal_ma tro_ve_rà, bel la cal_ -
turn to joy an- - oth- er day, turn to joy
f
bel_ la cal_ma tro_ve_rà, bel la cal_ -
turn to joy an- - oth- er day, turn to joy

cal - - ma tro-ve-rà, bel-la cal -
joy an-oth-er day, turn to joy
cal - - ma tro-ve-rà, bel-la cal -
joy an-oth-er day, turn to joy
cal - - ma tro-ve-rà, bel-la cal -
joy an-oth-er day, turn to joy
- - - ma tro-ve-rà, bel-la cal - - - -
joy an-oth-er day, turn to joy
- - - ma tro-ve-rà, bel-la cal - - - -
joy an-oth-er day, turn to joy
- - - ma tro-ve-rà, bel-la cal - - - -
joy an-oth-er day, turn to joy
- ma tro-ve-rà, si tro - ve-rà, si tro - ve -
an-oth-er day, an- - oth- - - er day, an- - oth- - - er
- ma tro-ve-rà, si tro - ve-rà, si tro - ve -
an-oth-er day, an- - oth- - - er day, an- - oth- - - er
- ma tro-ve-rà, si tro - ve-rà, si tro - ve -
an-oth-er day, an- - oth- - - er day, an- - oth- - - er
- ma tro-ve-rà, si tro - ve-rà, si tro - ve -
an-oth-er day, an- - oth- - - er day, an- - oth- - - er
- ma tro-ve-rà, si tro - ve-rà, si tro - ve -
an-oth-er day, an- - oth- - - er day, an- - oth- - - er
- ma tro-ve-rà, si tro - ve-rà, si tro - ve -
an-oth-er day, an- - oth- - - er day, an- - oth- - - er

End of the opera